The Last Day

The Last Day

a novel

JAMES LANDIS

STEERFORTH PRESS
Hanover, New Hampshire

For information about permission to reproduce
selections from this book, write to:
Steerforth Press L.L.C., 45 Lyme Road, Suite 208,
Hanover, New Hampshire 03755

Library of Congress Cataloging-in-Publication Data
Landis, James David.
The last day : a novel / James Landis. — 1st ed.
p. cm.
ISBN 978-1-58642-165-6
1. Iraq War, 2003 — Veterans — Fiction. 2. Snipers — Fiction.
3. New Hampshire — Fiction. 4. Psychological fiction. I. Title.
PS3562.A4767L37 2009
813'.54--dc22

2009024562

SECOND PRINTING

For Denise
who believed

For comfort and aid,
the author is grateful to
Leslie Gardner, Pamela Malpas,
Roland Pease, Chip Fleischer

One

The Isles of Shoals

I MEET JESUS on the day I get home from the war. I'm on the beach, but I don't know how I got here. My mind is as dark as the night.

I walk, but only back and forth. New Hampshire has a tiny coastline. A lot of it is rock, sent down from Maine when God made the Earth, to keep us on our toes down here. I walk where the sand is wet and hard and cold. It holds my toes, and my toes hold it. In the desert, where I fought, the sand was inhospitable.

The darkness is a gift. I would tell my little baby girl when she woke up in the middle of the night, "Dodie, there's nothing to be afraid of." I've always loved the dark. In the dark, you light up inside. Things become clearer the darker it is.

Out here, on the beach, I'm alone. I always have been. Or as long as I can remember. As long as since my mother died.

I'd come here in the middle of the night to find myself and to get away from others. The beach is a place of memories. When you come here, you take your life with you. When you go other places, like the city or the desert, you leave your life behind.

I remember everything.

Except how I got here.

I spend the whole night on the beach. But when the sun's faint light begins to bend around the Earth, I see him.

Out there, ten miles out in the ocean, are the Isles of Shoals. There are nine of them. On the clearest day you can see five at most. They sit like flat gray stones on the skin of the water. If it weren't for them, your eyes would disappear into the horizon.

I've never been to the Shoals. I'm not a sailor. I'm a soldier. I've been content to stand here looking out at them. When there's haze or fog, or night has set in, I imagine them. They're always there for me. They make the ocean safe.

They sit off to the east, of course. New Englanders are always looking east. To where we came from. To where we go to fight for freedom. From this coast, the only coast I know, the sun always rises behind the Shoals. Its first light brings them up out of the darkness of the ocean. One by one they begin to glow.

There, coming toward me, out of the light, is a man. He seems to step on the islands one by one, the way I would cross the slippery stones of the Swift River by the Kancamagus Highway up north to try to reach my father.

Behind the man a faint curtain of light rises to the sky out of the ocean. He wears the light like a robe, though I see he's dressed like me. Jeans and a T-shirt, no shoes. And that he's older than I am, a lot older, maybe midthirties.

He walks right toward me. He walks right into my eyes.

In the war, we were taught to be suspicious of strangers. That's what they called it: *suspicious*. What they meant was *fearful*: we were taught to be afraid of strangers.

But I'm not afraid of this man. I'm home now. I still don't know how I got here. But I feel that nothing, and no one, can hurt me.

Still, I want to be alone. I'm thinking, *How come on an empty beach if one person puts his chair down and another person arrives, he puts his chair down right near the first person?*

He comes right up to me.

"I know you want to be alone, Warren," he says.

"Do I know you?" I ask.

"You do now," he says.

"Well, you don't know me," I say. "Anyone who knows me knows I don't call myself Warren. Nobody calls me Warren."

"I do," he says.

"Fine," I say. "Call me Warren. Who are you?"

"Will you believe me if I tell you?"

"How do I know?"

He laughs. "That's just the right answer."

I don't know what he means by that. But I'm flattered.

And then I know.

It's Jesus.

"My name is Raphael," he says.

"Yeah, right."

He smiles. "I like to name myself after painters."

"I don't know much about painting," I say. "But I like poetry."

"You should," he says.

"Is that an order?" I ask.

He laughs. He has a nice laugh. His eyes laugh along with his voice.

"You probably had enough orders," he says. "In the Army, I mean."

I look down at myself to see if I'm wearing a uniform. I'm not.

"There's a hole in your shirt." He touches it. I can feel the tip of his finger just over my heart.

I expect the hole to close up. It doesn't, but I suddenly feel wonderful. Immortal. It's not a new feeling. It isn't even all that unusual. It's the feeling you get when for a moment you're in harmony with time and space. It's the feeling of being alive. It's the warmth of life.

"Let's change shirts," he says.

I look around. "I guess I didn't bring my duffel."

He smiles. "I meant, let's *exchange* shirts."

I put on his shirt.

He puts on mine.

The hole is still there.

"Tell me the truth," I say. "How did you know my name?"

"A friend of a friend."

"And who might that be?"

"Me," he says, and turns and starts to walk away.

"Wait," I say.

He keeps walking. I'm surprised to see that his feet make prints in the sand.

"Raphael!"

"Call me Ray," he says back.

I follow him along the beach.

It isn't hard to keep up with him. Even for me with a limp. I realize I don't remember this either: getting my right leg wounded. They used to tell us that if you get hit, you won't remember getting hit. They used to tell us that the mind is self-correcting. Or was it self-protective? The body remembers; the mind forgets. Something like that.

I don't even know I have a limp until I start to limp after Jesus.

He's easy to keep up with because he keeps stopping. He's like a little kid on the beach, turning everything into a mystery. Or turning every mystery into something simple.

The tide is halfway in. The sun is halfway up on the distant horizon, balanced for a moment on the edge of this wondrous planet. It frightens me to see it. I know it's made of fire. I fear the fire. And I fear the fire going out.

The beach is covered with everything the last tide brought in and the new tide has not yet taken back. Empty shells, stones, wood, a couple of bricks, nautical rope in neon colors the lobstermen now use, some of the s—— stupid people throw in the ocean, like beer cans, and all the living things that come in with the tide and hope not to get trapped in the sun or eaten by the crying seabirds.

Jesus likes to step on empty shells. He even goes out of his way when he sees a shell, whole or half, lying on the sand, tempting him. So he zigzags a bit as he walks up the beach. This also makes it easier for me to catch up.

"I like to hear them crunch," he says when I finally reach him.

"It's kind of destructive," I say.

"We call them 'shells' for a reason," he answers, and leaves it at that.

"But this . . ." He kneels down and digs two fingers into the wet sand. He feels around in there like someone doing trills on a little keyboard. Sure enough, he comes out with a little muddy ball that looks like a dirty marble. He moves it around his fingers in a circle. The wet dirt begins to fall off. Then he kind of scrubs the thing in his hair. I think how he's getting all this dirt in his hair until I have a memory of Bethie inviting me into the shower with her and when I get in there she's got mud all over her hair and I say, "What the heck is that?" and Bethie laughs and says, "It's clay." She reaches for the plastic bottle. She reads, "Australian Kaolin Clay." Sure enough, after the shower, when we were laying on the bed because we'd had to get out of the shower quick not to leave Dodie alone in her crib for too long, and now we have Dodie cuddled between us, Bethie's hair was so beautiful you'd think it was shining with some inner beauty.

Jesus has perfectly nice hair. But I can't see that it gets all shiny from the mud. It's short hair, not like in the pictures of him. Short like mine. Mine is military and his is short, probably because summer's coming. I know he knows the number of hairs on my head. And probably on his own. Everybody thinks, *Oh, New Hampshire, it must be nice and cool there in the summer.* It can be a furnace. A wet furnace. Not like the desert. Here the sun comes through the haze and leaves you lathered with sweat day and night. There it doesn't separate heat from light.

Bethie's hair is long. Or was. I haven't seen her in more than a year and a half. I don't know if I could bear to see her ever again.

"Look," says Jesus.

I've been thinking so hard about Bethie I expect that Jesus has produced her there for me on the beach.

But when I look, it's at the little marble he's got in his hand. All clean.

"A snail," I say.

Jesus takes a few steps toward the water, where the waves are less waves than they are a blanket being drawn up gently to your chin by your mother tucking you in at night. The sun is almost whole in the sky. It sits on the edge of the Earth held up by nothing but faith. There's a straight line of white light all the way from the sun to Jesus' hand in the water. He rinses off the snail and shakes the water off and presents it to me with another "Look."

"A snail," I say again.

He nods. "A mud whelk. Isn't it beautiful? Look. It's black when it's wet. But when you dry it off it's brown until you look more closely and you see the red, here, along the bulgy part of the whorls. Like people's hair sometimes, you see it in the right light and it has that beautiful red tinge. And look inside, Warren!" He holds it up close to my eyes, like I was an old man. "See the foot in there? The little guy sticks that out when the coast is clear, so to speak, and he walks along looking for algae to eat. There are probably thousands of these right where we're walking. Sometimes there's a strong wave and you're suddenly walking on a carpet of mud whelks."

"I know what you mean." I always tried to avoid stepping on them. I think about how I didn't mind killing people, though. It's hard enough to live in the world. I'm glad I didn't make it.

"Say goodbye," he says, and drops the snail into the water.

"Goodbye," I say, though I feel kind of stupid.

"I was talking to the mud whelk." Jesus smiles at me before he walks back onto the sand and toward some of the rocks that I picture dragged by the glaciers out of Maine and released like animal droppings in long narrow clusters of granite. When the rock is wet it gets dark and slippery. With the tide still out, and the sun just up, and the air clear, the granite is almost pale.

Jesus squats and puts his hand on the rock. His nails are no cleaner than mine. But his fingers are longer. The veins on the back of his hand are the kind guys envy. His hands are almost too strong.

"I love rock," says Jesus.

"I should think so," I say. I'm not being sarcastic, exactly, but I know there's that question about whether the rock the church is built on is Jesus or Peter. I'm ready to vote for Jesus, if he wants me to.

"See this?" He points to pink specks in the granite. "Feldspar. But what I really love is this."

He reaches down between the slabs of rock and picks up a small, darker piece of granite that has a vein of quartz running all the way through its center. "Here." He hands it to me. "Put this in your pocket."

I stick it in there. I go to arrange it in the deepest corner of the pocket the way guys do and I feel something else there. I pull out a couple of what look like little gold rocks.

"What are those?" asks Jesus.

"Bullets," I say.

"Where did you get them?"

"From a woman I met."

"Somebody's mother," says Jesus, like he knows.

"Somebody's mother," I say.

I put the bullets back in my pocket. While I do that, Jesus puts his fingers right into the sand again and comes out this time with what looks like a worm.

"This guy's like you," he says.

"Thanks a lot." Not that I'm bothered by worms. I just don't want to be one.

"They like to be alone," he says.

"Oh."

How does he know? He found me alone. But I think he sees in my soul that I'm a soul alone. I think he knows that everyone's a soul alone. Until we die.

The worm's about three inches long. He holds it from one end. It fights against the air, dancing. "See how it's like the rock," says Jesus.

"It has these little dark eyespots. It's also like that mud whelk, with these bands. It's named after these bands."

"What?"

"Banded. Banded feather duster worm."

"Why feather duster?"

"I have no idea!"

Jesus drops the worm back onto the sand. It wriggles against the hard rock before it slides its soft, gummy body beneath it.

I wonder how many worms this rock has eaten.

Jesus finds a beer bottle. It's got sand in it. He picks it up and shoves it in the pocket of his jeans. "Maybe you need a bottle-deposit law in New Hampshire," he says.

"Whaddya mean, *you*? You're not from *here*?" I ask him, sort of playing around.

"You got me there," he answers.

We walk until we come to our shoes. Two pairs.

Mine are Wellco Schwarzkopf combat boots. Used to be tan. Now they're nearly black with old sweat and for all I know sweet crude Arab oil that's hard to tell from blood, as it should be. We all coveted the Oakley Assault Elite Special Forces boot. They were black to begin with and you could tuck your Army Combat Uniform cargoes under the tongue and look cool. Heck, they're literally cooler than the Norms, and their laces are fire-resistant. But they're shorter too and let the sand in. They were "new soldier" when at least a few of us wanted to honor the "old soldier." Old soldiers are like old gods. They shouldn't be traded for new ones. Not even in the deserts of Kedar.

I don't remember leaving my boots here. I don't know why Jesus' shoes should be next to mine. Or how they got here.

"Are you ready to leave the beach?" he says.

"Not really," I say.

"Why not?"

"It hurts to walk," I lie. I mean, it *does* hurt to walk. But that's not the reason I don't want to leave the beach. I love the beach. I don't know how I got here. But this is the only place I want to be right now.

"Maybe wearing your boots will help," says Jesus.

"I don't think so."

"Sit down." It's an order. As a soldier, I'm used to orders. What I'm not used to is someone who gives an order and then holds out his hand.

I take Jesus' hand and lower myself onto the sand. He kneels down before me and takes one of my boots and pulls out my white PT sock and shakes sand out of the boot and the sock. Then he slips the sock onto my foot and pulls on the boot and ties it just tight enough. By the time I stop to think, *Hey, Jesus is putting on my boot,* he's tied it and is doing the same with the right one.

"Stand up." This time he doesn't give me his hand. This time, when I think I need it more.

But I don't. I stand up, and I realize my right leg doesn't hurt anymore. I take a step, two steps, a few more, away from Jesus and then right back toward him. I'm not limping. "You healed me," I say.

"I think all you needed was to put on your boots."

"I don't think so," I say.

"You just needed the support."

Yeah, I'm thinking, *your* support.

Jesus puts on his own socks and shoes. They aren't sandals, which is just as well, because guys around here who wear sandals with jeans are not guys from around here. But Jesus' shoes aren't either those dainty slip-ons some men wear that leave half the top of their foot exposed and all of their ridiculousness. He's wearing Timberlands. A local product. From Stratham, New Hampshire. Jesus is no fool.

"Let's go," he says. Before I can say anything he adds, "Now that you're healed."

I can't very well refuse now. "Where to?"

"Follow me," he says.

But then he gets behind me.

I know where he wants me to go.

It's not to church.

The dawning of the new day follows us as we leave the ocean and walk into my old life that's my new life. It's dark before us and light behind. We seem to carry the light on our feet, one step at a time.

It isn't far to Bittersweet Lane. But it seems to take forever. I don't want to go there. And there's no place else on earth I want to go more.

The tiny house is dark. But there's a light in the lone kitchen window. We never had a light in the window. But we had lights everywhere else. Bethie never bothered turning them off. I don't like seeing things have changed. Even though I know things have changed completely.

The light isn't a light. It's Bethie. Her face. All I can see is her face in the window. It's the most beautiful face I've ever seen. It always was. But I never told her that. I'm not sure I ever knew it. I'm not sure I ever looked at her before, except to make her disappear. Inside me, I mean. I never looked at her apart from me.

She looks neither happy nor sad. She looks intent on something. It isn't me. She isn't looking at me. She isn't looking at Jesus. She's looking beyond us. Her pale eyes are like pearls beneath the shell of her eyelids. You can't see the ocean from here, though it's not far. But she looks like someone looking out to sea. Looking for someone. Trying to see the visible in the invisible.

She's so young. I never realized how young she is. Or maybe it's that my eyes have grown old. That I've seen too much in the time since I saw her last. Or that, in that time, since she's left me, I've left her too.

What is she doing up at this hour?

Dodie got us up at all hours. But not this hour. By this hour, when the night turned into day, we were always asleep. Finally. We used to joke that a baby lets you go to sleep just in time for you to wake up.

And where is her boyfriend, Ryan? He was my one and only friend and then our friend and then he was hers. How can he let her out of his sight? I would never let her out of my sight. She's been out of my sight for too long.

"Do you see her?" I ask Jesus.

"Who?"

"Bethie."

"I don't see anyone."

"She's like a vision," I say.

"I don't see visions," he says.

"Just snails under the sand."

"That's a good way of putting it."

I look at him, to see what he wants me to do.

He looks at me, to see what I want to do.

I don't know what I want to do.

That is, I know what I want to do. I don't know if I can do it.

Jesus takes my hand. He puts it up to the front door.

We knock.

Softly.

"Come in."

It's the first time I've heard her voice since I left for Fort Bliss. I direct-deposited her my paycheck, including my uniform allowance, but I never called her. Not once over the past year. When I went off to war, I knew I might never come back. So I never looked back. I didn't want to miss what I might never see again. Who I might never see again.

The guys in my unit weren't like that. They were always calling and e-mailing and IM'ing their wives and girlfriends. First from the training at Fort Bliss. Then from sniper school at Fort Benning.

Then from The Mess. I saw one guy get killed by shrapnel while he was IM'ing his wife. His laptop was fine. He had a hole in his neck. I looked at his computer and saw his wife still typing at him. HONEY? HONEY?? HONEY!!! And everybody heard the story about a young female Marine who was webcaming her boyfriend when her body opened up, but nobody believed it.

The Mess is what we called Iraq after they told us in Sensitivity/Diversity Training that it used to be called Mesopotamia. The Mess. Then people began to make up things that The Mess stood for. Aside from The Mess we were all in. There was My Enemy Seems Stupid. Which was kind of lame. My Enemy Seeks Surrender. Which was much better, because the word *Islam* means *surrender*. Not surrender to us, of course, but to the will of the god they worshipped. MESS also meant Miserable Ephemeral Sorry and Sad. I liked that one too, but most soldiers didn't know what *ephemeral* meant, though some of them learned the hard way. And of course there were the dirty ones, which I can't say because I don't, but a lot of them had the word *suck* for the first *S*. I can say that because *suck* is in the Bible. The righteous people suck the hidden treasures out of the sand, like us in The Mess. Or they suck honey out of the rock, which even God says is oil. Or one of those things that's the same in all the Gospels, "Woe unto those women who are with child and who give suck, for there is great sorrow in this land and wrath upon this people." The chaplains loved to preach that because it's the way it was in The Mess and why I was there, so it wouldn't be the same here and Bethie and all the other American mothers could feed our babies without fear or sorrow.

But I just couldn't look back at Bethie and Dodie. It's the wrong way to go to war. Good soldiers have no pasts. Every war destroys the past to save the future. Good soldiers look in only one direction: toward the enemy.

My father taught me that. He was the only one I wrote to. Letter after letter. He was the only one who wrote back. Once or twice. Twice.

I open the flimsy door. The only thing protecting anyone inside is the American flag decal on the cloudy glass. It's faded, like the subdued shoulder-sleeve insignia we wore on tactical, so as not to glow in the dark or the light. The flags we wore we wore reversed, so what the enemy saw coming toward him first would be the shrapnel of our stars.

There's none of those SUPPORT OUR TROOPS magnets either. Magnets come off too easy. Besides, your troops want more than your support. Support is for jockstraps. Soldiers want your blessing. BLESS OUR TROOPS.

The door leads right into the kitchen. It's that small a house. The front door is the back door. *In case of fire, use the winder*, as they say in New Hampshire.

It's warm the way it always was. It smells the way it always did. Like her and her. Bethie and Dodie. There's nothing of Ryan in the air.

There's a light on in the kitchen. Faint, like always. It's one of those lights that hangs from the bottom of a fan. Two-in-ones for people who can't afford one-and-ones. Our little TV had a VCR built in. Lucky I didn't send her the kind of murder tapes I couldn't watch but did watch over in The Mess.

The vision of Bethie's face in the window must have dimmed the light and made the house look dark and empty from outside. She's sitting at the kitchen table. Alone. In an old bathrobe. She has a cup of tea. Her hands are wrapped around it, the way she would in winter. But I can see it's my cup. Or what I used to call "my cup." We had only four cups. One was hers, one was mine, two were for visitors. I know it's my cup because the handle's broken. You have to wrap at least one hand around it to pick it up. Two hands if you're a girl.

Her hair is short. She's cut her long hair off. It's not as short as mine or Jesus'. But her long hair is gone. I imagine it falling to the floor of the tiny bathroom. I think, *That's me.* Falling away from her.

Her face isn't as beautiful as it was in the window. I like it more, because I recognize it. She's an American Northeast girl: dirty-blond hair, pale blue eyes, small nose, a scary mouth, because of how tempting her lips are and how she never put up with any bull. I never looked at other women in the army. I was afraid they might look back.

A terrifying feeling comes over me. It's a feeling of such great love that I don't know what to do or what to say. I never felt this way before. I was afraid to. I never knew her enough to love her like this.

Bethie looks up at me. "You can't be here," she says.

"But I am."

She looks puzzled.

"He's here with me," says Jesus.

Bethie ignores him.

"Go away, War," she says.

"Were you looking for me?"

"When?" she asks. "Where?"

"At the window." I go to the window, not to look out it but to have something to look at that's not her.

"I wasn't at the window. I've been right here the whole time."

"Couldn't sleep?" I ask.

"Don't flatter yourself," she says.

Then she looks at Jesus.

"Who's your friend?" she asks me.

"This is Ray," I say, because that's what he wants me to say. I figure those who know him will know him.

"How come you're wearing War's T-shirt, Ray?" she says.

"I couldn't let him see you with a hole in his shirt," says Jesus.

"You actually remember my T-shirt?" I say to her.

"Don't flatter yourself," she says again. Then she adds: "I remember everything about you. Everything. You never had holes in your shirts."

"Well, I still don't. Look. Ray gave me his shirt."

Bethie shakes her head. That's to let me know she doesn't think there's more between me and Jesus than there is. Though of course there's more than she can imagine.

"Were you on the ground there too?" she asks Jesus.

"On the ground?" says Jesus.

"In *Iraq*." Jesus doesn't know but I do that she's getting exasperated.

"In a manner of speaking," Jesus answers.

"What the hell is that supposed to mean?" says Bethie. I recognize *that* tone. I'm kind of glad it's directed at him and not me.

Jesus handles it pretty well. He laughs. "I know it's not a very direct answer. But it's the best I can do."

"Intelligence?" says Bethie.

"Are you asking, 'Do I have it?' or 'Was I in it?' " Jesus says.

"What a wise guy!" That was always one of Bethie's favorite sayings. It cut both ways.

"I'll take that as a compliment," says Jesus.

"Don't," says Bethie.

"Then how about a cup of tea?" asks Jesus. "I'll take a cup of tea instead."

I hope she gives it to him.

I remember the story from Bible-study group of Jesus visiting Martha, and Martha complaining she has to do all the work. Mary and Lazarus just hang around. It was like living together. Not relatives, I mean, but a woman and a man. Bethie and me. *Who does this and who does that*. I sometimes think we never bothered to get married because we never figured that out: *Who does this and who does that*. The things you have to do in life between the times you do the things you love in life. Also, I wanted to wait so I could take total care of her. I wish I'd told her that, instead of just being quiet about the whole thing. I was good at being quiet. Sometimes it's good to be good at saying the important things.

I also remember the Iraqi Army soldiers with their chai-stained teeth and their sweet breath.

"What kind?" Bethie asks Jesus.

"What are you drinking?"

"Chamomile."

"Couldn't sleep?" Jesus asks the same question I did.

"Never," she answers, and gets up to make the tea.

"What about you?" she asks me.

"I could never sleep either," I answer.

"Wise guy," she says and waves a tea bag at me.

Now I know I'm home.

I watch her at the stove. She turns on the gas with one hand and with the other takes a wooden match out of the old box hanging on the wall and strikes it against the side of the box. The head of the match explodes. I hate the sight but love the smell. The smell is like home, not war. She brings the match down to the burner cap. The stove is so old that only one part of the ring flames up. A thin arrow of fire finds the bottom of the kettle. It moves against it like a feather. Bethie stands there waiting for the water to boil.

"You have the patience of a saint," I say to her, and look over at Jesus and give him a wink.

Bethie says to me, "And you could never stay put, you son-of-a—"

"Monica," says Jesus, as if he'd been thinking about it. "Saint Monica."

"Never heard of her," I say gratefully. I didn't want him to hear Bethie swear at me.

"b——," she finishes up anyway. Except she uses the whole word.

I say to Jesus, "She's angry with me because I went away."

She turns around from the stove and looks right at me. "I was angry with you because you were always going away. Every day you went away."

"It was just to the d—— beach," I say.

"That was every night," she says. "And then when you really went away I never heard from you."

"I had my paycheck sent to you," I say.

"Like I wanted to sleep with George Washington!" She shakes her head. If only she had laughed, I would have laughed too. She could be funny or sarcastic and sometimes you never knew which.

"Where's Jody?" I say, like I was changing the subject but not really.

"Who?"

I was hoping she'd ask. Now I'll get to sing the song I've been rehearsing ever since I heard from my father that Bethie'd took up with Ryan: "Ain't no use in goin' home. Jody's got your girl alone."

"Very funny," says Bethie. She has a tear in her eye. She turns back to the stove.

I explain to Jesus, "They don't call them Dear John letters anymore. Probably because the army's filled with people named Felipe and Malik and Jessica. It could be Dear Anybody. It would be politically incorrect to say Dear John. So it's always about Jody. Jody's always the one who steals your girl. Or, if you're Jessica, your man. That's why it's Jody. Jody could be a woman or a man. So where *is* he?" I ask her.

Bethie turns around with the kettle in her hand. It's steaming. Jesus must have performed a miracle to get the water to boil this fast. Bethie pours water into the two guest cups. You can tell they're the guest cups because their colors haven't faded as much from washing. I hate being given a guest cup in my own home.

When I see this tea's not chamomile but the same old Salada, I don't feel as bad.

I walk up to her to get mine.

"How's your leg?" she asks.

"See!" I say to Jesus.

"He thinks I cured him," Jesus says to Bethie.

"Are you a doctor?" Bethie takes Jesus his tea. She puts it down in front of him but doesn't slide it toward him. She's not sure of this guy yet.

"In a manner of speaking," he says.

"Someone has to kill the enemy," she says. Bethie was always more patriotic even than me. When I told her I was going to enlist, she told me that she would go and I could stay home with Dodie. Now I wish she had. That way, I'd be here waiting for her. Instead of this. Her not waiting for me.

"And the enemy's enemy," Jesus says.

"There's only one enemy," Bethie says.

"Those who kill the innocent," says Jesus.

"The ones who would hurt the ones I love," says Bethie.

Once that was me. Now it's Dodie and who knows who else.

"Who told you?" I ask her.

"About your leg? That was your father. You wrote to him but not to me."

"I just couldn't," I said. "I was afraid."

"You should have been." I know we're talking about two different things.

"He's at the pharmacy." She changes the subject back, either to get away from my father or toward Ryan. Bethie's the kind of girl who faces things. Directly. She knows we have to deal with Ryan. It's Ryan who stands between us.

"He works the night shift. So many drugstores opened around here that instead of having shorter hours they have longer ones. First Walgreens was open twenty-four hours. Then CVS. Rite-Aid. Brooks. Osco opened in the supermarket, so the supermarket started staying open twenty-four hours. The funny thing is, you drive by them in the middle of the night and the parking lots are still half full. If you go inside them, there are always people there walking up and down the aisles. They stay for hours. They're like ghosts. Ghosts looking for medicine."

"Or deodorant," I say.

Bethie laughs. She says, "Oh, War." She almost puts her head on my arm, the way she used to when I'd make her laugh in the school corridor between classes and we weren't even going out.

"So what time does he get off?" I ask.

"Jody?" she says sarcastically.

"Ryan," I say. I've been rehearsing his name in my head ever since I learned from my father's letter that he'd moved in with her. "Nothing to stop him," said my father. "You never married that girl."

"He gets off at eight."

I look at my watch. It's the Timex Military Quartz. Ugly and simple. Other guys preferred the Black SWAT that said MIL-TEC on its face or one of those huge Casios that protected you against every shock except looking into the eyes of an enemy with ordnance strapped around his chest and a wire wrapped tight around his middle finger.

My watch has stopped. Who knows when that happened.

"What time is it?" I ask.

Jesus doesn't wear a watch. What if he did?

I look at his wrists for one of those WWJD wristbands. That would be even stranger than a watch. But not as strange as the WWWD wristbands some guys wore. That stood for What Would Dubya Do.

"It's five fifty," Bethie says.

"So early," I say.

"The longest day of the year," says Jesus.

"Just like every other day," I say.

"It's the first day of summer," says Bethie. "You always loved summer."

Oh God, I want to hold her in my arms. How could I have known that there are parts of us that are taken in by other people? And that they become us, and we become them? I was brought up to think that a man stands alone. Is alone. There was only you and God.

My father didn't cry when my mother died. Maybe because he didn't realize that part of him had died too.

I didn't cry when my mother died. Because I didn't want my father to see me crying.

Such a little thing: that Bethie would remember a little thing I loved.

"Don't," she says and holds up her hands.

That makes two of them who can read my mind.

I met Bethie junior year of high school. We were in the same English class. English was the only subject I liked. I was good in it. I was terrible in everything else. My father said he would rather I failed everything than pass only English. He thought English was for people who thought that words spoke louder than actions. He said words accomplished nothing good. A man should be known by what he did, not by what he said. Or read.

My English teacher was Mr. Smith. I met him and Bethie on the same day. I saw them for the first time at the same moment.

I walked into class that first day of school and there was the teacher, an old guy, I thought, a kind of dumpy man with a round stomach and half-moon reading glasses perched near the end of his nose and white hairs flying off the sides of his head like they wanted to escape to wherever all the other hairs on his head had disappeared to.

He was talking to a girl. She had long hair then and had her back to me so what I could really see was the way Mr. Smith was looking down through his glasses into her face. He looked like he was memorizing her. He had his mouth shut but his eyes were open and dancing and blinking and staring straight down into hers.

He didn't care he had a class to teach and that dozens of the rest of us were filing in and trying to figure out where to sit so he would or wouldn't call on us. All the others sat in groups, two or more here, two or more there. I didn't care where I sat, so long as I didn't have to sit next to anyone I knew. I'd always wished they had desks in schools that didn't have other desks near them.

I loved to be alone. Especially in English. I didn't want people interrupting my thoughts. I didn't want anyone watching me read or write. I don't know why; maybe it was because I always had to read in private at home, because my father said he didn't want to catch me with a book, the way other fathers said they didn't want to catch their kids with a beer. When my father said, "You can't shoot a book," he didn't mean at it. My father knew that the world got purified by guns more than by books. And damaged by books more than by guns. The sword was mightier than the pen. He liked it that way. At the same time, he would tell anyone, especially anyone who wanted to ban guns, "Guns don't kill people. Books kill people." He meant books of belief. He was right. One reason I was in The Mess was because different people believed different books. So far as my father was concerned, there was the Christian Bible. Everything else was a novel. He hated novels. He used to tell me, "Don't go into any house that has more books than guns. You could get badly hurt."

I didn't take a seat. That was normal for me. I always waited for everyone else to sit down first. But this time I wasn't waiting for the others. I was waiting to see what it could have been about this girl's face that made Mr. Smith stare into it like it was the sun and he didn't care if it blinded him.

Then he smiled. He smiled at her, even as he looked up from her over his strange little glasses and then up over her head, which wasn't very hard because she was even shorter than he was. It seemed to register with him for the first time that there were other people there. But he just kept on smiling. I knew it wasn't because he saw the rest of us. I knew he was smiling at us because of whatever joy this girl had brought to him. She was part of him already.

"Take your seats, please," said Mr. Smith.

Actually, the only two people still standing were me and the girl. She turned around then to look for a seat. I saw her face for the first time.

She had that American girl face, round and soft and a little mean, mean in a good way. I had a narrow face with just enough stubble even then not to look stupid wearing it. Though I would have looked stupid trying to shave it off. My hair was short. Hers was long.

She walked down the aisle toward where I stood at the back. She looked at me and she didn't look at me. I couldn't tell her eyes from mine. I saw her seeing me for the first time and thought I was seeing myself for the first time. Not in a mirror. In the air. In the world. In my life.

The two empty desks weren't in the last row, which was where I always liked to sit. They were in the next-to-the-last row. Worse, they weren't next to each other. They were separated by one desk. A guy I didn't recognize sat there. He was playing drumrolls on his arm with his fingers and looking out the window at the butt-end of summer vacation waving goodbye to him.

"Would you mind?" said the girl.

I got out of her way.

"Not you," she said to me.

"You," she said to him.

The guy got up out of his seat. Just like that.

"Thanks, Elvin," she said.

"Oh," I said, "you know him?"

"Not really," she said, and sat down where Elvin had been sitting.

"Have a seat," she said to me, and pointed at the desk next to hers.

I sat down.

"Good," she said.

That was all she said until class was over. She never even looked at me. Or tried to. She listened to Mr. Smith and took some notes, while I couldn't hear a word he said and looked at her the whole time out of the corner of my eye, which meant I couldn't really see her at all. She was not the sort of person you could get anything out of if you didn't try to get everything.

When the bell rang she stood right up and hugged her books to her chest. She reached into the middle of them and pulled a piece of paper out of a notebook.

"Here." She handed them to me. "You're going to need this."

It was the page of notes she'd taken during class.

I followed her out of class. She seemed to know I would. She looked over her shoulder for me.

Our school was so overcrowded that all corridors on all floors were one-way. It didn't matter if your next class was right next to the class that just ended. If it was not in a counterclockwise direction, you had to walk around the entire school to get to it.

So there was only one direction we could go. We walked next to each other. There were no people coming toward us, but some of the people coming from behind were running like crazy to try to get to a distant class. It was usually impossible for two unclenched people not to get separated, which is probably why so many people in the high school hooked up on the first day: not because they were in love, but so they had someone to hold on to in the corridors between classes. Yet no one came between me and this girl. We didn't talk to each other. Even our sleeves didn't touch. All we did was walk next to each other. While around us, flying past, went what seemed like the whole school. The entire population of the world.

Pretty soon there was no one left. All was quiet. We were alone in the corridor, right back where we'd begun. In front of Mr. Smith's classroom. The door was closed. The bell had rung. Next class had begun.

"So you have a free period too?" she said.

"No," I said. "History."

She laughed. As she laughed, she leaned toward me, the way you do toward something that makes you happy. She leaned toward me until her head was on my arm. She wasn't tall enough for her head to reach my shoulder.

That was how we touched for the first time.

That night I looked at her notes from Mr. Smith's class.

> *"Don't think of this class as English. Think of it as Language."*
>
> *"Language is not life. It is the expression of life."*
>
> *"All words are beautiful. But not all words are used beautifully."*
>
> *"Think before you write."*
>
> *"Don't think before you talk."*
>
> *"Except to me."*
>
> *Mr. Smith is the greatest teacher ever.*
>
> *The boy next to me is not paying attention.*
>
> *Except to me.*

Reading her notes was the only homework I did in any of my subjects. I read them over and over. Then I folded them up and put them in my wallet. I carried them in my wallet to Iraq.

Now I don't have a wallet. I don't know what happened to it. I don't know how I could have paid to get here or how I got here. I have nothing in my pockets. Except for the little golden bullets and the piece of granite Jesus gave me with the vein of quartz running through it.

I take the rock out of my pocket. I say, "Look, I have a present for Dodie."

Jesus reaches over and touches my hand. "Not now," he says. "Put it away."

I can't believe he's telling me I can't see my own child. I feel the way I did in the war, like hurting someone who wants to hurt me. I stand up the way men do when they're angry. I knock over my tea.

"Ray's right," says Bethie. "Let Dodie sleep."

"Oh," I say. "Sleep. I forgot how early it is."

I sit back down. I put the rock back in my pocket. In that order.

"Thanks, Ray," says Bethie.

She comes over and mops up the tea with a dishcloth.

"Such a slob," she says to me.

I didn't see her again until Mr. Smith's next English class, two days later. I looked for her everywhere. I hunted her through the corridors of all the floors of the main school building. I peered through the windows of the annex trailers used as auxiliary classrooms. I stood stock still and waited for her like the sniper I would become.

I even went to all my classes in case she might be in one. Then I skipped my math class before English so I could be the first one there. So I could save her the desk next to mine. So we could sit where we had sat before. So I could feel I was alive again.

My heart leapt when I saw she'd arrived there before me. But she wasn't saving me a desk. She hadn't even put her own books down. She was up there again with Mr. Smith. He was looking into her face through his glasses as he had before and as I realized I wanted to look into it, with wonder and pleasure.

The bell rang. The other students started coming in. Mr. Smith looked over the girl's head again and then looked back into her face with a kind of regretful smile this time.

"Take your seats, please," he said.

This time the girl touched his hand before she turned around.

But this time she wasn't looking for a seat.

This time she was looking for me.

I knew that because when she saw me, she made a little gesture with her head as if my arm was right there next to her. Then she spread open the first two fingers of her right hand like a peace sign and pointed at our two desks. Our same two desks.

I put my books down on one of them and my backside down on the other. I watched her walk down the aisle. I tried to think of what to say to her.

"You'll do anything for an A," I said, and gestured with my head toward Mr. Smith. I tried to say it like it wasn't necessary for me to give Mr. Smith the benefit of the doubt.

"He's my father," she said.

When Bethie mops up the tea, she bends over the table. Her bathrobe spreads open at the top. I can see she's wearing an old flannel nightgown that's white with pink flower petals. Even when I'd left, way more than a year ago, it was worn so smooth I sometimes mistook it for her skin. I know she always puts it away for the summer. This is the first day of summer. She wore it right up until the last minute. Or she wore it for me. But I can hardly bear to see it. If her body were to disappear from inside it, that nightgown would still be her. So would everything else she touches. Or that touches her.

I put my hands flat and hard down upon the old kitchen table. To keep from reaching out just to touch her nightgown. But also to put my hands where her hands had been, here on the table.

It's a sad way, I realize, to get to hold hands.

Jesus knows. He may not have much experience with women . . . I mean, with girlfriends. But he knows women. He knows women will be there when all the men have run away. The only ones left when he died were women. It was women who got to hear him say the last words he said. I used to think my favorites were "Today you will be with me in paradise." But the words I always kept hearing in my mind were "Woman, behold your son." Every time I did something I was proud of, I would say silently, not to myself but to my mother, "Woman, behold your son." Is there anything we want as much as for the dead to be able to see us?

Jesus leans over. He puts his hands flat on the backs of my hands. When he does that, I can actually feel beneath my own hands not the old tabletop where I've been imagining I could feel Bethie's hands, but Bethie's hands themselves. Bethie's hands are all I can feel. The small bird bones, the soft skin between her fingers, the curve of her nails and the way at least one of them always had a nick in it, for scratching my back, she would say. I don't feel Jesus' hands at all. But I can see them, hiding mine.

Bethie can see them too. She stares at our hands together. But she doesn't say anything. She knows that I'm touching her through Jesus.

We all know it's the only way I'm allowed to touch her.

The strangest thing about Mr. Smith being Bethie's father was not that he actually *was* her father, and not that I sometimes wondered who I loved more, Bethie or him, but that even though I got to know him really well, and even though he's Dodie's grandfather, I always called him Mr. Smith.

That day, when she first told me he was her father, I was so surprised I didn't know what to say. And by the time I figured out what to say, I couldn't say it, because Mr. Smith had called the class to order.

He said, "Well, class, I know you'll all be very happy when I tell you that we're going to be reading and discussing some poetry."

Groans from the boys. The girls didn't groan. What they did was worse. They rolled their eyes and looked at each other with that kind of *duh* expression girls use when they want you to think they find other people stupid, and they don't know just how even stupider they look doing it.

Mr. Smith smiled. He looked delighted.

"Who," he said, "can tell me what language is?"

One guy put up his hand and said, "Words?"

"Dear me, dear me," said Mr. Smith. He was still smiling; I didn't know why.

I knew that Mr. Smith's daughter knew the answer. But I also knew that because she was his daughter, she wasn't going to be the one to give it.

I raised my hand.

"Yes." Mr. Smith pointed at me. I didn't usually speak up in class. I didn't like teachers pointing at me. But I wanted Mr. Smith to notice me.

"Language is the expression of life," I said.

"Yes!" Mr. Smith just about leapt out of his little shoes. He had small feet. It's true. So did his daughter. He was short too, like her. "Yes!" he said again, and this time he smiled at me. "Language is the expression of life. And life is nowhere more beautifully expressed than in poetry. Remember, class, how I told you that all words are beautiful but not all words are used beautifully? Well, in poetry, good poetry, all words are used beautifully. And in poetry every single word supports every other word. Poetry is the way humanity would be if humanity were as beautiful as poetry. A great poem is not the expression of life. A great poem *is* life."

He picked up a book from his desk. It was an old book. I could hear it when he opened it, creaking and sighing like an old man getting out of a chair. The boards that held its pages together were wrinkled like an old man's face. Mr. Smith held the book in one hand and tried to smooth his hair down. Then he held the book in the other hand and tried to smooth down the hair on the other side of his head. His hair didn't obey him any more than I figured the class would when it came time to read poetry.

He looked down into the book through his little glasses. A smile spread over his round, rosy face. He shook his head, the way you do when something's too good to be true. Then he nodded his head, the way you do when the thing too good to be true turns out to be true.

"Oh, class, you're gonna love this!" he said. He turned that smile of his out of the book and onto us. His smile made me smile. It made his daughter smile too. But from what I could see from where I sat, it made the rest of the class look at him with that dumb look kids share with each other when they don't understand something and want some company in their ignorance.

Mr. Smith knew. He said, "Hey, relax. I'm not going to test you on this. You don't have to read anything yourself. I'm just going to read to you. You can listen or not listen. Or you can start not listening. I guarantee you, everyone's going to be listening before I'm done."

He held the book up in front of him, in one hand, so it was spread open like a piece of music he was about to play.

He cleared his throat.

He smiled over the top of the book at us, his class, spreading his smile from one side of the room to the other.

Then he said, "Oh, by the way. This poem doesn't have a title. Titles are nothing more than advertisements. This poet *never* used titles. And she certainly didn't use the numbers I'll tell you about some other class. So when we refer to this poem, we refer to it, as we will with all this poet's work, by its first line. Or part of its first line. So what we call this poem is . . ." Mr. Smith took a breath and opened his eyes wide behind his small, round glasses. "We call this poem WILD NIGHTS!"

That's how he said it. WILD NIGHTS! He just about shouted it. *WILD NIGHTS!*

The combination of his shouting and the words themselves, WILD NIGHTS, made the whole class jump. The people who were sitting there with vacant expressions on their faces now opened their eyes wide. And those who were pretending to be about to doze off, to show how bored they planned to be to have poetry read to them, they jumped the highest.

Mr. Smith was no fool. WILD NIGHTS! He knew how to open eleventh-graders' hearts, or some other part of their bodies, in order to find his way into their tiny brains.

"Wild nights! Wild nights!
Were I with thee,
Wild nights should be
Our luxury!

"Futile the winds
To a heart in port,
Done with the compass,
Done with the chart.

"Rowing in Eden!
Ah! the sea!
Might I but moor
To-night in thee!"

When he finished, Mr. Smith looked up at us over his half-glasses. I realized he never took off those glasses. They were a part of his face. He was always ready to read something. A book. His daughter's face. A poem out loud. And he was always ready to look up over those glasses. At the world that books and people came from. Mr. Smith could see everything. He made you believe that he could understand everything.

He kept looking at us as he closed the book. It was so old you expected to see dust fly out of it. But all it did was make a solid pop, not like paper and not like the wood the paper was made from, but like granite, hard and final.

Then, silence.

"No," said somebody finally.

"More," said somebody else.

Mr. Smith grinned triumphantly.

His daughter next to me smiled only at me, with tears in her eyes.

It was a short poem, but it had seemed to last forever. I looked at the clock. Class was almost over. The little poem had absorbed eternity. How long had we been sitting there in silence?

"I'm not going to ask you to say what the poem means," said Mr. Smith, "because nobody knows what it means. People have been arguing about what this poem means for more than a century. They can't even agree on who the *Thee* is at the end — is it the lover or the sea? they wonder. To me, it's God. But no one knows for sure what the poet meant. And the poem itself is almost a hundred and fifty years old. It was written by a thirty-year-old woman who lived not far from here, over in western Massachusetts. She wrote almost two thousand poems. Only half a dozen were published, and those without her knowledge. She had no desire for fame, if it's possible for any of you to believe that someone who could have been famous chose not to be. Now, of course, she's probably the most famous American poet who ever lived. I think you might be interested in some of her other work. Poems that begin like this: 'I'm Nobody! Who are you?' 'I dwell in Possibility.' Here, you're gonna love this one: 'I felt a Cleaving in my Mind — As if my Brain had split . . .' and believe me, class, she wasn't talking about having too many beers. I think you know better than I what she was talking about — 'I felt a cleaving in my mind, as if my brain had *split*.' You know *exactly* what she's talking about, don't you? And how about this! 'I felt a Funeral, in my Brain.' Probably the way you felt when I said we were going to be reading some poetry. And *this*! 'I like a look of Agony.' That's definitely about looking in the mirror after a night of too many beers. But here's a more optimistic one: 'The Brain — is wider than the Sky.' No, that's not about drugs. It's about God.

"Speaking of God, He's about to ring the bell for the end of class. Sometime I'll read you one of her poems about Jesus. I know we're not supposed to talk about God and Jesus in a public school. Well, tell your parents Mr. Smith is going to read about Jesus. Tell them that today you discovered the work of Emily Dickinson. And for that you can just thank God."

At that moment the bell rang.

Mr. Smith looked up at the ceiling the way a ballplayer looks up at the sky when he's just hit a home run. But he didn't seem grateful. He didn't want the class to end.

Neither did anyone else.

Except for me. I wanted it to end. Not because I hadn't loved it — it had been the best class I was ever in, in my whole life. But I desperately wanted a chance to say what I'd finally figured out to say and hadn't had a chance to say to the girl next to me after she'd told me that Mr. Smith was her father.

Now, with the class over, I got a chance to say it: "So you must be *Miss* Smith."

She looked at me. Then she looked at her father. Then she looked back at me. I could see she was working very hard not to laugh. I've always blessed her for that.

"That's right," she said. "Bethany. Bethany Smith."

"I've never known anyone named Bethany," I said. "What do people call you?"

"People call me a lot of things," she said. "Cute. Stuck up. Cold."

"Cold?"

"Cold," she said again. "As in hot."

"Hot?"

"Haven't you ever noticed that the only girls boys call cold are the ones they first call hot?"

"I don't listen to what boys say about girls."

"How come?"

"Because the things they say have no relation to the things they feel."

"Bethie," she said.

"What?"

"That's what people call me. Bethie."

. . .

Jesus says to her, "Do you have anything to eat?"

"Like what?" says Bethie.

I have to laugh. This is just like her. She'll do anything for you until you ask her to. If you say, "Where's dinner?" there won't be any dinner. If you don't say anything, there will probably be dinner. Bethie can cook. But not to order.

"Anything," Jesus answers.

"No," says Bethie. "Nothing. I didn't have a chance to go shopping." She looks at me like it's my fault. "Besides," she says to Jesus, "you don't look like you eat much."

"Oh, no," says Jesus. "I'm hungry all the time."

"You men are all the same," says Bethie.

Jesus nods.

I know what he's doing. He's telling her he's real. He did the same thing when he came back from the dead. He's not going to ask her to touch him. I know from seeing him when we changed shirts that he doesn't have any wounds to show her. He's just going to ask for something to eat.

"Check out the fridge," Jesus says to her.

Bethie shakes her head, but she does get up.

The refrigerator is shorter than she is. It's old and almost round on top and it's so nervous about dying it never stops shaking. When Bethie opens the door, I expect to see food falling out the way fish fell out of the disciples' nets in the sea of Tiberias. A miracle! Of course . . . Jesus standing on the beach, just the way he had when he came to me and I didn't know at first who he was.

Except the refrigerator's empty. Or almost. There's one egg in the egg tray. A little milk. Butter pads from some restaurant. Yogurt, because Dodie always loved yogurt.

"What did I tell you?" says Bethie.

"You told me there was nothing," says Jesus. "How about I make an omelet?"

"Yeah, Ray," says Bethie, "make yourself a one-egg omelet."

Jesus takes the food out of the refrigerator. He finds the spatula and a frying pan. He holds up the frying pan and says, "Do you have anything bigger?"

"It's one egg, Ray," says Bethie.

"But it's an omelet," says Jesus.

"Forget about it," says Bethie.

"Do you have a bigger frying pan?" Jesus asks me.

"I don't live here anymore," I say.

"You never knew where anything was even when you did live here," says Bethie.

"Only in the kitchen," I say. "I knew where other stuff was. I knew where all the gardening stuff was."

"We never *had* a garden," says Bethie. "We never had room for a window box, let alone a garden."

"I still knew where the gardening stuff was."

"Yeah, under the bed," says Bethie.

"Hey," I say, "you knew where it was too!"

She laughs. She doesn't want to, but she laughs. I think for a moment, *I have her back. I have her back.*

She gets up. She bends to the low shelves next to the exposed pipes of the kitchen sink.

"Here." She hands Jesus a giant frying pan.

"When did we get that?" I ask.

Then I realize I shouldn't have. I'm afraid it's something from when she began to live with Ryan.

"We had it the whole time," she says. "You *ate* out of it, War."

"Such a slob," I say.

Jesus strikes a match. The light fills the room.

A couple of weeks after I met her, I got up the courage to ask Bethie out. It was after school. We were sitting in my truck. I was about to drive her home.

I said, "Will you go out with me?"

"Out where?"

"Out on a date."

"I don't go out on dates."

"Neither do I," I said.

"Let's keep it that way," she said.

"But —" I began.

"War," she interrupted, "we're together all the time. When exactly did you want to have this date?"

"I don't know," I said. "I just wanted to have it. I want you to be my girlfriend."

She leaned over the gearshift and touched her head to my arm. "I'm something better than your girlfriend."

"What's that?"

"I'm your friend."

"I have a friend," I said.

"Now you have me too," she said.

While Jesus makes his omelet, I sit there at the little kitchen table with Bethie. I can't think of anything to say. So I say, "We're like some old married couple. We don't have anything to say to each other."

"But we're not married," says Bethie.

"That's my fault," I say.

"Mine too," says Bethie.

"How do you figure?" I ask.

"Did you think the only way to get married is for the guy to ask the girl?" she says kind of fiery.

"I never thought about it."

"Then I guess it's your fault after all," she says. "Besides, War . . ."

"What?" The way she hesitated, I know, just know, she's going to be asking me to marry her. Better late than never.

"I'm going to marry Ryan," she says.

"When?" I ask, like an idiot. Like knowing the date will help make it never.

"I don't know," she says. "Soon. Any day now. We have the license. We just have to pick a time and place."

"Doesn't sound like much of a wedding," I say.

"I never wanted a wedding," she says. "I just wanted to get married."

"I was going to marry you when I got back from the war," I say.

"And who did you tell that to? Certainly not me. And not your father. Or my father. Who did you tell that to, War?"

"God, I guess," I say.

"Well, I never heard from either of you."

Jesus turns around from the stove with the huge frying pan held out in front of him. "Who's ready for some omelet?"

My friend was Ryan. He was the one real friend I had before I met Bethie.

Or after.

You don't have friends in the Army. During training, there's too much competition. In war, there's too much loss. And fear of loss.

I met Ryan the same day my mother died.

I got called down to the principal's office. I was in fourth grade, nine years old. It was my favorite grade ever. The girls were reading about Fudge and Superfudge. The other boys were reading about hatching dragons. I was reading about a boy in the girl's bathroom and about how a man named Ulysses came home from the greatest adventures ever and killed all the men who wanted to marry his wife and then killed all their relatives who came to kill Ulysses for killing *their* relatives.

I was a good boy and a lousy student. If all the lousy students got called down to the principal's office, the principal's office would have to be about as big as the whole school.

So I figured I was being called down to the principal's office for being a good boy. I believed in Jesus and in my country and in my parents. Not that the principal could have known that. He didn't know me. But then, I didn't know him either.

His name was Mr. Strone. He looked different from the way he did up on the assembly-hall stage. There, he was like the president or something. In his office, he looked small. His suit was the same brown color as the walls. He looked like he wanted to disappear.

"Your father wants to talk to you," Mr. Strone said.

I looked around. There was only Mr. Strone and a lady whose name I didn't know who had followed me into his office and was standing so close behind me I scared her when I turned around.

"On the phone," said Mr. Strone.

He looked at the phone on his desk. There was a red light blinking on it. Mr. Strone seemed afraid of the phone. He pointed at it, for me to pick it up. His finger was shaking when he pressed the red blinking button.

"Hello," I said into the phone.

"Oh, War."

"Dad?" It didn't sound like him.

"Mom," he said.

I was confused. It was a man on the phone. Not my mother. Who was it?

"Hi," I said.

"She's dead. Your mother's dead."

"Oh, Dad." I still didn't know it was him. But what else could I say?

"By her own hand," he said.

All I could see was my mother's beautiful hand, near my face. All I could hear in my head was Paul sending his greetings to Jesus, with his own hand.

"What does that mean?" I asked my father.

"She took her own life." he said.

"Where did she take it?" I asked.

"To Heaven," he said.

The lady behind me put her hand on my shoulder. I realized she was there to catch me. I didn't want her to catch me. I didn't want her to touch me.

I didn't want to touch another human being for the rest of my life.

I started to walk away, out of the office.

"Mrs. Witherspoon will give you a ride home," said Mr. Strone.

"I want my father to pick me up," I said.

"He's in no condition to drive," said Mr. Strone.

"How do you know?" I asked.

Mr. Strone looked around his big office for an answer. "Because of what happened," he said.

"I want my father," I said.

Mr. Strone shook his head. "He told us to help you get home."

"His truck must have broke down," I said.

All the other ladies who worked in the office outside Mr. Strone's office were standing up. They must have been waiting for me. They looked at me the way they must have thought my mother would have looked at me if she could have known I'd got the news I'd got. But she must not have known. Otherwise, she wouldn't have done what she'd done.

"You poor child," one of the ladies said.

I was not the kind of kid who swore. Not out loud. Sometimes I swore inside. I wanted to swear at that lady. But I swore to myself.

"Screw you!"

It was loud enough to make all the ladies instantly lose their expressions of sympathy. They looked slapped.

I thought maybe the words had leaked out of me until I saw another kid sitting there. He was small and looked like he'd been eating chalk.

"Thanks," I said to him.

He nodded at me before one of the ladies grabbed him by the arm and pulled him into Mr. Strone's office.

Mrs. Witherspoon was more gentle with me. She tried to hold my hand on the way to her car in the principal's-office lot.

She couldn't think of a thing to say as she drove me home. She even had the directions all written down.

"Who was that kid?" I asked her.

"Not somebody you'd want to know," she said, and then she didn't say another word until she saw police cars and an ambulance in front of my house. "This must be it."

We had a large American flag flying on a tall pole in our front meadow. As we drove up, my father was standing with its ropes in his hands. His hands were high over his head, adjusting the ropes. He was so tall, and his arms were so strong, that I thought he was about to tear the flag from the pole and the pole from the sky and the sky from Heaven. He was looking straight up. I couldn't see his eyes but could follow them. They were empty and angry and dry with pain. He moved both hands delicately. A little on this rope, a little on that, he brought the flag down. He brought the sky down with it. The clouds came together and the wind kicked up and the clouds swarmed toward the earth. The air darkened.

When he had the flag at half-staff, he secured the ropes. His forearms knotted as he knotted the ropes. His forearms had always excited me. They would have made me afraid if my father had been someone to be afraid of. But he wasn't. He was the strongest man in the world. His arms had made me want to lock myself within them.

He took a step back and looked up at the flag and shot a hand to his head and saluted the flag.

"There," I heard him say as I approached him. "There."

I went up to him and wrapped my arms around his waist and put my head on his chest. I waited to feel him put his arms around me. I wanted him to pull me into him so hard that I would disappear. But he didn't. I guess he couldn't.

I let go of him. I stepped back to look at him. He was staring up, not at the flag but at the ever-darkening sky.

"Rain," he said. "Goddamn it, rain!"

It got as dark as night.

But it didn't rain.

. . .

The omelet Jesus made not only fills the giant frying pan, it hangs over the edge like the brim of a yellow hat.

"Are you kidding me?" says Bethie.

"We don't have to eat it all," says Jesus.

"That can't be one egg," says Bethie.

"Sure it is," says Jesus.

"Give me a break," says Bethie.

"Where are the plates?" I ask.

Bethie shakes her head and laughs.

Jesus points to a cupboard and says, "I'll bet they're there."

They are. I set the table. I'm glad to have a chance to do something. I want this to be my home again.

I find a knife. Jesus puts the frying pan down on the counter. I cut the omelet into three pieces, like a peace sign without the fletching shaft. I put a piece on the three plates.

Bethie stares at her omelet. It looks like a giant slice of golden pizza. "Tell me the truth," she says to Jesus.

"I used Eggstender." Jesus bows his head, as if he's embarrassed and kind of proud to be telling his little secret.

"I don't get it," says Bethie.

"*Eggstender,*" says Jesus. He backs up his chair and reaches behind himself to get a bottle between the burners of the stove. It's the beer bottle he picked up on the beach. It's filled with what looks like sand. He hands it to Bethie.

"Never heard of it." Bethie licks her finger and sticks it into the neck of the bottle and turns the bottle on its side. "Who cares about making eggs more tender anyway?"

"Not *tender,*" says Jesus. "Egg*stend*er. Like *extend*. It makes the eggs go further."

"Oh," says Bethie. "Kind of like Hamburger Helper."

"But without the cornstarch," says Jesus.

Bethie licks her finger. "Still too much salt," she says.

"Taste the actual omelet," says Jesus.

Bethie takes a forkful. "Very tender," she says.

"I was *afraid* I gave it the wrong name," says Jesus.

"It's absolutely delicious, Ray," says Bethie. Egg is hanging over her bottom lip.

"Warren?" says Jesus.

I'm sitting there thinking about two miracles: how he's kind of tenderized Bethie and made her happy and content with our presence. And how he's fed us with manna that we didn't know, to make us understand that everything we live by comes out of the mouth of the Lord.

"Fantastic," I say.

Jesus is just like any other cook.

"Do you really like it?" he says to both of us.

My father had my mother buried in the old broken-down cemetery off Spring Hill Road instead of in the big Greenland Cemetery on Cemetery Lane. This didn't have anything to do with how she died. He loved her more than ever. He wanted better things for her in her eternal rest than he believed he had given her in her earthly life. He just didn't want her buried so close to the Bramber Valley Golf Course.

My father didn't believe in golf. The only sport he believed in, for himself, though he didn't call it a sport, was hunting.

Our little farm was well over the Rye border, closer to Great Bay than to the Atlantic, in Greenland. My father enjoyed telling people not from here that he lived in Greenland. "Isn't it cold there?" they would usually ask. "Not really," he would say, and they would look at him like he was exactly the strong man he was. Or had been, before my mother died.

There weren't many people at the funeral. This didn't have anything to do with how she died. My father didn't want to share her, not even with me. He rode alone with my mother in the hearse. I had to ride with a neighbor, who kept saying, "You poor thing. You poor thing."

"It's okay," I finally said to her. "I don't mind riding with you that much."

She never spoke to me after that. Not ever.

The cemetery was old. Everything in it was old. The headstones were mostly small and thin and bleached white by the sun and maybe cleaned by all the snow that buried them in winter. I wandered among them and looked at the old, faint names like Ebenezer and Adelia and Enoch and Fanny. Everybody else had died two centuries ago. My mother was going to be a visitor from their future. I thought about everything she would have to tell them. They weren't going to believe their ears. I thought of my mother standing there every night surrounded by everyone else, listening to her. I could hear her saying to me, "I'm like the new kid in school, War, but I'm from another planet. They love me."

I could see why my father chose this place. There were no Peases here, from his family. There were a couple of Gookins, which was my mother's name before she became a Pease. But that's not why. He chose this place because no one would ever bother her here. He would have her all to himself. He and the ancient dead around her.

He didn't ask me to stand near him when my mother went into the ground. But I went up to him anyway. We were both wearing our dark church suits. The spring sun was shining brightly. We stood there together like two black marks against the perfect white of eternity, to remind the world of sin and suffering. I leaned against my father so we would be one dark, sad sight. He was as hard as a rock. I didn't fit into him.

Our pastor said, "There is no understanding this in God's way."

My father said, "This *is* God's way."

Our pastor said quickly, "We say goodbye to our sister, Dorothy Gookin Pease."

My father shook his head. "Wife," he said. "We say goodbye to my wife."

"My mother," I whispered, as she disappeared into the dark shadows of the cold, quiet earth.

I thought everyone there had left by the time a couple of men put the headstone in place. It said:

Jesus softly whispered to thee
Come to me, I'll give thee rest

The words made me cry. I hadn't cried before. All my sadness had been locked up inside me. Now it came out with the words my father had had carved on the headstone. I hoped he didn't see me. I looked around for him. He wasn't there. I thought I was all alone. But then I saw, on the other side of the cemetery fence, the same boy who had been waiting to see Mr. Strone.

"C'mere," he said.

I walked over to him. "What are you doing here?"

"I heard about it," he said. "It's tough."

"Not *that*," I said. "Hey, you're missing school!"

He laughed, like it was the biggest joke of the year.

"So are you," he said.

"I have a good excuse," I said.

"The best," he said.

"How did you get here?" I asked.

"Walked. You?"

"I got a ride with another lady who called me a poor something."

"Screw her!"

"You don't have to talk like that," I said.

"Okay," he said, like now we might have an agreement.

"Where do you live?" I asked.

"Not far," he said.

"Me neither."

"Where's your father?"

"I guess he took off."

"That would be weird," he said.

"Usually."

"I know what you mean," he said.

Just then my father showed up. Out of nowhere. It was like he'd been hiding in my mother's grave.

"Who's this?" he asked.

"I'm Ryan." He held out his hand to my father. Or held it up. My father was very tall. Ryan was very short. It didn't matter. I'd never met a kid who just came out with his name and stuck out his hand.

"He's my new friend," I said.

"That's good," said my father. "You'll need a friend."

My father let go of Ryan's hand and turned away from us.

"I'm War," I said to Ryan. I figured he knew my name from school and all the talk about what my mother'd done. But I wanted to make my father jealous.

I didn't know if he was jealous, but he did turn back. "You need a ride?" he said to Ryan.

"With both of you?" Ryan asked.

"Certainly," said my father.

The hearse drove us. My father sat in the front seat next to the driver. He stared out the window at the side mirror, like he hoped to see my mother coming after us. If he did see her, she was getting smaller and smaller before she disappeared and my father, I could see in the mirror, closed his eyes.

When we got to Ryan's house, my father told me to get out too. I did. That's when I knew that I lost my father when I lost my mother. She had taken him away from me. Almost sadder was that he didn't get to go with her.

When we finish the omelet, Jesus says, "It's time to go."

"Where are we going?"

"Where do you want to go?"

"I don't know."

"That's where we're going."

. . .

Of course, I do know. Not where I want to go but where I have to.

"I don't know if I'm ready to see him," I say.

"He's ready to see you," says Jesus.

"Does he even know I'm home?" I wonder out loud. I can't imagine him answering the door to notification officers.

"Sure he does," says Bethie.

"Did you phone him when I wasn't looking?" I ask.

"Your father and I don't talk that much," she says.

"He doesn't talk that much to anyone," I say.

"Neither did you," she says.

"Talk is cheap," I say.

"Yeah," she says, "but silence is expensive."

She's right. I know it is. But sometimes it's just too hard to say what you want to say. Because you're afraid of what you'll hear back.

"How's *your* father?" I ask only now, because I *was* afraid to ask it earlier.

Bethie just shakes her head and gets up to start clearing the dishes. I know Mr. Smith either must have told Bethie what he'd told me, or he was sick enough now for her to notice it.

"He has eternal life insurance," I tell her.

"So he says," she says. Which, I can't help it, makes me smile, because he once said the same thing to me and it makes me feel closer to her.

"Let *me* do the dishes." That used to be my job. When I remembered to do it.

"That's a good one," she says. "Get out of here. Go see your father."

"But I haven't seen Dodie yet," I say.

"It's still too soon," says Jesus.

"Don't you mean too early?" I say.

"That too," says Jesus. "Let's go, Warren."

"Do you have a car?" Bethie asks Jesus. "You could borrow ours, but Ryan took it —"

"We'll be fine," says Jesus.

He goes to the door. I follow him. Bethie follows me.

"Thanks for making breakfast, Ray." She moves her hand slowly toward him. She touches the shirt he's wearing, my shirt. She traces the hole in it with her fingertip.

When she turns to me, she has tears in her eyes.

"Can I come back?" I ask.

"I don't know," she says. "Can you?"

I look at Jesus. I don't know if I'm seeking his permission or his power.

"Ask her the right way," says Jesus.

"*May* I come back?"

I remember how Mr. Smith taught us that there are some things you can do but may not, and other things you may do but can't. I never realized before that this was more than a lesson in grammar.

"You better," Bethie answers.

"May I have a hug?" I ask.

"Go!" She laughs, but still she pushes me out the door.

I can hear the door on its noisy spring close slowly behind us.

"So how are we really getting there?" I ask Jesus.

"How's your leg?" he asks.

"Fine."

"We're walking," he says.

"Walking!"

He's already ahead of me.

When I catch up to him, I stop and turn back. I can see Bethie's beautiful face at the window again. This time I know it's a vision.

We go back to the ocean and walk up the beach toward Rye. The sun seems to have waited for us. It hasn't risen much more at all, until we step out toward it onto the sand and then it almost bolts off the ocean. It leaps into the sky, dripping light like seawater. It's at the height of my shoulder. His too. It moves north with us, hanging off the sleeves of our T-shirts.

"How did you get it to do that?" I ask.

"It's the first day of summer," he explains.

"That's not all it is."

"That's never all it ever is." Jesus quickens his pace, so I won't ask him what he means when he says things like that.

"You know Green Day?" I ask him instead.

"Is that like Earth Day?" he says. "I know Earth Day."

"It's a rock group," I tell him.

"I know a lot about rocks," Jesus says.

"I know," I say. "You told me how you love rocks. But this isn't *rocks*. This is *rock*. The *music*."

"I love music too," he says.

"Yeah," I say. "Hymns."

"Don't tell anyone," he says.

"Don't worry." Like who am I going to tell? "Anyway, there's this group Green Day. We used to play them in Iraq. But before I went there, when I thought about the first day of summer I used to hear in my mind one of their songs. *Summer is coming fast*."

"Yeah," says Jesus. "But you got the words wrong, Warren."

"I *know* I do!" I say. "But how do you know that?"

"As you said—I love hymns." Jesus stops walking. He puts his hand on my arm. "In the song, summer isn't coming. Summer is gone."

"I like my version better," I tell him.

"So do I," he says.

He starts walking again. I follow him.

We're walking in our shoes. I miss the feel of the sand on the bottoms of my feet, between my toes.

"Take off your shoes if you want." I don't know, or care, if he's reading my mind or my body.

"What about you?"

"I walk faster in mine."

"Are we in a rush?"

He stops and puts his hand back on my arm. "Yes," he says.

"Then why did you stop walking?"

"So you could take off your shoes." Now he holds my arm to balance me. But I don't want to take off my shoes. I don't want to lose any time. But I like his grip on me. It makes me feel like I could take off both my shoes at the same time. That I could leave the Earth.

Jesus seems to realize this. Even as we walk on, he keeps his hand on my forearm, tight at first, only slowly releasing me, like it was the most natural thing on earth, two men on the beach, one holding the other as they walk.

As we continue up the shore, the Isles of Shoals are always there, to our right, to the east.

"Is that where you came from?" I ask.

"I've been there," he says.

"I never have," I say.

"You don't know what you're missing," he says.

"Well, that's better than *knowing* what you're missing," I say.

"You're right about that," says Jesus, like he never thought of it that way. It makes me feel good, that I could teach him a thing or two.

"Besides," I say, "I kind of like having a place I always want to go to and never do."

"You wouldn't be disappointed," he says.

"You sound like a travel agent."

Jesus laughs. "Hey, I *am* a travel agent," he says, like he's never thought of that before either.

We leave the beach when we get to Eel Pond and follow Bailey Brook up past Burke Pond and then Locke Pond. We have to cross Love Lane, where the early-morning traffic is beginning to move. Jesus likes to keep to what woods and fields are left, given all the housing developments where they seem to think houses look bigger and better without trees around them so they cut down all the trees. It's impossible not to hear cars groaning in the distance. They don't grumble here like the pathetic five-tons and the up-armored Humvees and the eight-wheeled Strykers and the huge Frankensteins streaking, bouncing along the Damascus/Baghdad road, crashing through the Nahrawan desert, kicking up light and sand, exploding now and then from mines or roadsides, steering wheels pinwheeling off toward the sun with someone's hands and wrists attached.

You tell people you come from New Hampshire and they think you raise animals and you learned to walk by stepping over cow pies. Actually, my family did have animals, not to raise them but to save them. This is New Hampshire by the sea. This is the artery between Boston and Portland, Maine, not that I've ever been to either one. This is where there are more cars and pickups than people, and there are getting to be too many people. Over on Portsmouth Avenue and Epping Road you can buy any kind of car in the world. Except an Infiniti. I never knew why you couldn't buy an Infiniti. But everyone knew you couldn't. Nissans, yes. But no Infiniti. Nice cars. And I always loved the name, though I knew Mr. Smith would hate the way they spelled it.

"There's a car called Infinity," I say to Jesus, and I spell it that way in my mind because he's Jesus.

"I knew that," says Jesus, who if he did know that knew that only because he knows everything. Otherwise, he didn't know that.

"But not one called Eternity."

"Well," says Jesus, "*infinity* makes people think they can drive forever. And *eternity* makes people think they're going to die."

"Do you like cars?" I ask him.

"I've never understood them." He's looking both ways before crossing Love Lane.

"You mean mechanically?"

"That too," he says.

"Do you have a driver's license?"

"I was never taught to drive."

"That's not what I asked you."

"Okay. Yeah. I have a driver's license."

"Can I see it?"

"Sure."

He takes a wallet out of his back pocket. He hands it to me. I think, *Jesus has a wallet. And I'm holding it.*

It's a beat-up thing. It's made of thick, wrinkled leather that looks as old as he is. And I don't mean midthirties. This could be made of camel hide. But the wallet's light and kind of spongy, like it had once been full. Now, I saw as I opened it, it was almost empty.

"How come you don't have any pictures in here?" I ask. "Girlfriend or something?" I kind of tease him.

"It's not big enough to hold them all," he says.

"*Girlfriends*?"

He shakes his head. "The people whose pictures I would have in there if I had pictures in there."

"You know a lot of people?" I ask.

"Just enough," he says.

I finger the cash. "Just enough of this, too."

"You can't have too much money," he says. "Or too little."

"Is it better to have too much money or too little?" I ask him.

"Too much," he answers right away.

"I was hoping you'd say that," I say, though I'm surprised he did.

"The more money you have, the more money you have to give away."

"Then what's so good about having too little money?"

"There's only one good thing about having too little money — giving it away feels even better."

"Everybody should just give their money away?"

"To everybody else," he says, and smiles and picks up speed.

I take the money out of his wallet and put it in my pocket.

"There's more where that came from," he says.

I look in the wallet. It's empty. Of money. That's what we say when a wallet doesn't have any money. It's empty. It doesn't matter what else is in there.

"So where's your license?" I ask.

"It's in there," he says.

I dig my fingers into one of the pockets and feel what could be a license or a credit card.

"Is this a credit card in here?"

He shakes his head. "I've always had a problem with borrowing."

"And lending," I say.

"Tell me about it."

He's a very difficult person to get a rise out of.

I tighten my first two fingers around the card and pull it out.

It's a New Hampshire driver's license.

Mine.

"Where did you get this?"

I wonder if he's a thief. Not the kind we know he is, who will come in the night to save us. But the kind who died next to him. The kind I would become myself if I could hear him say to me, *Today you will be with me in paradise.*

Jesus touches my picture on the license with the tip of his long finger. "Well, you didn't think I'd have one in *my* name," he says. "I told you I was never taught to drive. You can't get a driver's license if you haven't been taught to drive."

"Oh yes you can!" I joke.

"That's why I try to stay off the roads," he says, and looks at his feet as we walk through a meadow I've never even seen before.

"Hey, was that my money too?" I ask.

He looks at my pocket. "It is now."

"Here's your wallet back."

"It's not really mine. I found it."

"It's not mine, either."

"What it holds is yours," he says. "So it's yours."

I never thought of that before. A wallet is really what's inside it. The way a glass of water is more water than glass.

All that's left in the wallet is a piece of paper. It's as wrinkled as the wallet's skin. I take it out and open it up. I don't have to read what's on it because I know every word of what's on it.

"Don't think of this class as English. Think of it as Language."
"Language is not life. It is the expression of life."
"All words are beautiful. But not all words are used beautifully."
"Think before you write."
"Don't think before you talk."
"Except to me."
Mr. Smith is the greatest teacher ever.
The boy next to me is not paying attention.
Except to me.

When Bethie became my friend, because she refused to be my girlfriend, that meant I had two friends: Ryan and Bethie.

Ryan was my older friend, which meant I spent more time with my newer friend. Life isn't fair that way.

Ryan and I had been inseparable since my father left me with him so my father could go the rest of the way home alone in the hearse and mourn my mother.

Every day, after school, I went to Ryan's house with Ryan. When it got dark, I'd go home to my father. My house was always dark when I got there. It became my job to turn on the lights. My father would be sitting there in the dark. When I turned on the lights, he would say, "Thank you." I don't know if he was grateful for me or for the light.

One Saturday I asked my father why my mother had killed herself.

I did it while he was working. My best chance to get my father to talk was when he was busy.

He was tending to our two pigs. Edith and Ethel. They were English Black sisters, with coats the color of night and snouts the color of pink carnations. We had no other animals. My father was a mostly livestock veterinarian. He said he had enough of animals to want to own them. But he loved those pigs. He got them when they were little and were suffering from scours, which is diarrhea. He treated them with sheep's milk and antibiotics. Then he bought them for what he said was bacon. Now they were grown up but still gilts, which is the name for lady pigs who've never had a litter. He was planning to breed them. I found him in the shed he was building for them to have their babies in. He didn't believe in farrowing crates. He said farrowing crates didn't allow pigs the freedom to be piggy, so they got antsy, which was about as far from piggy as pigs could be. Instead, he was building a little fence that didn't quite come to the floor. He would move the piglets there through the creep space so maybe they wouldn't be overlaid. That's what they called it when the mother crushed her babies when she laid down. It was hard to keep mother pigs from crushing their babies. They got restless from having too many babies or not enough water or achy breasts or just from having people around. Mothers never meant to hurt their children. But sometimes they couldn't seem to help it.

I made sure my boots were clean before I went into the shed. Vets are even cleaner than regular doctors, except maybe baby doctors. Animals are made simpler than people and die easier. Who knows how they might ask God why this should be. Because I was raised around animals, I always assumed they had their own way to pray. Maybe their prayers even got answered easier, because they couldn't talk. Words are like a shield sometimes to protect what's under them. Maybe that's why I like poetry, where words are weapons and wounds both. So are the sounds that animals make. They can mean only one thing. We just don't know what that one thing is. But God does.

"Hello, Edith. Hello, Ethel," I said.

Pigs talk to each other but not to people. So when they grunted, both of them, I figured they were telling each other that the kid was here.

"Anything I can do to help?" I asked my father.

He was a farmer and a doctor and a hunter and a patriot and a widower. He was all the first four before he became the last.

"No," he said.

"When are you going to breed them?"

"Got a boar coming next week."

"How long will it take?"

"It better not happen before I get this barn together. Boars can get pretty feisty."

"That's not what I meant," I said.

"I know." My father laughed.

It was so rare a sound, I didn't know what to make of it.

"Why did Mom kill herself?" I asked.

My father was even taller than me. And I'm six feet exactly. He was also a lot handsomer and a lot stronger. He got handsomer all the time. His grief was carving him down into a beautiful statue. More and more ladies were bringing him their animals that weren't sick. One of them went out and bought a bird and brought it right here from the pet shop. It still had the price tag hanging off its foot. My father told the lady the bird was fine but she was sick. She started to cry. My father stroked the feathers of the bird.

He never talked about her, my mother. He was hiding her from me, inside himself. That's the only place aside from Heaven she was alive. So when I prayed to her, or just tried to talk to her, I was praying to him too. But he never answered. So she never did either.

He stopped laughing. He took his hand off Ethel or Edith, I can't remember which. He rose to his full height and came around the pigs and walked up to me. I thought he was going to hit me, though he'd never hit me in his entire life. He put his hand behind my neck. He pulled my face against the side of his so I couldn't see him.

"Your mother killed herself," he said, "because she couldn't have another child."

It was worse than hitting me. I cried as he held me and he didn't let go until his eyes began to burn red from my tears running into them.

I spent more time with Ryan than I did with my father, if you don't count time sleeping. I never slept over at Ryan's. I always slept at home. My own bedroom was the only place I talked to my mother. I knew it was the one place in the house my father never entered. It wasn't my privacy he was respecting. It was his own.

Ryan was like the brother I never had. Mr. Smith would say that's a trite thing to say. But after what my father said about why my mother had killed herself, I made Ryan into my brother to give my mother what she wanted. And to try to stop feeling so bad that I hadn't been enough for her myself.

I used to think that my mother was looking down at me and Ryan and thinking, *That's the most ridiculous thing I've ever seen. They can't be brothers. They don't look anything alike.*

It always bothered Ryan to be short. I was tall and skinny, so I didn't know what it felt like to have to have to look up at everything and everybody. I think it was being short that had made Ryan so angry and use foul language. He was cursing something beyond his control. Of all the things to curse, that makes the most sense. A curse is a kind of negative prayer. But it's definitely a prayer.

I knew being short bothered him. So I told him, "You're going to shoot up someday." It was like that expression my mother used to use on me: *You're going to fill out someday.*

"That's all I need," said Ryan. "To be the world's shortest drug addict."

"You know what I mean," I said, laughing at this little joke.

"If only," he said. "If only."

Some of the saddest words I ever heard began with *If only.*

But Ryan said *If only* the way some people said, *From your lips to God's ear.*

Definitely a prayer.

Like a lot of small guys, Ryan started lifting weights. He started when he found some at a yard sale on Breakfast Hill Road. He went into the people's house and called me at home. It was a Saturday. People have yard sales on Saturdays. And I stayed home on Saturdays in case my father needed me to help with the animals. Or he might want me to go hunting with him. He almost never did. But I always stayed home on Saturday.

"I need you to get the hell over here to help me carry some weights," said Ryan.

"Well," I said, "since you're always carrying mine . . ."

Ryan had saved me. I didn't know from what. But I knew he had.

When I got to the yard sale, Ryan was standing on the lawn with the weights around him in a circle. He looked like a small version of one of those husbands guarding something while the wife pays.

"Did you bring any money?" he said.

"Money!" I said loudly, because I didn't have any. "What I should have brought was a wheelbarrow."

It was a huge set. Like 480 pounds. The guy who sold it to us was fat and looked embarrassed. He said, "I bought this for my wife."

Yard sales are the best places to buy exercise equipment. It's almost always brand new and dirt cheap.

"Fifty bucks seems like a lot for this," I said.

"How about thirty?" said the guy.

"How about we pay them to take it away?" said his wife. "You never even —"

"Twenty!" the guy interrupted her. He'd turned red. That was a lot of red to turn.

"See," I whispered to Ryan. "I did bring money."

"Yeah," he said. "Invisible money."

We carried the weights piece by piece to Ryan's garage. He got his father to give him the twenty bucks. His father was short too. He gave Ryan twenty ones. "Guilt money," Ryan called it as he fanned himself with it on our way back to the yard sale.

Ryan's family didn't own a wheelbarrow. They didn't need one. They lived in one of those houses attached to other houses, like blocks that little kids play with, all interchangeable. They had a garage but not a front yard and not a backyard and just one short little tree growing up from between the flagstones of their short front walk. The tree wasn't supposed to be there. Ryan loved that tree and watered it and in the winter he put a blanket over it. No one knew what kind of tree it was, so Ryan called it an oak, which it certainly wasn't.

Without a wheelbarrow, just carrying the weights to Ryan's garage was an amazing workout. It took us so long that the people who sold him the weights took in their yard-sale sign and folding tables and ate dinner. But Ryan still insisted we set up the bench.

"Spot me," he said as he lay down. He was so short his feet didn't come close to the garage floor.

I didn't know what he meant.

"Stand behind me so I don't crush myself to death."

He put so much weight on the bar the first time he couldn't even lift it off. We couldn't even lift it off, the two of us.

Finally, we got the weight down far enough so Ryan could do a few presses off the bench.

I helped him with the last one.

He was smiling down there on the bench.

"What did you mean when you said I was always carrying yours?" he said. "You never bought any weights."

That's when I realized, a couple of years before I even met Mr. Smith, that I was a poet and Ryan wasn't.

. . .

In those two years, Ryan lifted weights. That's all he did. With his spare time, I mean. He lifted for between two and four hours every day. He could do so much because he learned to break his body down into parts. For lifting purposes, I mean. Shoulders one day. Chest another day. Legs another day, until later he began to have thigh days and then calf days. He also learned to alternate between push muscles and pull muscles and never pushed or pulled two days in a row.

I know how long he lifted because I was there with him for every minute of it.

He wouldn't lift without me. He told me he needed me to spot him. I said, at the beginning, that I could understand why he might need me to spot him when he was doing bench presses. But bicep curls?

No, he said, he needed me to spot him. For everything. If I didn't spot him, he wouldn't lift, and if he didn't lift, he would stop growing, and then he would shrink down into nothing. Into nothing, he said. That was in the days before he would say that all his muscle would turn to fat.

"I need you to spot me," he said.

So I was there every day, except Saturday, in case my father wanted to do anything. I found an article in one of Ryan's bodybuilding magazines that said everyone should take off at least one day a week. That's how I got him to take a day off. So I could have one too. He said it was the worst day of the week. I said it was for me too. But I had to be there for my father.

I knew Ryan never cheated. I knew he believed that if he lifted weights without my being there, something terrible could happen to him. It wasn't that he needed me to spot him. He needed me to be there to spot him. He needed me to watch over him, sometimes literally.

I actually enjoyed it. I could see my only friend, my best friend who was my best friend not just because he was my only friend, change before my eyes.

In those two years, Ryan got huge. Not tall. Just huge. He looked almost as wide as he was long. His shoulders were like two large rocks balanced on the top of an ancient monolith. There's something eternal about a body made of muscle. And something the opposite.

Ryan looked indestructible. But he felt temporary. No matter how much he lifted, he didn't get taller. He barely grew taller as he got older. He thought he was trapped in time. He thought he would die if he didn't lift weights. He wanted to grow, and the only thing he could grow was muscle.

The two of us were together a lot. Not just when he was lifting. We took the bus to school. Then when I got my license I would drive us to school in the little Ford Ranger my father bought me because it was a member of the 200,000-mile club and because he didn't want me asking him ever again for a ride anywhere.

Ryan and I hung out at school when we weren't in our classes. We ate lunch together. Then at the end of the day we went home together because that's when I spotted Ryan, every day after school. And Sunday afternoons — Ryan liked to lift weights while most other guys were sitting in front of TVs watching football games, growing fat while he grew hard. All we did was listen to classic rock on The Shark except when they canceled it for Patriots' games. Which we never listened to because real athletes like real soldiers got no time for games, video or radio or on some field or otherwise.

People couldn't figure me and Ryan out. I kept getting taller, but even when I lifted a few weights of my own at Ryan's house, I didn't fill out any. And Ryan just grew sideways.

It was like we were eating off each other.

People kind of laughed at us when we walked around school together. We didn't care. We were kind of in balance.

I wanted him to get tall and be happy. He wanted me to have someone to talk to aside from my dead mother. And people being spotted love to be talked to. It takes their minds off the pain.

• • •

Even though we were so different looking, sometimes I thought Ryan saw himself in me and me in him. How else to explain that when I asked him why he didn't have a mirror in his garage — "Everyone who lifts weights has a mirror," I said — he answered, "I can look at you, War. I have you to spot me."

Or was it that he didn't like what he would see in a mirror?

The day I'd met Bethie in English class I went home with Ryan as usual. I was spotting him for real that day, since he was doing bench presses. Ever since he'd learned not to lift straight up but to use a J-lift he'd increased the weight until he got to just under three hundred pounds whether it was one rep or six slow and was stuck there. He did everything right. He squeezed his shoulder blades together. He tucked in his elbows. He grabbed the bar hard enough to grimace — I mean, for the bar to grimace. The only thing he didn't do, because he still couldn't, was to use his legs. He couldn't press his feet into the floor because they still didn't reach the floor.

I stood above him with my fingertips on the barbell. I'd gotten so used to this over the years, standing there with my palms up. It was like a form of prayer, except instead of having your hands together, you had them apart. And instead of praying for your own life to be saved and to mean something, you were praying for your friend to be safe. And for his life to mean something because he worked so hard to have his body take the place of his soul.

"I met a girl today," I said.

"What's her name?" Ryan asked.

"I don't know."

"I see you're your old suave self."

Ryan and I often talked about girls. We talked about them instead of talking to them. That's what friends were for.

"She talked to me," I said.

"What did she say?"

"Well, her first words to me were, 'Not you.' "

"That's encouraging." Ryan smiled his usual upside-down smile when he was laying there and motioned with his eyes for me to get ready to guide the weights down. He had one forty-five-pound and one thirty-five-pound and one twenty-five-pound plate on each end of the GOB-86 bar, which weighed exactly forty-four pounds. He closed his eyes as he pushed up against the bar. This was always my favorite moment in spotting him. My own hands rose as his did, but I was exerting nothing. His strength passed into me, even as I watched over him.

"Well, that's better than what I thought she said. I thought she said, 'Would you mind?' "

"Would *you* mind," said Ryan as he lifted the bar off the catches.

I let my hands float free as the bar left them and then I lowered my hands as Ryan let the great weight come down toward his chest.

"She said it to a guy named Elvin. She made him move his seat so she could sit next to me."

I looked down at Ryan for his reaction to that. But I'd forgotten that he didn't talk when he was in the middle of a lift. All his breathing went into his work.

"It's not what she said to me," I went on. "Even before she said one word I felt this strange connection to her. When I looked at her I thought I was seeing myself. Not *me.* But *myself.* I know that sounds crazy. I mean, what the difference is between me and myself. I think the *me* part is my body and the *myself* part is my soul. That must be it. I looked at her and I saw my own soul. I know what you're going to say. If you could say anything. You're going to say, 'When you look at a girl, man, you're supposed to see the girl.' And you're right. But that's what I mean. I did see her. I thought she was very beautiful. But I couldn't tell her from me. Not that I mean to say I'm very beautiful. I just felt this kind of connection. I felt like I was giving myself up to her and at the same time that I was finding myself."

"Oh, my God!" screamed Ryan.

"It's not that big a deal," I said.

"My feet!"

I looked down. His feet were flat against the floor.

Ryan pushed the bar up onto the catch.

"Load it up," he said. "Give me two tens and a five each."

I found the little weights and released the spring clips and slid the weights onto each end of the bar and clipped them on.

"Now," said Ryan.

He lifted the bar so quickly I couldn't even put my hands under it.

Down it went, three-hundred-plus pounds, down to his chest, which seemed to fan open with muscle as his triceps trembled and pulsed and turned from flesh to stone.

Up it came, all three hundred four pounds of it, up. Ryan had his eyes open for once, looking right into mine, a smile on his face. He lowered the bar again, raised it yet again. He did three reps and then he lowered the bar to his chest, and this time, and for the first time ever, because he never worked quite to failure, he couldn't lift the bar. He nodded to me, so I put my hands under the bar and together, him pushing, me pulling, we brought the bar back up and into the catches.

Ryan sprang up from the bench. "We lifted more than three hundred pounds!"

"Did you hear a word I said?" I asked.

He nodded, smiling, though whether for me or for himself I didn't know. "You're in love, man."

From that moment on, when Ryan's feet finally reached the floor from the bench in his garage, Ryan began to grow. Taller, I mean. Every time I saw him, he seemed taller. Maybe that was because I didn't see him as often. He stopped lifting weights. I never knew if it was because he'd started getting taller or I wasn't there to spot him.

It's not that I gave him up for Bethie. I gave myself up for Bethie. I had less for Ryan — less time but mostly less of me. She crowded him out inside me. Not on purpose. It wasn't her fault. It wasn't mine either. She filled me up.

I even got bigger. I started to fill out.

Ryan got taller. I got at least a bit more muscular.

We both noticed it, Ryan and me.

"It's weird," he said. "It's like we're trading off."

"It's Bethie," I said.

"She's just a little thing," said Ryan.

"It's not physical," I said.

"War," he said, "all my pants are too short!"

Ryan, even when he no longer lifted weights, was a physical creature. I was something else. Ever since my mother died, part of me was always somewhere else. Floating free but lost at the same time. I couldn't feel myself inside.

When I met Bethie, that same part of me was still floating free, but I started to feel it, getting ever closer.

"She's inside me," I told Ryan.

He didn't know what to make of that. He said, "If I weren't getting taller, all my muscle would be turning to fat."

"Then I'm glad we're not trading off," I said.

"But we are," he said.

Jesus takes us north, until we're halfway between the ocean to the east and Great Bay to the west. Because it's turning out to be such a clear day, with the air so pure it's empty of everything but light, I can smell how the salt of the sea mingles with the mold of the earth. I can even see the fragrance on the breeze. In the desert, I could see the heat, running in streams of crimson from the sun.

Packer Bog is drained into Great Bay first by Packer Brook and then by Pickering Brook, which got channeled when they built I-95. No one built on the bog. First because it was too wet and then because it got protected from the same kind of developers who offered to buy my father's farm to put up houses and he told them, "My wife is buried here." He didn't mean Mom's body.

Jesus walks right into Packer Bog. His Timberlands must be waterproof.

"What do you think," says Jesus, "is this a bog or a marsh?"

"It looks like a swamp to me."

He dips his finger into it and then sticks his finger in his mouth. "Salty," he says. "But not too."

There's moss on everything. But out of it here and there grows long grass. I follow Jesus, and it's like walking on rubber. Though it probably looks like we're walking on water.

He tells me the long grass is actually a reed called spartina.

I say, "Have you read *The Odyssey*?"

Jesus shakes his head. "Before my time."

"Did you ever hear of Helen of Troy?"

"Of course!" He looks at me like he might think I consider him an idiot.

"Did you know that before she was Helen of Troy, she was Helen of Sparta?"

Jesus picks up some grass in his hand. Brown water runs down the veins in his forearm. "I did not know that," he says.

"She ran off from Sparta to Troy with Paris, after her husband trusted her with Paris and Paris with her."

Jesus knows what I'm getting at. "But you're not Bethie's husband," he says.

"In everything but name," I say, like I'm challenging the teachings of his church. Which I guess I am.

"There are some things that are nothing without the name." He looks at me sternly. He has a kind face that stays kind except for his eyes. They darken. I've heard that expression before — eyes darkening — but I've never known what it meant until now. His eyes darken, and I feel the darkness spread over me. I feel invisible.

He takes immediate pity on me and changes the subject by shoving the grass at me. "Feel how thick this is," he says. "It has to die to become food. Everything in here eats it. See over there. That's a wrack."

"What!"

"A wrack," he says. "The good kind. It's a carpet of grass over the moss. It lies down and dies and everything in here eats it. Or everything that eats it eats it, and then someone else eats them. Spiders, mostly."

I shake my head. "I thought you said *Iraq*. What's the bad kind?"

"Ruin," he says. "Wrack and ruin. You know."

"Hey," I say, "like someone wracks up their car."

"Still on cars, I see."

"Still on Iraq," I say back.

Jesus puts his hand on my hand. I think it's to comfort me, but then I see he's got a tiny turtle in his hand. He holds my arm from underneath and puts the turtle on the top, so I've got to hold my arm out like a fancy waiter with the little turtle sitting on it looking up at me. It's about three inches long. It has orange head markings and a black shell.

"What is it?" I ask.

"A turtle."

"No kidding."

"It's a bog turtle, so this must be a bog. Except it also lives in swamps. So maybe you were right."

"Is it a baby?"

Jesus touches its shell with his long finger. "It's one of the smallest turtles in the world. This is a full-grown female. You can tell from her small red head."

"It's orange," I say.

"Whatever."

"Whatever!"

"Whatever." Jesus smiles. Then he says, "She's three years old. You can tell from these annuluses on her shell."

"Like rings on a tree." I run my fingers over them. "Except they're raised." So I keep running my fingers over them.

"We're lucky to find this little lady," says Jesus. "These are the most covert of all turtles."

"*Covert?*"

"Hidden."

I know what the word means. I was just surprised to hear him use it. It's the same word they used for us snipers. It was always one of my favorite words. It could mean *hidden*. It could mean *secret*. It could mean *a sanctuary*. It could mean *camouflage*. It was a great word for snipers and for God.

It was also the name of a Dark Ops Stratofighter spear point some guys carried. I preferred the trusty old Olsen four-inch my father had given me, which made it my most treasured weapon.

"Why?" I ask Jesus. Not about God. About the turtle.

"Because they're draining most bogs and filling them in. And because the females are nesting now."

"How do you know all this stuff?" I ask him.

"I live here," he says.

"In the swamp?"

"On the Earth."

"Can I ask you something?"

Jesus takes the little turtle off my arm and turns it over in his hand to look at it before he puts it down on the moss, and it disappears so fast I touch the place on my arm where it had been. "I've always lived here," he says.

I laugh. He probably thought I was going to ask him about the Second Coming or something. But it isn't.

"Is this the only one?" I ask.

"Bog?" Now he laughs.

"World?" I say. "Planet? No, I don't mean planet. I mean, is this the only place where there are people? Life? Is this the only place where there's life? As we know it? Life. Is this the one and —"

"Yes," says Jesus. "Yes. This is the only one. The one and only."

My father would take me hunting here on the bog. He'd be impatient, so we'd come out here via Buckminster Way during the week and a half of the muzzleloader season. When that ended, the second week of November, the regular season would begin. The only weapons they ever allowed in Greenland for deer anyway were muzzleloaders. It was the same for Portsmouth and Stratham, which bordered the bog. We could have waited and shot with any sort of rifle in Exeter or Rye. But my father wanted the deer early, and the deer in those other towns were the kind that read books, he said. If we got our four, then the rest of the season we'd hunt for other animals, going up north in his truck. To the Kancamagus Highway where, when I was a little boy, and my mother was alive, I would wade in small rapids of the Swift River. When my father would hold out his arms to me, I would run to him over the slick rocks and not care how wet or bruised I got trying to reach him.

There were always white-tails in the bog, but not as many in November as later in the winter, when they'd hang around in herds of almost a dozen and when you shot one the others spun out like rays of light from a red sun. My father would show me how they'd browsed the white cedar so much that there were no young white cedar. There were red cedar, but they were getting chewed up too. No one liked the deer except hunters and little kids in car windows. The deer would leave the bog in search of food and go out in the developments among all the big ugly new newcomer houses and eat whatever they could find and then not find their way back to the bog because they got confused what with all the houses looking and smelling exactly the same. The deer would stand there like lawn ornaments.

Hunters loved the deer because they killed them. My father said that those who kill are those who most respect life, because they know that the taking of life is life's most profound act. He felt this way before my mother took her own life; he felt it even more strongly after. Killing didn't make you happy; it made you human. And what made you human made you holy. God was with you every step of the way, but you met Him only when you died. As the soldier was mankind's greatest representative, so was the hunter, whether man or animal, the highest in the animal kingdom.

Killing animals was not ecology, my father said. It was theology.

His muzzleloader was an old .50-caliber inline Gonic Arms 87. It had a blued barrel, because my father didn't like stainless or plated steel, and a maple stock that came from a tree that had grown in Gonic, New Hampshire, where the gun was grown too, my father said, because he liked to think of guns as growing, not out of the soil but out of the hands and brains of men, who made no more beautiful machines than guns.

He used only about 125 grains of loose powder in it and a 370-grain maxi ball. This way almost all his powder charge got burned.

My muzzleloader was a cheap good little Hunter .50-cal from Connecticut Valley Arms with a laminated camouflage stock I thought was a little embarrassing. My father taught me how to neck down the case to accept a 7mm-08 Remington. He said I'd get less recoil from this on my skinny shoulder and I'd still carry about twelve hundred foot-pounds at 350 yards.

"Three hundred fifty yards!" I said.

Most deer around here got taken at thirty to forty yards. It was always what my father called a humane kill.

He scaled the scope to my rifle and told me I had a good eye.

So different from the Knight's Mark 11 mod 0 Stoner SR-25 they gave us in The Mess before they got some Knight's SR-47s and then the killer Barretts. I'd stick a 7.62 x 39 round in an AK-47 magazine and with one shot turn anyone's soft tissue into liquid tissue and my shoulder black and blue. When the Russians used the 7.62 x 39 in Afghanistan, not that it did them all that much good, the Afghans spared called that ammo *poison bullet*. The poison was pure. It was in the heat and spin.

In The Mess, the Sunnis got hold of Russian Dragunov SVDs. Some of our guys would stick an optic sight on their M-14s so they could see the enemy in their crosshairs and then let the little red aiming dot dance on their chests or their foreheads before they misted them. I didn't like using aiming dots. No more on humans than I would on deer.

One early-November Sunday morning me and my father walked into the bog with our guns and our identical Olsen knives strapped to our thighs. It was the first time we went out together after my mother died. He didn't even ask me to go hunting. He just handed me my muzzleloader. He liked to hunt on Sundays because New Hampshire allowed it and Maine and Massachusetts didn't. My father called them heathen states. The best way to observe the Sabbath was to hunt. Hunting kept God's order in the world. Hunting, and, until my mother died, going to church. After she died, when I went to church I went alone.

We walked into the wind the way he'd taught me we always must. So we could smell the animals and they couldn't smell us. It was also raining a bit, which my dad said was like God's fingertips all around you on the forest floor covering up the sound of your own footsteps. You'd think the deer would have learned to fear the rain instead of basking in it.

The first deer we came on was a buck. It had huge antlers, but they were ugly because they'd begun to lose their velvet. You could see some velvet hanging like a bald man's halo hair from the bark of red cedars, where bucks had rubbed it off. Muzzleloader season here was always just before the deer's peak breeding season.

I saw my father was just watching it so I raised my gun.

"No," said my father. It was the first word he'd said to me since he'd handed me my gun at home. "Wait for the doe."

Sure enough, the ladies came around. Bucks will mate with them all, but one at a time. This big buck picked one out and off she went with him. She was losing her summer red and turning gray, but in the morning sun she still had that beautiful red tinge. She raised her tail the way they do when they're scared and running off. Her soft white backside was displayed.

My father shot her dead.

The buck looked surprised. He looked around until he found us. The wind no longer hid us from his indignation and concern. But I think he wanted to see us. He shook his head at us, and I imagined the tips of his naked antlers writing something in the air. Then he went off and found another doe right before our eyes.

"Shoot her," my father said.

"No," I said.

The buck mounted her. My father said, "You're a fool."

I didn't know if he was talking to me or to the buck.

We retrieved our doe and hauled it to our truck and off to the check station at Suds-N-Soda on Portsmouth Avenue.

All of a sudden, the bog starts to shake. You can see it moving like waves on the ocean. Except I'm not standing on the shore the way I always would, looking out at the Isles of Shoals. Instead, I'm riding on this strange wet landscape, half earth and half ocean. It rolls beneath my feet. I wonder if I'm going to sink in and drown.

Jesus loves it. He stands next to me smiling and lets his body go with the movement of the earth and water. I stand next to him stiff with small fear. I reach out to him at the same moment he reaches out to me. We don't hold hands, exactly. But I've got him by the wrist. His other arm he raises and moves slowly, pointing with his finger until I see little animals popping up on the surface of the bog, wood frogs and two jumping mice that bounce one after the other, like kids on a trampoline, and salamanders slithering about with their tails in one another's mouths.

"Bog quake," says Jesus happily. "Check it out." He directs my gaze to the path we'd made behind us through the reeds in the wet marsh. It's gone. Swallowed up.

"The Red Sea," I say.

"Ha!" says Jesus.

"Are you laughing at me?" Not that I would mind.

"There's no Red Sea in the Bible," he says.

"What about . . ."

"Sea of reeds," he says. "Just like this. Probably a place in Egypt called Bitter Lake."

"Hey," I say, "I live on Bittersweet Lane."

"Not anymore," he says.

"Don't rub it in."

"I would never," he says. "Though it is a nice coincidence — Bitter Lake and Bittersweet Lane."

"Do you believe in coincidences?" I ask him.

"Of course not," he answers. "It wasn't a coincidence the Egyptians were swallowed up. It was a bog quake. Like this one."

"So it wasn't a miracle," I say, like he's some kind of scientist.

"Warren," he says, "we're standing here and the ground is shaking under our feet and we're hanging on to each other riding on the surface of the Earth. Of course it's a miracle!"

I grab him harder. "I see what you mean!"

"I know you do."

At that very moment it's over. I'm disappointed. Just when I'd started to enjoy our miracle.

Out of the last shudder of the surface of the Earth, between a white cedar and a tamarack, comes a single orchid. It's the most beautiful flower I've ever seen. It has white angel's wings spread over a pink cup. Not a miracle. Not a coincidence. A natural event. I do know what Jesus means.

I let go of him and reach down to pick it.

"No," he says.

I think of my father telling me not to shoot the buck.

"A lady slipper won't last long enough for you to take it to her," he says.

"I never brought her flowers," I say.

"You should have," says Jesus.

"What are you, an authority on dating?"

"On love," he says, and reaches down and plucks a green stalk out of the bog and holds it out to me. "Hungry?"

"How come you can pick that and I can't pick —"

He sticks the ugly green thing with its prickly flower scales into his mouth and takes a bite. I can hear the thing crunch in his front teeth and then as he chews it.

"Give it a try," he says.

He holds it up toward my mouth. It doesn't look particularly good, but I like the idea of eating something Jesus just took a bite out of. I wonder if it's a sacrament I never heard of.

So I take a bite.

"Salty," I say. "What is it?"

"Glasswort," he says. "If you burn it, you can make glass out of its ashes."

"Glass!" I stop chewing.

"Glass*wort.*"

"How do you spell that?"

"W-O-R-T."

"That's a relief," I say. But I still spit the stuff out.

I remember how my father came home one night just in time to sit down to dinner after he handed my mother the wildflowers he brought her every summer evening, and my mother kissed him on the cheek and asked him, as she always did, "How'd it go, Fido?" That's what she called him, Fido, a nickname because he was a vet and she loved to call him that and he loved for her to call him that and neither of them knew what a hopeless turn of events FIDO stood for in the Army. Come to think of it, I never heard her call him by his real name, Wesley. I never heard anyone call him that. I only read that on his mail. Otherwise I would never have known that was his name. People other than my mom called him Wes. But until I was older I thought they said "West." I was always grateful my parents didn't name me East.

So he said to her, “I was called over to Nottingham to check out some hairy heel warts.”

“Omygodwashyourhands!” my mother just about screamed.

My father went to the kitchen sink. “Don’t worry,” he said. “It wasn’t another woman.”

“I kind of wish it was,” said my mother, and I could tell from her holding back her smile that she was thinking about some lady with hairy heel warts.

“Just my luck,” said my father. “But it was cows. First these idiot farmers didn’t drain their freestalls and then they waited long enough to call me so there was hair growing out the lesions. It hurts like hell. Poor little things. Some calf heifers. Imagine cows walking around on tiptoes.”

With that, and with his hands still wet, my father got down on all fours right there on the kitchen floor and pretended he was a cow walking on tiptoes. He was so strong he could walk on his own fingertips and toes. He walked like that right up to my mother and stuck his nose on her knee under her dress and said, “Moo.”

“I don’t go out with men with hairy heel warts,” she said.

“Thank God for small favors,” said my father. “What’s for dinner?”

My mother couldn’t help smiling with what Mr. Smith would later teach us was the irony of the whole thing: “Beef tenderloin.”

My father went up on his knees and grabbed her around the waist and pressed his face into the middle of her.

The two of them were laughing to beat the band, as my father used to say.

Jesus and I wade through some Floating Heart. They have yellow leaves and little white flowers on the top. But just below the surface they’re veined and the kind of purplish red that blood is when it meets the air. It’s Jesus who tells me the name, Floating Heart, and I go soft over it. Then he says they're a noxious weed and they invade and take over from other plants.

So I love the name even more and wish I'd known about it in Iraq. That's exactly what we were, all us soldiers: Floating Hearts, Purple Hearts, bleeding and misunderstood.

At the edge of the swamp there's a single tree, giant; it must be seventy feet. It looks like a hickory, but it doesn't have braided bark, just smooth gray armor gashed from top to bottom. Hanging off its branches are little yellow flowers. They give off a strange smell, a flowery decay, moldy and sweet at the same time. I'm tired and lean back against it and sink slowly down until I'm sitting. Jesus kneels before me. He says, "Your boots are wet." He puts his hands around one of them and squeezes. No water falls off it, but my foot feels warm and dry. He does the same with the other boot. I close my eyes and let the tree hold me up before him.

He says, "This is a tree-of-heaven."

"I should have known." If I could open my eyes, I would wink at him.

"Also known as paradise tree," he adds.

"No wonder it feels so good." If I could turn my arms around, I would wrap them around it.

"Or stinkweed."

"What!"

He enjoys his little joke. I open one eye and see how merry he looks.

"You seem to get a kick out of how nothing is the way it seems."

"Everything is the way it seems," he says. "But nothing seems to be the way it is."

"That's a contradiction," I say.

"Yes, it is."

He sits down next to me, leans against the tree. We're two guys relaxing on an early-summer day. Like we have nowhere to go. That's the way it seems, anyway. But not the way it is.

"My father's a vet," I say, "who hunts."

"Yes."

"I never really got it."

"No," he says by way of agreement.

"I'd watch him taking care of animals. So gentle. Then he'd go out and shoot them. Talk about a contradiction. Do you know what I mean?"

"My father's the same way," he says.

"How so?"

He won't tell me. He gets up. He says, "Come on." He doesn't even offer me a hand up. I wonder if I offended him by asking about his father. We all know who his father is. Jesus probably doesn't want to talk about him any more than I want to talk about mine. Because he doesn't really understand him.

I put my hands behind me against the tree and push myself up. I pat it goodbye.

"This tree can't be here," Jesus says.

I've still got a hand on it. "But it is."

"It's the only one left then," he says. "New Hampshire cut them all down and sprayed the stumps with herbicides and pulled out all the saplings. They should have planted black locust reclamation trees. This tree is poison."

"I love this tree," I say.

"Me too," says Jesus.

On the day after our pigs, Edith and Ethel, had their babies, my father said, "I'm going to see your mother."

I got all excited. "Is she alive?" I said. And I was thinking, *They played a trick on me. I don't care. As long as she's alive.*

I figured she had to be alive. Not because he said he was going to see her. But because he had just talked about her. He never talked about her.

"I'm going to the cemetery." He kicked his muck boots against his truck before he got in and closed the door and drove away.

I didn't ask if I could go with him. I was scared to see her grave.

I was afraid that I would feel worse than I felt at home all the time with her gone. But as soon as I was alone at home, I longed to be with my father at the cemetery. I knew then that he lived with her more than he lived with me. If the cemetery was her home, it was his too. Where he lived with me was the true graveyard.

I was alone at the house for the first time ever. I had no one to talk to. Even when my father was there, he didn't say much to me. But I still had him to talk to. I could still ask him questions, even if he rarely answered. Or even if I never asked the questions out loud.

I used to imagine being home by myself. I used to want to be. But now that I was, I didn't know what to do. I was frightened. I wanted there to be a ghost in the house, and there wasn't. I couldn't find my mother anywhere.

I went to my room. I closed the door. I got down on my knees at the side of my bed, but I didn't pray to Jesus. I said, "Mom, it's War. I know you're probably talking to Dad right now. I'm sorry to interrupt. But I wanted to ask you a question. How come you wanted to have another child? Dad told me about that. He said you wanted to have another child. Why did you want that? You already had me. What was the matter with me? Why did you want another child?"

The problem with talking to the dead is they don't talk back. If you hear them talking back, it's just you talking to yourself. And I didn't hear anyone.

When I heard my father get back that day, I was so grateful not to be alone that I ran down the stairs and followed him out to the pig hut. One of the pigs, I didn't recognize which one, had rolled over on its litter after they'd finished feeding and had crushed them all. Or should I say overlaid. They were little flat black clouds in a sky of golden hay.

"Oh, War," my father said when he realized I was next to him. For the first time since my mother had died, he had his own tears in his eyes.

• • •

Jesus and I walk out on Breakfast Hill Road. I turn around and take one more look at the tree-of-heaven standing alone on the edge of the bog. It's a sentry, you don't know if it's going to shoot you or shade you.

In The Mess, the trees didn't have water to grow tall like this. They had to ship us Fraser firs from Stateside for Christmas, dry, crackly things that soldiers would hang grenades off as ornaments. Everyone thought they were the M69s, which were for training. But someone hung a real M67 off one tree by its pin. When it went off fortunately no one was less than twenty meters away and so the worst thing that happened was a few soldiers ended up wearing Fraser fir needle flechettes in their eyelids.

Most Iraqi trees were fruit — lemon and orange and date palm and what they called *tooki,* which our guys called dookie. When we bulldozed all the orchards in Dhuluiya we went in blasting Green Day. 'Cause I got outvoted for "Ballad of the Green Berets." Green's green. But the tooki juice turned us into a bunch of redheads screaming along with "Welcome to Paradise" and "When I Come Around." What we were really there for was for when the insurgents came around. But tearing up their trees didn't bring them out of the ground. The soldiers, I mean. The trees lay there with their roots spread. The tooki juice off our faces was sweet and sour together. But the lemon in the air made the whole place smell as clean as a bathroom back home so we got real homesick.

I think I can understand why Jesus might love a tree that's called paradise and stinkweed. It's the perfect tree for this one and only world of ours. Jesus better than anyone knows how painful it is to get happy.

He stops walking when we get to the overpass on I-95. He watches the cars like a kid. Northbound, they're shooting out from the Hampton Tolls. Everybody knows about the Hampton Tolls. In The Mess I'd say I was from New Hampshire, and people would say, "Yeah, the &$%#*!@ Hampton Tolls." Southbound, the cars are weeping smoke. They approach the Hampton Tolls like it was a checkpoint and they could leave their lives there. The rising sun blackens the driver-side windows.

Suddenly the sky darkens. The sun disappears. Jesus looks up before I do. A huge KC-135 Stratotanker is moving in from the southeast to land at Pease, its base, a few miles north-northwest in Portsmouth. The plane's shadow, grayer and larger than the aircraft itself, glides right over me and Jesus. I close my eyes and let the shadow pick me up and carry me off into the air. Jesus says, "Wow!" I realize he's right there with me, floating above the Earth in the shadow of a plane that moves so slowly into landing it doesn't move at all but surrounds us like a house in which we're safe from the danger everywhere around us. In The Mess, KC-135s that might have made their way from right here to the 92nd out in Fairfield in Washington State and then on to the Mideast would refuel F-16s. They'd release the flying boom and stick their shuttlecocked drogue into the probe of the fighter that floated beneath it just the way Jesus and me were now. We're little planes getting fed by the big momma plane. No one made sex jokes while it was happening; they were scared of blowing up in midair. I don't make one now either. Not my thing.

I always liked clouds. Shadows. Darkness. Even when there were no lights on in my bedroom, I loved it when my mother would come in and pull my blanket up to my chin. The minute I heard her footsteps with one ear I'd take the crystal earpiece out of my other ear. My father had built me a crystal radio set like the kind they called foxhole receivers in the Second World War. He used a piece of galena crystal from Australia. He told me the diode was a cat's whisker. I used to ask him to show me the cat a whisker like that could have come from. It must have been the biggest fiercest cat he ever treated. He'd say he would but he never did, and I never wanted him to really because there was no such cat and I wanted to believe there was and he'd healed it anyway. All I could ever hear when I made contact between the cat's whisker and the crystal was faint static. My father said that was the sound of God breathing in the universe. I could listen to it for a long time in the night before it put me to sleep. I could sometimes hear words in the static. Or what sounded like words. Someone talking far away so you hear a voice but you don't know what he's saying. You don't need to know. You just need to know someone's talking.

My mother didn't mind that I was listening to the radio in the dark. Most kids watched TV. I didn't. I just listened to static on a radio my father'd made. My mother loved that radio even though she never tried to listen to it. It was like she could see me and my father connected by a wire that was real. So maybe she thought he and I would never, could never, be separated. Even when she had left us.

She'd raise the blanket toward my chin. "Higher," I'd say. So she'd smile and raise the blanket to my lips. Her hands were so beautiful, because they brought such comfort. I would shiver when the tip of her finger touched the top of my top lip. "Are you cold?" she'd ask, which is how a lot of people in New Hampshire say, Hello. "More," I'd say, and she'd raise the blanket to my nose. "More." Finally to just under my eyes, when I'd get one last faint look at her smiling down at me. Then she'd pull the blanket up over my head, because that's where she knew I liked it. She'd kiss me through the blanket on the forehead. "Good night, my one and only," she'd say. I'd listen to her leave. Her footsteps were so soft I'd imagine them the beats of angel wings. The angel would be flying away. But I knew she would always come back. I pulled the blanket up around my head and fell asleep in utter happy darkness.

The KC-135 releases me and Jesus. We float back down to the asphalt of the bridge over I-95. We watch the plane float down and away toward Pease. Its vapors don't quite reach us. We both breathe deeply, not to lose the loss of Earth we'd so enjoyed together. We'd gone flying, Jesus and me. I'd seen my mother. And Jesus had been with me all the while.

The plane disappears beneath the bank of trees surrounding Pease.

"It's landing," Jesus says.

His body tenses. I can feel it next to me.

He's no different from anyone else. He wants to know a plane is safely on the ground.

My father was born the year that Portsmouth Air Force Base got renamed after a distant cousin of his from up north. Though the Greenland Peases didn't even know the Plymouth Peases, my father's parents took him to the opening ceremony, September 7, 1957. My father was only six months old. But he always told me he could remember that day. He didn't know what anyone said about his cousin, because he was too young to talk. But he could see the Thunderbirds flying in formation above the airfield. He said he thought they were little pieces of God moving back and forth in the air to get his attention.

"Imagine that," he said. "I didn't believe in God until I was already six months old."

When I was about the same age, he started telling me about my cousin once removed, Harl Pease, Junior. He called him my cousin once removed because my cousin was dead. Harl Pease, Junior, was a lot more removed from me than that as a cousin. But as a person, he was once removed. My father taught me that about the difference between the living and the dead. Once removed.

Of course I didn't understand what my father was talking about until I learned to talk myself. My father told me I learned to talk before other kids because he started to talk to me when I was too young to know what he was talking about. I don't remember what he said to me when I was six months old. But I remember him talking to me the way he remembers the Thunderbirds in the air. Your father's voice is the voice of God.

Harlan Pease Jr. was born just a few days after America declared war on Germany in World War One. He died in 1942 as a prisoner at the Japanese camp at Rabaul, on the Gazelle Peninsula in the northernmost part of the island of New Britain in Papua New Guinea. He was by that time a captain in the Army Air Corps. The Japanese at the war camp called him Captain Boeing. On October 8, 1942, Harl and five others were taken into the jungle on a work detail. They were ordered to dig. One by one they were beheaded and thrown into the grave they had just dug.

On December 2, 1942, Harl was awarded a posthumous Medal of Honor for heroism in combat. President Franklin Roosevelt presented the medal to Harl's parents. The citation honored what it called Harl's "complete contempt for personal danger."

My father made his name my middle name. He told me your middle name is protected by the names around it, the way all of us are protected by those who have died for us.

He told that story of Harl Pease, Junior, over and over. That's the way it is with family stories. You're always trying to bring the people to life. Especially when they're dead.

He especially liked to tell me the story when he was doing something he didn't like doing. One time my mother and me heard some terrible screaming coming from the hospital barn. It didn't sound like human noise. My mother said, "I think your father's finally lost his patience with some poor baboon. Go see what's happening, War."

I knew he didn't treat baboons. My mother liked to joke about things having to do with my father's work. I think it made it easier for her to live in a place where there was so much suffering. No one ever taught animals, the way they teach kids, not to cry. My mother often walked around the house with her hands over her ears and tears in her eyes.

I ran out to the barn. There I found my father watching a small red-haired pig trying to walk toward him. He had it in the weaner pen, though it looked just big enough to be in the grower pen. The poor thing's back legs kept falling out from under its body, so it would drag its legs and then it would pull them up to where they were supposed to be and then the legs would give way and the little pig would drag them behind it as it moved toward my father. He stood there with one arm over his chest and the other reaching out toward the pig, like he couldn't decide if he wanted to ignore the pig or tickle it under the chin. While the pig limped and pulled itself along, it screamed. It screamed so loud I got worried about my mother. More than about the pig. I didn't want my mother to worry about some baboon that she knew didn't exist in the first place.

"What a cute little pig," I said.

My father shook his head. Half at me and half at the pig. "It's called a potbellied pig," he said.

"I can see why," I said.

"Somebody's pet probably." My father shook his head again and knelt down and let the pig drag himself or herself into his waiting arms. I felt bad for the pig getting a head shook at it. Not once but twice. Parents should never shake their heads, whether at pigs or at kids.

My father loved animals but he hated pets. He would have hated people who had pets, but he was a good Christian so he couldn't hate people. He couldn't hate animals either. So he hated pets. Not animals. Pets. Pets, he said, were not animals. Pets were an idea of animals.

Animals were not playthings. They were put on Earth to serve man. And because they serve man, man has to serve them. That's why my father was an animal doctor. To help animals help man. Animals were for food and labor and in the winter they kept people warm, which is why some people had houses where the animals lived on the ground floor and the people who lived up above them could feel their warmth spread through them and all winter they must have thought they'd died and gone to Heaven.

I always wondered how they got used to the smell. Even this little potbellied pig smelled to high Heaven, which I'd never realized before was an expression that must have come from people living happily above warm smelly animals in the winter.

I said, "It really stinks."

My father almost laughed and turned the pig over and showed me its penis. "They didn't barrow the poor thing. You're too young to notice this in yourself, but male hormones smell."

"What's the matter with it?" I asked.

"Dippity pig," he said.

I started to laugh, but before I could say anything my father said, "That's not his name. That's a disease."

"It must hurt," I said, because the pig not only hadn't stopped screaming, it seemed to scream even louder when my father told it it had dippity pig. "What is it?" I asked.

"Nobody really knows," he said.

"Why's he screaming?"

"It hurts."

"Do something," I said.

My father got a syringe. He sucked some medicine into it from a small bottle and unscrewed the needle and handed the syringe to me.

"What's in it?" I asked.

"Aspirin."

"How come?" I said and moved the syringe around in my hand. He usually gave regular-size pigs aspirin ground up in peanut butter sandwiches. I always got to lick the spoon.

"The smaller the pig, the smellier the farts."

Even the pig seemed to laugh. Or at least it opened up its mouth even more as it screamed so I could stick the syringe right between its lips and feel the plunger thaw beneath my thumb.

"Now what?" I said, because the pig was still screaming its head off.

"You know how your mom feels when she's taking her allergy medicine?"

"No pain," I said, because that's what Mom always said when her medicine made her just about pass out.

"Exactly," said my father.

He washed out the syringe and needle and screwed the needle back on and took out a silvery vial of diphenhydramine. Those little bottles always made me stare at them. I loved how clean they looked and how the medicine melted into the needle, but they also made me shiver because I didn't like needles any more than pigs did.

"How much do you figure?"

My father nodded at the Alley Weigh Scale. We got the pig onto the scale together. It didn't scream as much. Maybe it was proud of being a pig and getting weighed. The first thing people usually asked about a pig was, "How much does it weigh?" My father used to say, "God made scales first for pigs. And then for women."

He weighed about forty kilograms. My father said that would make him maybe two years old. "I'm going to go about a quarter over," he said, and drew a hundred milligrams of diphenhydramine into the syringe. "This'll sedate him enough so I can work on him and maybe it will also help stop the pain. Move his ear."

The pig had only one whole ear. The other one was ripped halfway off. It was a little ear to begin with, not like big pigs' ears that looked like bats. This was more like a misshapen leaf half devoured by beetles. It made you want to comfort the pig for its suffering.

My father stuck the needle in behind the whole ear I was holding up. I had the other arm wrapped around the pig's head, because I knew that when the needle went in the pig would try to look me in the eye and bite my head off. This way it only screamed louder than ever, "What the h——!"

"It hurts more there than in the buttocks," said my father, "but you need a bigger needle back there because we all got more fat in our backsides, or at least pigs and ladies do; it's only males who are fatheads, and the hind fat slows up the medicine and look at our little friend now it's already working."

Sure enough, the pig had a smile on his face. Or if not a smile, because if you look at a pig the right way it's always smiling, then a grin. A grin is a smile with the teeth showing and the eyes lighting up. This pig's eyes were lighting up and closing at the same time. It was like he was dying and getting a glimpse of Heaven all at once.

My father held the pig around the underline and folded up its short legs and lowered it to the floor. He moved aside some of the short red hair on the pig's back and sides. The pig must have blown his coat recently. On his flesh there were deep narrow ugly sores. The dried blood around them was almost the same color as his coat.

"Did he do that to himself?" I asked. I didn't believe he would, because at that time I didn't know about hurting yourself on purpose. But I did know that pigs who blew their coats would try to dig out their hair and old skin with their hooves and dewclaws.

My father explained, "It's the dippity pig."

He got down a large tube of cortisone and squeezed some onto his first two fingers and put his fingers right within the pig's sores. Very gently he rubbed the cream into the wounds. The pig lay there smiling.

"The thing about pigs," my father said, "is if you get them drowsy like this with an antihistamine or a sedative, you have to let it wear off before you put them back in their herd. The other males will sense weakness and attack the drugged one. That's probably how this guy here lost his ear. Somebody ripped it half off."

"I didn't know pigs had fights with each other," I said. It was hard to imagine. They were so round.

"Everybody fights," he said.

"Why?" I asked.

"Everybody has something to protect. The thing you need to

know about this world, War, is that there's more war than peace and more pain than pleasure. Every creature fights for territory. Maybe because every creature knows that there's only one world and it's a small one in the scheme of things. But only man fights for the territory of the soul. And in the end your soul is all you have. Literally. Your cousin Harl Pease, Junior . . ."

I lay down there next to the pig while my father told me Harl's story yet again.

Jesus says, "I want to go where that plane went."

So I say, "Do you want to fly there?"

"Wise guy," he says back. He starts down the hill to the highway. "Walk there."

So we walk along I-95 toward Pease. While we walk, I tell Jesus the story of the guy Pease was named after, my cousin once removed, Harl Pease Jr.

We're alone out there. Nobody walks along I-95, unless your car broke down. Or you wracked it up. But there we are, like two bums, walking north along the highway. The cars and trucks go by so fast they carry us along with them. Our feet go as fast as feet go when they're walking. But we also seem to fly through the air. It's not that the wind is at our backs. The wind surrounds us and so, yeah, we fly.

It's a relief to get to the airport, not just because I was afraid some cop was going to pull up to us on I-95 and we were going to get arrested and Jesus would end up in jail and the great New Hampshire State Police would end up looking like the Sadducees. I could see me and Jesus with the swords he told his guys to buy. That was every soldier's favorite part of the Bible. The chaplains made it a point to read it to us as often as possible. So we'd be sure not to turn the other cheek. Jesus and the two swords. Jesus said it was enough. That's all you need in life: side by side with Jesus, one sword each. And what boy doesn't want it said about himself, like what Jesus himself said was said about him, "He was counted among the outlaws"? So we'd take on the police and like Peter I'd cut off someone's ear. And just as the cops are about to shoot us both dead, Jesus would put the man's ear back on.

It's also a relief to get to the airport because we were wading through trash along the side of I-95. It was a lot worse than what was on the beach. But here at Pease even the runway overruns are paved and clean. We walk around a stub and onto the taxiway. I say to Jesus, "We're not supposed to be here." I expect him to say back, *But we're outlaws, Warren*. But all he says is, "I know that."

It's like we're invisible. Planes are taking off and landing. An Allegiant passenger. An Emery Worldwide cargo. Another air-shattering KC-135 from the New Hampshire Air National Guard. I can feel their heat and the wind they make. They roar in my ears like the voice of God.

Jesus talks to me. I can't hear him. He puts his lips up to my ear. I can feel his mouth make the words.

"Let's get some lunch."

"You're crying," says Jesus.

"They made Harl dig his own grave," I say. "They cut off his head and threw it into his grave."

"Graves are for bodies." Jesus turns on his bar stool and puts his hand against my chest. "He's buried here."

My father wrote me in Iraq that the last American to see Harl Pease alive had died. He was a Catholic missionary, a prisoner named George Lepping. He was supposed to be beheaded the day after Harl but was saved when the camp at Rabaul was bombed by American B-17s. My father had gone to visit him in Washington when Father Lepping finally returned Stateside from his mission work in the Pacific in 1991.

Harl Pease Jr. had been the last to die. He had comforted his gunner, Chick Czechowski, and had watched Chick's head fly off into the hole Chick had dug for himself.

That's what Father Lepping had told my father.

That's what my father told me.

I wonder who will tell people about me when I'm dead.

So I'm sitting there in tears at the bar in a pub at Pease (my cousin!) Air National Guard Base aka Pease (once removed!) International Tradeport when the bartender says to me, "You look like you could use a beer."

I look at Jesus. I want to see if he wants a beer. Wine, that I could see. That is, if he ever took up wine drinking again after he said he wouldn't drink it until that day when he could drink it with all of us in his father's kingdom. Maybe today is that day. It's such a beautiful day. If the world is ever to end, it should be on a day like this one.

But who knows if Jesus drinks beer. Also, I've never had a beer.

Bethie doesn't drink. When she was pregnant she told me I couldn't drink even if I wanted to, because it would hurt the baby. "If the *father* drinks?" I said. "This baby's growing in both of us," she answered, and that was that.

Ryan tried a beer once, but he said it was like swallowing weights instead of lifting them.

My father stopped drinking anything alcoholic when my mother died, like he didn't want to lose his ability to concentrate on her memory and he didn't want to be like other men, the ones who *start* drinking when their wife dies.

Most everyone drank in the army, whether it was at Fort Bliss or the Army Sniper School at Fort Benning or in The Mess. You don't have to be twenty-one to drink and die, unless you're in the Real World.

Jesus tells the bartender, "I'll have a Double Black."

I don't know what that is, but it reminds me of our twin English Black pigs.

"Sorry," says the bartender. "We don't make that anymore."

"Sure you do," says Jesus. "Just give a tug on that lever."

Jesus points to a handle that says BLONDE ALE. The bartender shakes his head. He takes a large glass and holds it at an angle under the faucet that the handle is attached to and as he pulls on the handle he says, "I'm telling you . . ."

Out of the faucet comes a thick dark liquid that looks like pudding with bubbles.

The bartender lets go of the lever and shakes his head even harder and pours the stuff out into the silvery sink. "No," he says. "Uh-uh."

He washes out the glass and sticks it under the same faucet and pulls on the lever that says BLONDE ALE.

"I don't believe it!" It's the same black liquid. Or should I say, double black. He cries out, "Who put Double Black in my Blonde?" There's no one there to answer.

"Please don't throw it out this time," says Jesus. "It's too good."

The bartender fills the glass and puts it down very quickly in front of Jesus. Some of it spills onto the bar.

"A coaster?" says Jesus.

The bartender slides one toward Jesus, but I can see that he doesn't want to lift up the glass and put the coaster under it. He's afraid to touch the glass.

"I'll have the same," I say.

"No," says Jesus.

"No?"

"No," says Jesus again. Then he says to the bartender, "Give him a Sunrye."

"I'll have to see ID," says the bartender. I figure he must be angry about being wrong about the Double Black. Otherwise why would he have said I looked like I needed a beer and then not give me one?

"Never mind," I say.

"Show him your license," says Jesus.

I take the camel-leathery wallet out of my back pocket. The first thing I notice is there's money in it. I feel in my side pocket and there's still money there too. "Where did this come from?" I ask.

"Someone has to pay for lunch," says Jesus.

I remember he said that there was more where that came from. More money, I guess. But also just more. Jesus provides.

"Come on, Warren," he says. "I'm thirsty from all our travel." He's too polite to drink without me.

"I'll have a Coke," I say.

"Show the man your license," says Jesus.

I take the license out of the wallet and put it down on the bar. I close my eyes. Maybe the real reason I never drank before was because I didn't want to be embarrassed. I don't like people calling me out. Or finding me out.

The bartender reaches for my license. But Jesus gets there first. The way he did on the beach, he touches it with the tip of his finger. He runs his finger over it. When it gets to my picture, I feel my body tingle. I shiver. The way they say you do when someone walks over where your grave is going to be. But if that's true, then why is it such an interesting feeling?

Jesus says to the bartender, "There."

The bartender picks up my license. He looks at it and looks at me and looks back at the license. He says, "Why didn't you tell me. Happy birthday! Today you are a man! I'm proud to serve you your first legal drink."

He sticks a glass under a lever that says SUNRYE. The glass fills up with sunlight.

"It's my first drink ever," I say.

"Happy birthday, Warren," says Jesus. He touches his glass to mine.

I watch Jesus take a swallow. When he takes the glass away from his mouth, the dark liquid on his upper lip turns into white bubbles. He licks it off with his tongue and closes his eyes and smiles.

"How come you like beer so much?" I ask.

"I like everything," he says. "I mean, do you have any idea what's in this? It's got wheat. And malt. And barley. Not just roasted barley. Carastan barley. And coffee! Do you like coffee, Warren?"

"I don't drink coffee." Bethie's father used to give me coffee. I never drank it. But he would always pour me a cup. I loved it that he did that. "But I like coffee."

"Me too," says Jesus. "Like I said, I like everything."

"Snails and turtles," I say.

"Of course." Jesus points at my beer. "Go ahead. Try it."

I'm afraid. Here I am, gone to war and killed people and been shot at by people who want to kill me and fell in love with a girl and had a child and quit school and gone to war, and I'm afraid to take my first taste of beer! It's not that I think it's a sin or anything. I think I'm afraid I won't like it. What will Jesus say?

"It's all right if you don't like it," says Jesus.

So I do it. I put the glass up to my mouth, and I take a sip in a way that reminds me of what I would do when my mother fed me medicine from a spoon. I try a little bit and prepare for the worst and let my mother's smile make the bitter sweet. In that moment, when I look at Jesus, I see my mother.

"How is it?" he asks.

"It's not that bad," I say.

Jesus laughs. "That's just the right answer," he says.

I remember that's exactly what he said on the beach this morning when I asked him how I would know if I'd believe him if he told me who he was.

This time I know exactly what he means. It's not that bad.

"So what's in this?" I ask.

"I have no idea," says Jesus. "I don't drink that light stuff."

The bartender must have overheard, because he comes over and he says, "This is our summer seasonal. And today, guys, is the first day of summer."

"Yeah, but what's in it?" says Jesus.

"Oh," says the bartender, "Mount Hood and Hersbrucker and a little bit of Kent Golding to hop the cask." He looks at us with a big smile on his face. "Hey, you guys want something to eat?"

Jesus looks at him with utter admiration. Me, I don't have a clue what he's talking about. Then Jesus orders a burger. When I say, "I'll have the same thing," he says, "Don't do what I do. You gotta try the Hefeweizen chicken."

"What the heck is that?" I ask.

"Chicken made with beer," says Jesus.

"Wheat beer," says the bartender.

"Why didn't you say so?" I play right along. "I'll have the hefe-whatever chicken."

When the food comes, Jesus doesn't even bother to put ketchup on his burger or wait for me to cut a piece of my chicken. He grabs that burger and opens his mouth and sticks the burger halfway in to its center and takes a giant bite and sits there chewing and smiling with burger juice running down his chin.

I realize he does this the way he does everything. Like it's his last day on Earth. And like there's no place he'd rather be.

I remember what he said to Bethie. I repeat it to him. "You're hungry all the time."

And he says back to me what Bethie said to him. "We men are all the same. Eat, Warren."

So I eat with him and he eats with me, just like I heard him knocking at the door and I heard his voice and I opened the door and he came in. It's like being in Heaven, one of those times when you feel wonderful and immortal and you know it's not because you're in Heaven but because you're on Earth and at that moment the Earth itself is heavenly. My Hefeweizen chicken is incredibly good. Something made the chicken not dried out. Probably the beer. But mostly I'm concentrating on what Jesus just said. "We men." He's not just trying to teach me to be like him. He's telling me I am like him. And he's like me. We men.

Like a lot of men, I guess, we eat without saying anything. Women talk when they eat. Men eat when they eat. Me and Ryan used to go to the all-you-can-eat pizza lunch at Pizza Hut on Portsmouth Avenue and the only thing we'd say to each other was, " 'Scuse me," when one of us got up to get more. I was brought up polite and I taught Ryan to be. I figure he's polite now with Bethie. He better be. And he better not be. With her, I mean. Forever, I mean. He must be with her now, at this very moment. I wonder what she told him about me showing up. I wonder if he's out there lifting weights again. With only my ghost to spot him.

I can't not talk so I say to Jesus even though we're both still eating, "It's not really my birthday, you know."

He puts the last little piece of his hamburger into his mouth. He's polite too. He waits until he's done chewing it before he answers.

"We all have two birthdays," he says. "The day we're born. And the day we die."

"Am I going to die?" And I'm thinking, *Is Ryan going to kill me the way I want to kill him?*

"We all die," says Jesus.

"Yeah," I say, "but we all don't come back." I look at him real closely to see how he's going to answer that one.

"Sure we do," says Jesus.

Two

Jesus in the Air

When Jesus and I walk up the long road to my father's house, the first thing I see in the front meadow is he's got his American flag flying again at half-staff. He kept it that way for years after my mother died. I mean, every night he'd take down the flag. And every morning he'd raise it halfway.

Before she died I used to go out with him most days and evenings to raise and lower the flag. But afterward he did it alone. He didn't have to tell me not to come. He just never invited me. I missed doing it with him. But I used to watch him sometimes from the window of my room, way across the front meadow, and I could see that for him it was like a time of prayer. I never heard him actually pray after she died. And he stopped going to church. But when he was out there with that flag, he did everything very slowly. He watched the flag go up in the morning, and come down in the evening, and each time it was like he was looking into the sky the way people do for God. Except my father would look only halfway, to where the flag would stop. He couldn't make it all the way to God.

Then one day he raised the flag all the way up again. It was a beautiful day, like this one almost. But instead of being at the beginning of summer, it was near the end. I was a teenager by then, but not old enough to drive. I took the bus to school with Ryan, like every day. He was still lifting weights then. It was before Bethie. So our plan was the same plan we had every day: we'd meet after school and take the bus and I'd get off at his house and spot him.

But on this day, something happened. I was sitting in some class. It wasn't English, so I don't remember what class it was. Probably my third class, because it was just after ten o'clock. The teacher was saying something, or doing something, or doing nothing, or saying nothing important. And I was sitting there wondering the way I always did what I was doing sitting there. All of a sudden, there's my father. He came in fast through the door of the classroom. The teacher said, "Hello?" in a scared kind of voice. Because you never knew what kind of crazy people might come busting into classrooms.

I had to admit, my father looked kind of scary. He had on a blue scrub that had what looked like bloody handprints on it, and one of his disposable polyethylene aprons, which was white so you could really see the blood. He hadn't even taken off his boot covers. He must have been operating on some animal, and he must have come here in a real hurry.

I was kind of scared and excited both. I worried he had something terrible to tell me, something even worse than the time he wouldn't come to school to tell me. But nothing could be worse than that. He was alive himself, and we had nobody else to lose. My mother had killed herself because she couldn't have another kid. I was alone in life with my father. But the way he was, I was just alone in life.

What excited me was just seeing him there. I knew the last thing most kids would want to see was one of their parents busting into their classroom. But for me it was special. My father had come to where I was.

He stood there at the front of the class near the scared teacher. His eyes searched the classroom, row by row. I wanted him just to fasten his eyes on me, to pick me out instantly from the other forty kids in the crowded room. But I realized that he didn't know me very well. If he had, he would have known just where to look. In the last row, as hidden as possible. Sniper position, now that I think of it. *Covert.*

The other kids were beginning to freak out. I don't blame them. A strange man with blood all over him busts into their classroom and looks them in the eye one by one. They had no idea who he was. He certainly wasn't wearing one of those visitor stickers they force on you at the school office. My father never came to my school after my mother died. Not even on the day she died.

I stood up. My father didn't exactly smile when he saw me. But he looked relieved. I wondered if he thought I didn't really go to school every day. Or if he was there because he'd heard something had happened to me.

He came right down the aisle to where I was. I couldn't remember the last time I didn't have to go to him.

When he got to me where I was standing at my desk he took my hand. Not my arm. My hand. He took my hand and he led me around the back of the classroom and then up the side wall and out the door.

I knew the last thing beyond the last thing any other teenaged kid would want was one of their parents holding their hand in the classroom. But I didn't mind. I mean, it was a little embarrassing his doing it. But what would have been even more embarrassing would have been if they all had known how much I loved it. My father hadn't touched me on purpose in years. I felt right then that I wanted him to hold my hand for the rest of my life. And I didn't care who saw it.

He was driving his clinic van. It was parked illegally at the end of the front walk to the school. He'd left the engine running.

He still hadn't said a word to me. But he did come around and open the passenger door, the way he always used to do for my mother. Then he did something he hadn't even done since I was a little boy, since before my mother died. He pulled the seat belt down and over my shoulder and reached over me and pushed the buckle into the clasp and pulled hard on the waist belt. For a moment my mouth was against the side of his face. If I had kissed him, it would have been the first time he'd let me kiss him in years. But all I did was take a deep breath, not to feel how secure he'd made the seat belt around me but to smell the nice smell of my father. No matter how many smelly animals he took care of, he always smelled like himself. He always overcame everything in the outside world.

I wished I *had* kissed him, when he backed off and pushed down the lock on my door and closed it with the handle up so it would be sure to lock. Then he went around to his side and got in.

I didn't know what he was doing there, but I was not particularly nervous about it. Not even when he'd belted me up and locked me in, like he was going to go very fast and drive recklessly. The thing was, my father got less reckless after my mother died. He got cautious. Like the whole world might explode any day, or he might inject an animal with the wrong medicine and hurt it without meaning to. Maybe he just wanted to take me hunting. Maybe he wanted to get me as far away from books as possible. I probably should have gotten him a copy of *On Killing.* I didn't need any conditioning to kill, but guys in my unit did. When you take life seriously, the way I do, you know you have to kill people who don't take it seriously. I don't mean jokesters. I mean suicide martyrs. I mean the enemy. My killology is, If you don't kill, the person you don't kill will.

"So where are we going?" I said as regular as possible.

"Home," he said.

"How come?"

"You're safer there than here."

"Yeah, with all the nuts running around."

"Flying around," he said. "They're flying around."

I didn't know what had happened until later. Until after we'd arrived home and my father stopped the van halfway down the driveway along the front meadow. Only when he threw open his door and jumped out did I realize that he hadn't fastened his own seat belt. Maybe he knew all along he was going to want to get out of the van in a rush. Or he'd decided that if we'd crashed on the way home he didn't care what happened to him. Which meant he did care what happened to me.

By the time I got my own seat belt unfastened and my door unlocked my father had run all the way to the flagpole. I didn't know what he was doing there, but I ran as fast as I could to get there too. His boot covers had come off and laid there to mark the way.

He had his hands on the ropes. He gripped them so hard it looked like it was them and not some animal that had bled on his apron.

The flag was at half-staff, the way it had been every day since my mother died. Every day for four years, five months, twenty-two days. But now my father was raising it.

He didn't do it slowly, like for my mother. He tore at the ropes so that the flag flew up like there was a wind around the sun on this late-summer day. But there was no wind. All was still except for my father's hands tearing at the ropes and the flag rising in its colors like a weapon shot into the sun. "There," I heard him say when the flag slammed into the bulb at the top of the pole. "There, you sons of bitches!"

He strangled the pole with the ropes so the flag could not come down.

It was September 11, 2001. While the rest of America was beginning to lower its flags, for the people murdered at the World Trade Center and the Pentagon and Shanksville, Pennsylvania, my father was raising his. It wasn't that he'd forgotten about the death of my mother. He would mourn and honor her for the rest of his life. But for the others dead on this day, he would mourn and honor them by raising our flag. And he would pray for them, the way he could not pray for her, with his anger.

I didn't know it then, but that was the day I joined the Army. That was the day I took my father's anger as my own and joined him in defense of my country and the family he was and the family I had when Dodie was born three years and three months and seventeen days later.

"The flag's at half-staff," I point out to Jesus.

"Yes," says Jesus.

"I wonder why," I say. "My father would never forget September Eleventh."

That's how I always say it: "September Eleventh." I hate it when people say "Nine-Eleven" and they write it 9/11. Numbers aren't words. Numbers take away from words. 3,000 dead in Iraq. 30,000 for a Dodge Ram. 12/7. That's Pearl Harbor Day. That's the day that ended up getting Harl Pease Jr. beheaded and buried far away in a grave he dug himself. We don't call it 12/7, and we can't call that day the Muslims came for us and my father came for me 9/11. We have to give that day a name. If we don't, it's going to end up 9/11 and it won't even mean as much as 911. It would be like if I called the day my mother died — 3/21.

"Your father's in mourning," says Jesus.

"But he raised the flag on September Eleventh. It's not like he stopped mourning my mother. He just decided that in the world it's more important to fight than to mourn."

"He's mourning you," says Jesus.

When Jesus says that, I feel for the first time that I want to see my father. That I'm not dreading it. "You're right," I say. Why should I be surprised that Jesus knows everything. "I never really thought about it before, but the day my mother died, I died to my father. He was never the same to me after that. I could tell that right away. But I never realized that I was dead to him."

"No," says Jesus. "He was dead to you."

"I know what you mean." Not that I lost my feelings for my father. Never. But that *his* feelings for *me* had died. He couldn't love me or touch me or even talk to me very much in a world my mother left him in alone. Alone with me. But now I'm home from war. I can only hope that he wants to see me and will be happy to. But I know how much I want to see him. I want him to be alive to me. And me to him.

I take off like a shot and run across the meadow toward our old farmhouse.

Mr. Smith was my father when my father wasn't. I drove Bethie home every day after school in my little red truck. We'd sit at her kitchen table on Trundlebed Road. We were supposed to be doing our homework. But I couldn't read or study when she was in the same room with me. Not even English. Every poem was about her. The poet's words got replaced with my own. I'd try and touch her, and she'd say, "Take it easy there, Lord Byron."

Soon her father would show up. It never felt like an interruption. I was always relieved, because Mr. Smith always gave me what I wanted.

"Good to see you, War," he'd say, no matter how many days in a row he'd seen me. "How's my new best student?"

He'd throw his book bag down on the table between us. He was the only teacher I ever saw who carried more books than the most book-carrying student. I never thought he was trying to keep Bethie and me apart by throwing the books between us. I think he was just trying to tell us that books were like love: they made new life.

One day Bethie said, "You know it's a waste taking two cars home."

From then on, Bethie and her father took the bus to school and I drove the two of them home. Sometimes we had to wait for Mr. Smith to finish up all the things teachers have to finish up when the students think school is all finished up.

Bethie would sit on her father's lap in my passenger seat. Good thing she's small. Still, the seat belt wouldn't fit around them. Good thing we don't have a seat belt law in New Hampshire. Live Free or Die Shackled. They were safe with me anyway.

Mr. Smith kept his promise. One class long before God rang the bell, he read us the poem about Jesus. He didn't say anything before he read it. Usually he did. This time he just pushed his glasses up his nose and slowly opened that old book. He didn't have to say anything. Everybody recognized the sound. It was like he was opening up the body of Emily Dickinson.

He didn't tell us how much we were going to love this poem. No smile spread over his face. He actually looked sad. He read the poem like someone was tearing it word for word out of his throat.

"At least to pray is left, is left.
O Jesus in the air
I know not which thy chamber is,
I'm knocking everywhere.

"Thou stirrest earthquake in the South,
And maelstrom in the sea.
Say, Jesus Christ of Nazareth,
Hast thou no arm for me?"

When he was done reading, Mr. Smith cleared his throat and said, "I want to dedicate that reading to War back there. War lost his mother, you know. I lost my dear wife a long time ago. This poem's about tragedy and redemption. It's about living on the earth and going to Heaven. Notice how the first stanza is about the poet, or about whoever the person is who reads it. The *I* person. You, me, anyone, War back there. And the second stanza is about the earth. The world. Some people think that 'earthquake in the South' is a reference to the Civil War. That terrible, necessary war was going on when this poem was written. I won't ask you the dates. It was 1862 Dickinson wrote this. You know what a maelstrom is — a storm. God gives us storms and earthquakes. God upsets the world and the people in it. He makes the ground rumble under our feet and the air swirl above our heads. But the air in this poem, this is the air above the world. Just the way the first stanza is about the person and the second is about the earth, the first stanza is about Heaven and the second is about our world. The world without end above, and the world that will end below."

Mr. Smith stopped talking at that moment. He pretended he did it to try to make his hair sit down on the sides of his head, first with one hand taken off the book of poems, then with the other. But he really did it so everyone could take a moment, as they say, to think about our world coming to an end. Teenagers loved to think about that. They never thought it would actually happen, so they loved to think about how it would happen. Just the way they never thought they would die, so they loved tattoos with skulls and movies with girls getting slashed to death.

No one said a word. You could hear the breathing in the room.

Then the bell rang.

Mr. Smith ignored it. He said, "As you know, Emily Dickinson didn't give her poems titles. So a scholar gave them numbers. This poem is number 502. I would never call it that. Numbers aren't words. Numbers are symbols. Words are divine. Words are sight and sound and smell and touch and taste and spirit. Words are the imagination made visible, the way human beings are God made visible. The Word was God, says the Bible. The Bible is the inspired word of God. What this means is that God breathed His Word into the people who wrote the Bible. The word *inspire* means *to breathe into.* And God didn't give up inspiring writers once the Bible was written. Every once in a while He chose someone else to inspire. Emily Dickinson was one of those writers. And if I were going to give this poem a title, I would call it 'Rapture.' *Rapture* is one of the most beautiful words there is. It means not just joy but ecstatic joy. It means not just ecstasy but joyful ecstasy. It also means *to carry off.* Not all carrying off is good. The word *rape* comes from the same root as the word *rapture.* I've told you many times that all words are beautiful. They're beautiful because we've made language out of the original Word of God. But the meanings of words can be completely opposite. Good and evil. Rapture and rape. At the Rapture, those who are alive on earth and who believe in Jesus will be carried off to meet him in the air. Yes, Jesus in the air! Just as she says. For you see, this is a poem about Emily Dickinson looking for Heaven. Knocking everywhere. Knocking on Heaven's Door."

Mr. Smith stopped to smile. A couple of guys in the class went, "Oh, yeah." One of them started to play air guitar like Slash in Guns N' Roses when they played that song. Knocking on Heaven's Door.

Me, I thought about someone standing at the door, knock knock knocking, and I hear him, and I open the door, and he comes in and eats with me and me with him.

I looked over at the door to the classroom. The glass part was filled with faces. I knew they were just wondering what was going on in here because it was time for the next class to begin. But they looked like people who had their faces pressed against the door to Heaven. Wondering. When they would get in. If they would get in.

For me, it was like being in Heaven. Mr. Smith was the greatest teacher in the world. He could take a mysterious poem and make you see how the mystery itself was the meaning.

"For you see, class," Mr. Smith went on, "the carrying off, the Rapture, is the ecstatic joy and the joyful ecstasy. No, we don't know which his chamber is. We live on earth and we aspire to Heaven. So we knock. And we pray. And we suffer the storms and earthquakes not just of our physical world but of our inner lives. But if we are good, and if we believe in Jesus, then we will all be raptured to meet him in the air. And from that time on, he will give us his arm. And wherever he goes, we will go with him."

Only then did Mr. Smith move his hands together on the covers of that old book. He had tears in his eyes. A few of them dropped down and hung onto the bottom rims of his little reading glasses before falling into the book. He closed it on them like they were ink and he was blotting them. I pictured them there forever in the book, true to form, the eyes' words.

With his hands together on that skinny book, he looked like he was praying.

My father isn't in the house. By the time I get out back to the hospital barn, Jesus is there.

My father has a gun pointed at Jesus. It's not a rifle but a captive bolt gun. It looks like a pistol. He uses it to kill animals. I remember he once told me, "Not everyone can be saved." He talked about animals like they were people. He said it made his job easier. He belonged to the Humane Slaughter Association. I used to think that would make a great name for a rock band. The only book I ever remember him reading was something they sent him all the way from England called *Farewell.*

"Who are you?" says my father.

"I'm with Warren," says Jesus.

"Warren?" says my father, like he doesn't recognize the name.

"I brought him to see you," says Jesus.

"No," says my father.

I want to run away.

"Yes," says Jesus.

"He can't be here," says my father.

"He's here with me," says Jesus.

"Where?"

I step out from behind Jesus.

My father puts down the bolt gun.

"I didn't think I'd ever see him again," he says.

"Talk to your son," says Jesus.

My father doesn't like to be ordered around. "Who are you?" he says to Jesus.

"Ask *him,*" Jesus says.

"Who are *you*?" my father says to me.

The school board fired Mr. Smith. I felt really bad for him, but he said, "War, they wouldn't tell me if they fired me because I talked about Jesus, because I mentioned rape, or because I kept the class late." Then he laughed. Mr. Smith was the only adult I knew who laughed. I don't mean at jokes or the stupid mistakes people make. I mean at himself.

"Aren't you going to fight it?" I said.

"*Fight* it?" Mr. Smith looked across his kitchen table and down through his reading glasses into my coffee cup. He always wanted to be sure I had enough coffee. Even though he knew I didn't drink the coffee he gave me. He nodded when he saw I had enough coffee. Only then did he answer: "But I won."

"You lost your job," I said.

"I got to teach my last class," he said.

"It was a great class," I said.

"It was," he said, "wasn't it?"

"It was," I said.

He smiled at me over his little glasses. "That was a rhetorical question, War. You weren't meant to answer it. But thank you. More coffee?"

"*That's* a rhetorical question."

He looked into my cup again. "You're right!"

"So what are you going to do now?" I asked.

"Homeschool," he said.

"Aren't you a little old for that?" I said.

At that point Mr. Smith also became the only adult who'd ever laughed at anything *I'd* said.

"As a *teacher*," he said. "Though they did take pity on me and left my pension. Or maybe it wasn't pity but fear I'd make a legal fuss. And I have Mrs. Smith's life insurance. Though I would rather have Mrs. Smith than all the life insurance in the world. Of course I also have eternal life insurance, if you know what I mean. And I may need that sooner rather than later."

I did know what he meant. About the eternal life insurance. Like Jesus says to Martha, *Whoever believes in me will never die.*

But what did he mean by sooner?

"I'm a bit sick," he said, either because he knew I was confused or he wanted to tell me.

"Does Bethie know?"

He shook his head. That's how I knew it was more than a bit. And that he didn't want me to tell her.

"I could still use some students," he said.

"Where do I sign?" I said.

"Right here next to Bethie."

He held out his hand, palm up, like it was a piece of paper. I put my hand upon his hand.

I touched her through him. And him through her.

I wished I could hold on to him forever.

Sometimes you look at a person and you might have known that person for years, or all your life, but when you look at him, you don't know who he is. Not really. You recognize him and you don't recognize him. He's a stranger. Just the way you can look in the mirror and see a stranger looking back at you. Sometimes you don't know who you are. Sometimes you don't know who anybody is.

My father doesn't know who I am. He recognizes me. But he doesn't know who I am.

I answer his question. "Warren Harlan Pease."

"How's your wound?" he says.

"He healed it," I say.

"Who?"

I point to Jesus next to me. "Him."

"You healed his wound?" my father asks Jesus.

"Talk to your son," Jesus says again.

"Who are you?" my father asks him.

This time I answer for Jesus. "Ray. My friend Ray."

"He healed your wound?"

I put my hand on my leg and walk toward my father. "No more limp," I say.

"Not your *leg*!"

I stop walking. "But you told Bethie about it," I say.

"Not your leg," he says. "Your other wound."

"What other wound?"

"Lift up your shirt," he says.

"Actually, this is Ray's shirt."

"Lift it up."

I do. I pull it up like a little kid so it folds up over my face. When I do it, I wonder how my father likes my abs. I'm pretty sure I toughened up over in The Mess.

"Who *are* you?" I can't see my father. But I know he's not talking to me.

The next thing I feel is my father's arms around me.

Mr. Smith never actually hugged me. I think he was embarrassed about being short and having a stomach he could rest a book on while standing up if he wanted to. But he did take me in. I started to stay over at his house with him and Bethie after our homeschooling sessions were done. Not all the time. Not every night. I'd always go to Greenland on weekends in case my father needed me for anything. And sometimes I'd show up there during the week. To get a schoolbook I might need or to pick up some clothes or do some laundry or to see if my father missed me.

My father didn't care that I left the public high school and took up schooling with Mr. Smith at home. I didn't hide it from him. I didn't tell him I was one place and sneak off to another. I didn't ask his permission either. I was seventeen years old. I could go to whatever school I wanted or no school at all.

When I told him, he said, "It doesn't matter where you go. You don't learn anything from school. You learn from life. Life teaches you that life teaches you."

"You went to vet school," I said. "Didn't you learn something there?"

"I learned to do things," he answered. "I didn't learn why I had to do them. I didn't learn why there's so much illness and injury done to God's creatures. And I didn't learn how to prevent it. Only to fight it. That's what doctors do. They fight. To the death," he added with a rare smile.

It's hard to know if someone misses you if they don't talk to you much. My father still thanked me when I turned on the lights. And if I watched him at work on some animal, he explained what he was doing. But he didn't talk much about people. Not about himself. Not about me. I sometimes felt the only person he ever really talked to was my mother. I think he sat there in the dark talking to my mother. Never out loud. I was the only one who talked to her out loud.

One day when I went to see him he said, "Where've you been?"

"At Bethie's."

"Your girlfriend."

"She's not really my girlfriend."

"What is she then?"

"She says she's my friend."

"And you want her to be your girlfriend?"

"I love her," I said.

My father looked at me with the saddest expression on his face.

It was Ryan who asked me, "So where do you sleep?"

"Not with her, if that's what you mean," I answered.

"I kind of meant, which room do you sleep in?"

"Isn't that the same thing?"

"Are you telling me just because you sleep in the same room as a girl you have to sleep *with* the girl?"

"You don't have to," I said.

"But you want to?" Ryan said.

"You more than want to," I answered.

I brought Ryan over to Bethie's. I figured it was time they got to know each other better. The first thing she said to him was, "That's where War sleeps. Have a seat." We were in the living room. She was pointing to the pullout couch.

Ryan gave me a look.

"Hey," I said, "I didn't tell her."

Bethie looked down at Ryan sitting on the couch. "He didn't have to tell me. You guys are all the same."

Mr. Smith came in from what he called his "study." It was a half bathroom so small that he could sit on the toilet and use the sink as a desk. With books on the toilet cover so he could reach the sink top and the sink top covered with a board. He had books piled in the corners. He'd had to take off the door so you could get into the room. He said it didn't need a door because it wasn't a bathroom. It was his study.

"Mr. Smith, this is my friend Ryan," I said to Mr. Smith. "Ryan, this is Mr. Smith."

Ryan did what he'd done that day my father and I buried my mother and Ryan met my father for the first time. He got up from the couch and held out his hand. "Hello, Mr. Smith."

Mr. Smith reached way up and took Ryan's hand. It wasn't that long ago that they were the same height. Ryan had kept growing taller since the day I told him about Bethie and he stopped lifting weights. He was almost the same height as me.

"That's quite a grip you've got there," Mr. Smith said to Ryan.

"I know," said Ryan with a big smile.

"Sometimes it isn't wise to show off our knowledge." Mr. Smith took his hand back from Ryan and shook it in the air between them. "Though look who's talking," he added, "I quote poetry at the drop of a hat. Do you know where *that* expression comes from? I'll tell you. It comes from when two men wanted to shoot each other and a third man would stand there and when he dropped his hat to the ground it was a signal for the two men to draw their pistols." Mr. Smith smiled like someone who just gave you a present and you opened it and he wants to know how you like it.

"No kidding," said Ryan.

That was good enough for Mr. Smith. He put his hand on Ryan's shoulder and said, "You should study with me."

"My parents want me to stay in school," said Ryan. Which meant he must have thought about it.

"This *is* school," said Mr. Smith. "Isn't that right, War?"

"It's the best school, Mr. Smith," I said.

"I love how you call me Mr. Smith," he said.

"Do you have a first name?" I asked.

"Of course," he said.

I waited.

"But I've been a teacher so long I've forgotten it," he said.

Ryan and Mr. Smith burst out laughing at the same time.

Bethie and I just looked at each other and shook our heads.

My father's hug isn't a love hug. It's a reality hug. He doesn't believe I've come home.

Still, I don't want him to let me go. I like the feel of me in his arms. He's such a strong man. Much stronger than the soldiers I fought with. They had bigger muscles, but he's harder than they were. I feel that all his strength has gone into his body. That his soul is as fragile as the little boat on Galilee in the hymn the Squids sing for good luck, "Jesus, Savior, Pilot Me." *Squids* being what the Marines disrespectfully call Navy sailors, which maybe they wouldn't if they knew that real squids are Marines themselves, aka marine cephalopods.

It's like when I first met Jesus this morning, who didst walk upon the sea, and when I beheld his form, safe I glided through the storm.

Not that it hasn't been a perfectly sunny day today.

"You're too thin." My father's digging his fingers between my ribs.

"I didn't eat."

"Lived on air," he says.

"And smoke," I say. "And the smell of blood. It's one long barbecue. War. Smells better than it tastes."

He puts his hands on my shoulders. "Whatever it was, you're broader in the shoulders." He grips them hard. "No more little Remingtons."

"M107," I say. "Barrett."

"It fires?"

"Twenty-five millimeter."

"Recoil?"

"You don't wanna know."

My father looks creased at me, like no one should tell him what he does and doesn't want to know.

"Beyond human limitations," I say.

"You say or they say?"

"They say."

"And you say?"

"It was my gun of choice."

"Until?" says my father.

"They had me test the XM109."

"In combat?"

"On the range."

"Target practice," he says, like it's beneath the Pease family.

"On bodies," I said.

"Human?"

"Not anymore."

"Recoil?" He's always more interested in guns than people. Guns never went off on you.

"Still more than advertised."

He squeezes my shoulder even harder. "Black and blue?"

"You said it, Dad." I smile through the pain.

"Hurt?" he asks.

"You bet!"

"I thought you were dead," he says.

"Once removed?" I say.

"Once removed." He doesn't smile the way I hoped he would — because I remembered everything he ever said and that would make him happy.

"Do I look dead?" I say.

He lets me go and looks at me. But there's no look in his look. His eyes are dead, his face is blank.

"What do you think, Ray?" he says to Jesus.

"Your son is tired," says Jesus. "He's come a long way to see you."

"All the way from Iraq," says my father.

"At least," says Jesus.

"And we walked here from Bethie's," I say.

"That's a long walk," says my father.

"Ray here walked from the Isles of Shoals," I say.

My father has to think about that for a second. Then he says, "That's a good one."

"He can walk on water," I say.

"*Salt* water," says Jesus, like it's a joke.

Jesus and I have a laugh over it. My father looks at us like we're a little crazy. Which maybe we are after walking so far.

"I'm kind of busy here," he says.

"What with?" asks Jesus.

My father looks like he wasn't expecting anyone to ask him that. "A possible case of CWD," he says.

"What's that?" I ask.

It sounds like something from the war. We had all kinds of IEDs, like BSIEDs, which were Bicycle Seat Improvised Explosive Devices, a variation on all-vehicle VBIEDs. And EFPs, which are IEDs that use copper melted into a beautiful golden gleaming slug that can pierce body armor, vehicle armor, even human flesh, that the Hajji actually learned to make by studying how the US Air Force, thanks a lot, guys, developed sensor-fuzed weapons that they used for the first time in Iraq. *Hajji* is Arabic for *pilgrim*, but we're not talking the *Mayflower* here. Meanwhile, my Army was making arrow-shaped MRAPs (Mine Resistant–Ambush Protected) and SADARMs, which is how guys from where I came from and from Boston pronounced the name of the late Saddam Hussein, though it stood for Sense and Destroy Armor Munitions. STFA stood for Shoot the F—— Arabs. But you got to kill more people with FIB, which stands for Firing Into the Brown, when you just shoot at people whose skin color is darker than yours. Which is not what my father meant when we'd go hunting for ring-necked pheasant where they'd been stocked on Post Road in Greenland or the Connor Farm in Exeter and we'd see them scurrying brown in the fine brown dust because they don't like to fly and we'd bring home a couple of cocks that my mother would cook and we would praise the Lord for his bounty. CAO was a Casualty Assistance Officer, aka Notification Officer, the *BIG NO* (because people screamed *NO!* when they saw a pair of them coming up the walk), who would go to the Primary Next of Kin (like my father) and to the Secondary Next of Kin (like Bethie) and tell this PNOK and this SNOK that you were DAD. DAD was Dead As a Doornail. Some guys from the South said *dead* that way anyway. "He's dad," so I'd look down and there would be a corpse in his ACU. CAD stood for Army Reg. 638-2, Care and Disposition of Remains. DAD and CAD made a little poem.

Maybe in war and medicine they're always trying to make things less frightening by calling them by letters. Things that make you bleed. Things that hurt. Things that kill you. I always hated abbreviations. Which Mr. Smith taught me are sometimes called acronyms and I started to think of as acridnyms, because they can be so bitter. Is it any wonder?

"Chronic wasting disease," says Jesus.

It sounds like something in the war.

"How do you know that, Ray?" asks my father.

"I like animals," says Jesus. "And if you didn't think we'd know what you meant, why did you use initials?"

"Because it's a terrible disease." My father gestures for us to follow him farther into the hospital barn.

There, not in a stall, just standing in the walkway, is a deer. A doe. It doesn't move when it sees us. If it sees us at all. It has a completely blank expression on its white-and-brown face. Usually a deer has live eyes. Fearful and interested at the same time. Kind of the way you'd expect your own eyes to be as you approach the gates of Heaven.

Which most deer are doing (deer Heaven) when I get close enough to see their eyes. But this deer's eyes are dead in its face. Its ears hang straight down. You'd think it was a statue of a deer if there wasn't spit dripping to the floor from the corners of its mouth. And if its skinny flanks weren't trembling like it was cold on this warm first day of summer when the sun lights up the world. For the first time in a long time I don't feel like I want to hide from it. The light I mean.

I look at my father looking at the deer. He has a kind of hopeless expression on his face. He looks at the deer the way the deer looks at him. And the way my father has looked at me since my mother died.

Then he goes right up to the deer and takes a big colored handkerchief from his back pocket and wipes the spit off the sides of the deer's face and kneels before the deer and stares into its dead eyes.

"CWD is a TSE that's related to BSE."

"Who are you talking to, Dad?" I ask.

"This deer here," he says. "I like to let my patients know everything there is to know."

Jesus laughs. I've heard him laugh before. But never like this. Even the deer seems to wake up.

My father smiles at Jesus. I wonder, what does Jesus have that I don't?

So I say to Jesus, "What do you have that I don't?"

He says, "I laugh at your father's jokes."

"That was a joke?" I say to my father.

"Thank you, Ray," my father says to Jesus.

The two of them talk disease. I learn from listening that the only thing I've heard of before is BSE, because that's Mad Cow Disease. We've never had that here. But I did once see a sheep with another TSE, which stands for something I can't quite spell. My father told me it was called scrapie. I loved that name, and I could understand that name, because the sheep scraped its fleece off against anything that would take it off. The trees out by the pen, the rocks in the ground, the wall of the barn, the fence around the pen, the chain saw, a snow shovel, the grille of a truck, my hand. My father said it was a horrible disease, because the sensation of itching was so intense. It wasn't satisfied by scratching. Not even by scraping. The sheep would have gone right through its skin when the fleece was gone. It would have ended up a single spot of flesh, dancing like sunlight on the barn door, trying to extinguish itself.

I like the name *chronic wasting disease* almost as much. Another good name for a rock band. Veterinary is full of them. Maybe because it deals with life and death. And most young guys think rock music is also about life and death. And that life itself is a chronic wasting disease.

I wonder if my father has it.

He seems to enjoy talking to Jesus. More than he does to me. I wonder what he'd say to Jesus if he knew who he really is. I wonder if he'd ask for my mother back.

They're talking about prions. To most guys it would sound like the name of a video game or someone in a *Star Wars* movie. To me sounds like Priam, the king of Troy. His son Paris carried off Helen from Sparta to Troy. Like all little kids, I used to dream my father was king and I carried off a beautiful girl. Obviously, my dream came true.

My father tells Jesus a prion is some kind of protein that infects the brain. That it converts healthy proteins into deadly proteins. That it's what causes chronic wasting disease.

Jesus says, "You learn something new every day." Which is something you'd expect Jesus to say.

My father says, "*I* don't." Which is something you'd expect my father to say.

Jesus says, "A prion is also a petrel."

"Where?" says my father. I don't think he believes Jesus.

"Antarctica," says Jesus.

"You've seen them?" my father asks.

"Yes," says Jesus.

"You get around."

"I have to," says Jesus.

"Restless, Ray?" says my father.

"One step ahead of the law," says Ray. I'm the only one who finds this funny. I guess because I'm the only one who knows what it really means.

"I know there's a Prion Island," says my father. "But there are albatrosses there. Is that what you mean?"

"No," says Jesus. "I mean the prion that's a petrel."

"What's a petrel?" I finally have to ask. It sounds like what the Brits fighting in The Mess called gasoline, which they always complained they couldn't get the way us Yankees could and they had to pay more than a thousand dinars a liter for it on the black market.

"A petrel's a bird," says Jesus. "You should see it. It flies just over the water. It moves up and down with the waves. Like it's part of the sea. You can't tell if its feet ever actually touch the water. It looks like it's walking on the water."

"Hydroplaning," says my father.

But I know exactly what Jesus is talking about. It's one of my favorite stories. Everything in it happens all at once. The way things happen in the Gospels. Especially Matthew. He's like Emily Dickinson. Only sacred — and clearer. Not a lot of adjectives. Not a lot of scenery or seasons. Bang bang bang. Everything happens in a few verses. I used to wonder if that's how the lives of the saints go by, even faster than ours. Mr. Smith told me no, it just seems that way, because poetry is compressed joy. No matter what it says, how terrible its events, it's a form of ecstasy.

I remember the first time I read that story. Herod hears about Jesus getting famous. So he arrests Jesus' cousin, John, which Herod figures will get a lot of attention since John has just risen from the dead. John gets Herod angry because he tells Herod he shouldn't have taken his own brother's wife away from him, kind of like Ryan and me, now that I think of it. Herod tells his stepdaughter she can have anything she wants because he likes the way she dances, the way cheerleaders in school usually have more nice things than the other girls. This girl says, "What I'd really like is John's head on a big plate." So John's head gets cut off. And this time he doesn't rise from the dead. This time John's body gets buried and his head ends up at the Umayyad Mosque in Damascus, Syria. That's where some of the people who were always trying to kill me came from. Insurgents were always crossing into Anbar province where Iraq and Syria meet like two snakes melted into one. When Jesus hears about John he gets so upset he goes into the desert. It's his place for suffering the way it's mine. But thousands of people follow him there. There's nothing for them to eat, so Jesus takes five loaves of bread and two fish and he makes enough food for everyone. Kind of like a giant serving of Eggstender. They eat and then he tells them to go away because he wants to be alone, like me again, to pray for his cousin John. So the people all end up going to the sea and sailing away. Jesus goes to the mountaintop. Four nights later he hears that the ships are in serious trouble. So he comes down from the mountain and he walks on the water toward all the scared people. His friends see him and they think he's some kind of demon. They start screaming in fear. Jesus says — and I always loved this, how he says it — he says, "Be of good cheer." *Be of good cheer. Don't be afraid. It's me.* But Peter doesn't believe him. He says, "If it's you, tell me to walk on water too." Like he needs to be told to do it. What he really means is, "If it's you, make *me* walk on water." So Jesus says, "Come on. Get out of the boat and walk over here to me." Peter does. He gets out of the boat and he starts to walk across the water. Just like Jesus. But then the wind starts to blow. Peter gets afraid. He thinks he's sinking, even though he already learned he could walk on water so what the heck is he worried about. "Save me!" he screams to Jesus. So Jesus does. What I like about it is that he reaches right out and saves Peter. He doesn't tell Peter, "Oh, you can do it." He doesn't say, "Give it another try." He just reaches out there and snatches him up. That's when he says one of the greatest things he ever said. "Oh, you of little faith. Why did you doubt me?"

The guy had already walked on water!

Just like the petrel.

That's what Jesus is telling me. Peter and the petrel are the same. Their names are the same. They both walk on water.

If my father wants to doubt him, fine. But me — no. I am to have faith.

I do have faith.

My father must be going to kill the deer. That's why he has the captive bolt gun to hand. It's used instead of a regular gun because it's safer. Not to the animal. To the person doing the killing and to anyone hanging around. It uses a blank cartridge and drives a spring-loaded retracted rod right into the animal's skull. The rod doesn't leave the head the way a bullet would. You get one clean dead animal and no gore-flecked dead people.

If this were a buck, my father would need a heavy-duty cartridge. But this is only a doe, and a weak, skinny one at that.

"Why do you have to kill her?" I ask.

I always asked that when my father killed animals in his office. This wasn't hunting. No one ever has to ask why you kill an animal when you're hunting. That's what hunting is. If you hunt without killing, you betray your history and worse than that you betray the animal's purpose on Earth.

But I could never get used to the idea of a vet killing an animal in the hospital. No more than I can over a doctor killing a person in a hospital. Or an unborn child in a clinic.

"Because the only way to test for this disease is on the obex tissue of the brain," says my father.

He places the pistol on the doe's forehead at the point where two imaginary lines intersect from the base of each ear to the opposite eye. Killing is an exact science when you do it right. He taught me that.

The deer dies as quickly and mercifully as the men I killed. It deserves this easy death a lot more than they did.

I was known for my quick kills. My nickname was *Mercy*. It might as well have been *Without Remorse.* I would have preferred *Juba*.

Juba was the most famous Iraqi sniper. I first heard his name in Haditha. But he worked in Baghdad. Some Shiites called Twelvers believed he was the long-lost Twelfth Imam, the promised Mahdi, who was going to return to Earth with Jesus and redeem mankind.

Juba'd take one shot and one shot only. He used a silenced Dragunov. He'd leave nothing behind but a single cartridge case and a note in Arabic: "What's been taken in blood can't be retaken except by more blood."

A man after my own heart.

I wonder what it felt. The doe. I see Jesus touch its head. I think about Mr. Smith the first time I ever saw him and he read to us, "I felt a cleaving in my mind, as if my brain had split."

My father has a poster on his wall from the American Veterinary Medical Association. It looks like a poem. It says in giant letters:

EUTHANASIA

Under that it says:

THE FOLLOWING ARE NOT PRACTICED IN THIS FACILITY:

DROWNING

ELECTROCUTION

FREEZING

THE FOLLOWING ARE NOT USED IN THIS FACILITY:

ACETONE
ARGON GAS
CYANIDE
MAGNESIUM SULFATE
NITROGEN
NITROUS OXIDE
POTASSIUM CHLORIDE
STRYCHNINE
SUCCINYLCHOLINE

Mr. Smith read me and Bethie a poem by Lord Byron called "Euthanasia." He said it was one of the rare poems about death that wasn't an attempt to seduce a woman by telling her how little time we have on earth. Instead, it was an attempt to seduce the reader. Not with love. With death. The poem says, whatever joys I've had, whatever I've been on earth, it's better to die and to go back to "the nothing that I was." It's better not to be.

Mr. Smith told us it was a soulless work. When he was young he'd written his own poem about our soldiers in Vietnam called *Youth in Asia*. It was a war poem, he said. It was an epic like *The Odyssey*. It was even longer than *The Odyssey*. Twice as long and less than a millionth as good, he said. "I'm not a poet. I'm the poets' puppet." I knew what he meant. I even knew where the apostrophe went. (Mr. Smith taught us things like that.) Out of his mouth came all the great poetry in the world.

The Odyssey takes place in Asia too. Asia Minor. Mr. Smith was thrilled I knew the story of Ulysses' adventures. We read it aloud to each other night after night, while Bethie sat there listening and then not listening but sleeping. Mr. Smith loved to say, "Bethie's sleeping." Sometimes he added, "Thank God." Because she could be a handful. She was not, for example, a big fan of Penelope, waiting all those years for Ulysses, who was off having the adventures of a lifetime. And I'm not talking just about hanging out with Calypso and Circe. I mean, the kind of adventures I had in Iraq. Which had nothing to do with women. The Queens for a Year used to say, "What happens TDY, stays TDY." TD being Temporary Duty, and Y being Yonder, otherwise known to the lady soldiers as The Middle Yeast. And Queens for a Year being women who spend their tour acting hotter than their looks and hooking up with the kind of men who would not have tossed them a cocktail nut back home.

I didn't want any other woman. But I sure did love to be the target of the enemy I took out before he took me out. I loved killing killers. It's the only way the world can be made pure.

When Bethie fell asleep, Mr. Smith would have me spread a blanket over her. I drew it from her feet to her head. I touched her through the blanket from her feet to her head. I think Mr. Smith wanted me to. He watched me, smiling. As soon as Bethie was snug under the blanket, he would start reading again. To me. To his sleeping daughter. She slept right through the great scene where Ulysses tells Calypso that Penelope may not be as good looking as Calypso but not a day goes by when he doesn't wish to get home to see her once again. And there I was sitting there wanting to be with a girl I'd never been with. I got tears in my eyes. Mr. Smith did too, I think not from Ulysses but from me. He knew I loved his daughter. He said, "That Ulysses, he certainly knew how to talk to a woman. He tells Calypso she's more beautiful than the wife he has the nerve to tell Calypso he'd leave her for in an instant. All Calypso hears is how beautiful she is. Quite a guy." That's how Mr. Smith made me feel — quite a guy myself.

Of course, little did I know I'd go to Asia myself to fight. To Asia Minor. The Turks called it Anatolia. Which means *the land where the sun rises.*

In Mesopotamia, it rises on death.

For Bethie and me, the sun rose on love.

I told her that I'd found her in another Byron poem. I told her she was

the nymph whose premature desires
Torment her bosom with unholy fires

She laughed and grabbed the book out of my hand and looked at the poem and said no, she was "the maid whose virgin breast is void of guile."

Her virginity was important to both of us.

But in opposite ways.

Enough said.

Jesus watches my father remove the deer's brain. I kind of watch. I got used to seeing parts of bodies in The Mess. You had to. So much of the killing was done on their side by explosives. They blew us apart. We took them down cleanly. All our commanders pointed this out. They said you could measure our civilization against theirs by looking at our dead and their dead. The people I killed looked alive and ready for Hell. The people they killed looked like meat. If you didn't believe in God and the soul, you wouldn't know what to make of war.

"Hold this open," says my father.

"Sure," I say.

I realize he's talking to Jesus. He hands Jesus two plastic bags, one inside the other. Jesus holds the bags open and stares down into them as my father holds the doe's brain over the opening with his hands together like a pastor making a point. Then he lets the brain not so much slide as drop gently into the doubled bag. I know it's not heavy, but I can see the veins in Jesus' arms tighten and swell. It's like he feels the whole doe is going into the bag. I wonder if he believes a doe has a soul and that by now it's flown away, weightless. And what's left is in his hands.

My father says, "Steady now," as he separates the tops of the two bags and presses his thumb and forefinger against the corner of the inside bag and runs them along the seal. Then he does the same with the outside bag. I can hear the bags zip closed. It's a sound like a sharp skate on clean ice. I can never fasten even a sandwich bag and always end up getting lettuce juice dripped on my pants.

My father gets a black Sharpie and writes on the outside bag, JANE DOE.

Then he pulls close a plastic gallon pail. "Put it in there," he says.

Once Jesus has done that, my father says, "Follow me," and walks to the sink. He has Jesus hold the pail under the faucet and fills the pail with water. I see that the brain is heavy enough not to float up to the top.

"Put this on it." My father hands Jesus the top to the pail. Jesus presses it onto the pail but he can't get it to seal.

"What good are you?" says my father. But he says it kindly. He was never the kind of father who humiliates people for their faults. He was tough without being cruel.

"Not much," says Jesus. "You try," he says to me.

"Thanks."

I take the top from him and fasten it straight onto the pail.

"War could always do that," my father says to Jesus. "You're the one trying to learn the ropes."

"As usual," says Jesus.

My father gets out a label and writes on it with the Sharpie: JANE DOE, VIA DR. WESLEY PEASE.

He slaps this label on the pail. Then he has Jesus hold the pail while he gets a ThermoSafe polystyrene cooler and a cardboard box that's got its own plastic lining. He puts the cooler into the box. He says to Jesus, "Now the pail."

Jesus lowers the pail into the cooler. My father goes to the freezer and comes back with a bag of ice. He hands it to me. Then he goes away. I stand there with the ice in my hands. I can feel it melting around my fingers.

My father comes back with some sealing tape. "How's that feel?" he asks me.

"Cold," I say.

"Good," he says, like he wondered if I could feel anything even after he squeezed my shoulder enough to make me wince if I was willing to wince. "Now pour it in."

I open the bag and pour the ice around the sides of the pail in the cooler.

"Why not dry ice?" asks Jesus.

"You're kidding, right?" says my father.

"If you say so," says Jesus.

"This is a brain we have here," says my father. "Not frozen lasagna. And we don't want frozen brain either. The USDA doesn't want frozen brain. And we don't want to have to vent the package. And if we didn't vent the package, the off-gassed CO_2 would pressurize the box and . . . *boom!*"

"Holy smoke!" says Jesus.

What a card.

My father smiles. Jesus gets my father to smile. I'm sure he did it on purpose. Jesus knows about dry ice. If he knows about mud whelks, he knows about dry ice. Jesus knows everything.

"Seal it up," my father says to me.

I attach the lid to the cooler. Before I can tape shut the cardboard box, my father slides a piece of paper into it.

"You know what that is?" he asks me.

"Pathology record," I say.

"Right," he says, and tries to smile at me too.

I rip off pieces of tape. It sounds like when you dry-skin a deer.

As I tape the box, my father kneels down and addresses it with his Sharpie to the USDA Contract Veterinary Diagnostic Lab at the University of Connecticut.

Beneath the address he writes: "Attn: Jane Doe."

. . .

In Iraq, when one of our soldiers got killed, he or she got put in two bags too. The first bag was black. The body went in there. The second bag was black too. The first black bag went in the second black bag. Then ice went in the second black bag around the first black bag. Then the two bags and the ice and the corpse got put in an aluminum box that ended up weighing five hundred pounds. The guys in the mortuary affairs teams always said they never got over how heavy a cold dead soldier was.

A lot more than a doe's brain.

The soldiers I saw die before I made it to Baghdad always went to Taqaddum. The soldiers I saw die in Baghdad went to Camp Anaconda, aka Mortaritaville, aka Mortalityville. Soldiers who died somewhere else went somewhere else. There were five Mess mortuaries in all. The mortuary affairs teams lived in white trailers next to their stations. They wore white gloves that looked like ghost hands on the black bags. They always carried our dead soldiers feetfirst, like they were walking. I always appreciated that, even though everyone knows you fly, you don't walk, to Heaven.

I want to show Jesus our big black pigs. I figure pigs are the complete opposite of chronic wasting disease.

"Are the pigs in the shed?" I ask my father.

"In the freezer."

"Edith and Ethel?"

"That's right," he says kind of defiantly.

"Bacon?"

"That's right," he says again.

"How come?"

"I couldn't take it anymore."

"Upkeep?" I ask.

"Overlaying," he says, and leaves it at that.

I picture the dead babies. Floating like clouds toward Heaven. I wonder how many litters there were while I was gone. I know sows have their babies in three months, three weeks, three days. 333, half the devil's number. Which to my mind makes them sacred.

Of course the number could be a coincidence. Or it could be intelligent design. Myself I don't call it intelligent design. It's too sacred to be intelligent. The brain can go only so far. There are mysteries beyond the brain.

I call it *divine design*.

Humans are sacred also, created by divine design, with babies coming in ten months exactly. Ten months by the moon. I always loved the moon. I would stare at it from the beach at night. I thought I could see my mother there. The moon belongs to women. Mr. Smith taught me that, before Bethie taught me the rest. He read Bethie and me Emily Dickinson's very first poem, where Adam is the sun and Eve is the moon. My mother's hair flows down through the Sea of Serenity. And she looks down at me from the Sea of Vapor. The moon is what we see of Heaven. My mother lives there. Look. You can see her.

I learned about women from Bethie. I learned about the moon from Bethie. I learned about women and the moon from Bethie. She was the mother I lost and the sister I never had. She taught me how women fly above the earth on the vapors of the moon. She taught me how the tides in women are controlled by the moon and their blood comes forth like the waters of the sea.

When she missed her period, that's what she said: "Hey, War, I missed my period."

"What does that mean?" I said.

"It means you're an idiot."

"Was I supposed to do something?" I said.

"You were supposed to come over here and say congratulations and hold me in your arms," she said.

I don't want to get into details, which are nobody's business, but we had finally made love one night when Bethie said to me, "It's about time."

I didn't know what I'd done so I said, "What did I do?"

"It's what you didn't do," she said.

"Like what?" I asked.

"Like this."

I had no idea.

I had no idea how beautiful she was.

I had no idea how beautiful she thought I was.

I had no idea how beautiful it could be for two people to share their beauty.

I had no idea what feelings there are hidden in our bodies that can be discovered only by someone we love.

I had no idea that God loves us so much.

My father takes off his scrub top and says to Jesus, "Follow me."

So Jesus does. And I follow Jesus.

We head outdoors toward the pig shed. The closer we get to it, the more the sky starts to darken. I wonder if it's some kind of reflection on how I'm feeling, walking toward the place where the pigs are no more.

My father knocks on the door of the pig shed. I wonder who he's got living in there that he has to announce himself to when I hear a great high squealing sound from inside.

I wonder if he was kidding when he said Edith and Ethel were bacon. But I know they were too giant to ever sound like this. Maybe they didn't crush all their babies. Maybe one was saved.

My father opens the door. The squealing gets even louder.

"Dippity!" my father calls out and hurries in.

The shed is now one big room. My father has taken down the useless creep space he built for the doomed little babies. He's dug a wallow in the middle. He's rigged up a hose to feed the wallow. And there climbing furiously up out of the mud is a red-haired potbellied pig just like the one he'd once treated except he's bigger. He's got a big smile on his face. This time it's not from medicine.

My father rushes over and kneels by the side of the wallow and hoists Dippity the rest of the way out of it. Dippity beats his front legs against my father's plaid shirt. Mud prints fill the little squares. The pig's back legs try climbing up my father's thighs. But my father has too hard a grip. The pig is climbing like crazy and going nowhere. He seems to find this funny. It's nice to see a pig that can laugh at itself.

"Ray, this is Dippity."

"Hello, Dippity," says Jesus.

Dippity doesn't so much as look at Jesus. He's only got eyes for my father.

"An indoor wallow?" I say. Edith and Ethel never had an indoor wallow.

"It's *hot,*" my father says. "And here it is only the first day of summer. *You* may sweat like a pig, but a *pig* doesn't."

"No sweat glands," says Jesus.

"That's right." My father nods at Jesus. "Can't have Dippity getting overheated."

"Is that a *pet*?" I ask him.

"Of course not," he says.

"Are you treating him?"

"He's all better."

"What's the matter with his ear?" says Jesus.

It's the same pig! He's bigger, and he smiles more, but his ear is still torn apart.

"Where did you get him?" I ask my father.

"I bought him."

"How come?"

"I had him back in. Not for dippity — something else. Some boosters and a mild case of St. Anthony's fire. You couldn't tell his red coat from the infection. But *he* could. The owners had put him back with the same pigs that did this." My father puts his hand behind the pig's ripped-apart ear. "I couldn't allow that. It's a wonder they didn't tear him apart."

"I thought they were territorial," I say.

"They are," says my father.

"So?" I say. My father is the one who taught me to accept the world the way it is with all its viciousness — more war than peace, more pain than pleasure.

"So I couldn't stand it anymore," says my father.

"May I?" says Jesus, like he doesn't want us to fight. But we're not fighting. I'm just trying to understand how my father has changed.

Jesus kneels down next to my father in the mud the pig had splashed up out of the wallow. He sticks his fingers into the wallow and scoops out some mud. He puts his hand behind the pig's half ear. Then he reaches his thumb around to the front of the ear. He massages the mud all over the ear with his fingers and his thumb. Dippity gets a stupid expression on his face. His eyes start going up into his sloped forehead. He seems to stop breathing.

"He's asleep standing up," says my father, like he can't quite believe it.

"Just like most of the rest of us," says Jesus.

"You got that right," says my father.

"Open your eyes," says Jesus.

I don't know if Jesus is talking to Dippity or to us. But I see him brushing the dried mud off Dippity's ear and I realize that Dippity's ear is pretty much like Dippity's other ear, a whole leaf growing off this fat little tree of life.

My father sees it too. He reaches down slowly toward Dippity's ear. He touches it the way you touch someone when you get out of your truck in the winter, like you're afraid of getting a shock. The quick tip of one finger. Until my father's whole large strong hand is holding Dippity's whole little ear from behind and his thumb is feeling it all over the way Jesus' thumb was.

"How did you do this, Ray?" he says to Jesus. He says it like half of him wants to know how, because he's a doctor, and half of him doesn't believe it could be done, because he's a doctor.

"With my hand." Jesus holds up his hand. The mud has dried on it. His nails are filthy. It looks like a real hand.

"That's not what I meant," says my father.

I like it when he talks sternly to Jesus.

"All I did was loosen up the cartilage," says Jesus. "The pinna was all twisted up in itself. Someone must have twirled this guy in the air by his ear. I just untwirled him."

"But not in the air," says my father.

"You're right about that," says Jesus. He puts his hand back in the mud. "Not in the air."

"I can't believe it," says my father. But I know he does.

"What's a pinna?" I ask.

"The auricle," says my father.

Jesus laughs. "It means *wing*." He takes hold of Dippity's two ears and flaps them to make it look like Dippity could take off right into the air.

"Hungry?"

What a strange thing for my father to say. He didn't make a single meal after my mother died. He never offered to feed me. It doesn't mean he didn't have food in the house. He just didn't cook it or serve it or want to eat except by himself. I think I knew that the one place aside from their bed that he shared every single day with my mother was the kitchen table. And he didn't want to share either place with anyone else ever again.

"We just ate," I say. "Over at the airfield."

"Always," Jesus answers my father.

"Good," my father says to him.

My father takes off his latex gloves and tosses them in the waste bucket and closes the door of the shed behind us. That's when I notice that he's carved into it two words: FOREVER HOME.

It's funny how you can recognize someone's handwriting even when it's done with a knife. Same thing when you cut the enemy up with one — every soldier leaves his own handwriting in the body. Same so far as I was concerned with a bullet. My shot left my mark. Every enemy corpse a work of art.

"What's that?" I ask him.

"Another name for sanctuary," he says. "The animal rescue people."

"Since when?" I ask.

"Since I realized Dippity could read."

Jesus laughs *again*. My father claps him on the shoulder. "Let's go eat," he says.

My father leads us into the house. He keeps his hand on Jesus.

The kitchen is neat, as always. It's a big country kitchen in a big country farmhouse. Ever since my mother died, it's been too big and too cold. Even on a summer's day like this one it's cold. Or at least cooler than outside. A kitchen's supposed to be warm. My kitchen on Bittersweet Lane was always warm. Winter or summer. So was Bethie, always warm to the touch.

"Have a seat," my father says.

Jesus holds up his hands. "I better wash up."

My father points back into the hallway behind us. "Second door on the left."

Jesus leaves. I realize that we've both been holding it in all day so far. After drinking beer even. I got used to that in the war — holding it in. Two things they say you always hold in combat: your urine (they use another word for it) and your breath. Both come out if you get shot. Now I've really gotta go.

I'm alone with my father. Standing there in the kitchen. Both of us are looking where Jesus just walked. Like he somehow inhabited the empty space.

There are so many things I want to say to my father. Maybe too many. I can't find the words.

My father surprises me by talking. Even though it takes a couple minutes of standing there together in silence. "Interesting guy. Ray."

"Yeah."

"I'm glad you brought him home."

"He brought me."

"The important thing is," says my father, "that he's here."

"Who?" It's Jesus, coming down the hall.

"You, Ray," my father says.

"It's all yours," Jesus says to me. Like he knows.

I head toward the bathroom. I can hear them talking right away. Both voices. But not the words. I don't have Jesus' hearing. Must be from what they call acoustic blast trauma. We all had it. It wasn't from *Headbanger's Ball*.

When I get into the bathroom, I see Jesus left the seat up. I know that because the rule my father had in the house after my mother died was the rule my mother had before she died: Put the seat down. I always thought it was a strange way for him to try and keep her alive. But I always put the seat down. For her. Not for him.

When I pee, there's a bit of blood. I don't care. I'm used to it. They used to tell us, "As long as you're bleeding, you're alive." Which is not true. As long as you can *see* your blood, you're alive.

The soap is wet. I'm glad to see it. Most guys don't wash their hands. You learn that in men's rooms. Not even when they do both things. Sometimes they wash their hands if you're washing yours. If they think nobody's going to notice, they don't. It's like doing something you shouldn't do, or not doing something you should do, because you think God doesn't see you. That's two sins in one.

I know Jesus didn't wash his hands the day he ate with the Pharisees. I think he did that on purpose, so they would say to him, *Hey, you didn't wash your hands*, and he could say back to them, *Hey, you're dirty inside and you're greedy and you're hypocrites and you honor your very ancestors who killed the prophets and the blood of those prophets is on* your *hands.* My *blood is on your hands.*

For a lot of reasons I'm glad the soap is wet. It's the same old soap. Camay or something. My father had been buying the same kind of soap my mother used. No man would buy Camay.

I'm twirling the soap around in my hands to lather it up when I feel Jesus on it. It's like the soap isn't just taking something off me, like dirt, but putting something into me. Or on me. I feel myself mixing myself up with Jesus on the soap. My skin and his skin. I feel him enter me and all over me. He's spreading through my body and on my body. I feel clean, of course. This is soap. But I also feel protected.

They used to ask who could endure the day of his coming. Who could stand it. Because he was going to be like fire or soap. You were going to burn one way or the other — from the fire or from the harsh soap on your skin and in your eyes. But for me it was never scary. I never thought I had a lot of sins to wash away. I had just enough to need him.

I don't want to put down the soap. I lather it up and lather it up until I can feel it shrinking in my hands and my hands aren't exactly whiter than snow but they're as soapy as I used to get Dodie all over to make her laugh in her little bassinet.

I guess I'm trying so hard to wear down the soap so there'll be no difference between Jesus and me that I try too hard and the soap flies out of my hands. It goes straight up in the air and I'm thinking, the way you always do when you drop something in the bathroom, like a toothbrush or your comb if you use a comb, *Not in the toilet! Please not in the toilet!*

I wouldn't call that a prayer. But whatever it was, it was answered. The soap landed on the little rug in front of the toilet. That was another thing my mother insisted on. A rug in front of the toilet. I won't go into why.

I bend down and pick up the soap and wash the little rug hairs off it and put it back into the soap dish.

I know this was my lucky day, because the soap didn't land in the toilet.

Not that I think it's also the day of his coming. This is my day with him. Not everyone else's.

I put down the toilet seat and dry my hands on the one small towel hanging there. It isn't wet. I picture Jesus waving his hands in the air to dry them. That would be something he'd do. It's strange how when you spend time with someone, you can understand how they would do something you never actually saw them do. It's kind of its own miracle, how we know people before we know we know them. Like when you catch yourself loving somebody and in that instant you can't tell that person apart from yourself. Like with me and Bethie.

As soon as I open the bathroom door I get hit with the smell of bacon. It's what you come home from war for, to open a door and get hit with something that isn't going to kill you. To get hit with the smell of bacon on the fire.

I follow my nose and hear them talking. I'm not used to hearing my father's voice. I'm getting used to hearing Jesus.

He says to my father, "I knew you could render fatback into lard, but I never knew you could cure it into bacon."

"Vastly superior to side meat," says my father. "Once it's cured, I wrap it in this cheesecloth here and —"

"You left the seat up," I say to Jesus.

My father doesn't look happy. I don't know if it's because I interrupted him or because Jesus left the seat up.

"I left it up for you," says Jesus.

My father nods at him, like Jesus can do no wrong, and he goes right on saying, "I cure it in the cheesecloth hanging off the fireplace chimney. Then I fry it up like here with some of this loin meat to balance out the fat. I've been waiting for someone to try it out on."

"I can't wait," says Jesus.

"Coming right up," says my father.

He picks up each piece of bacon with some tongs and shakes off the fat into an old mayonnaise jar that's been there since my mother was alive and drops the bacon onto our plates and his.

When we're all sitting there together at the table my father says, "Enjoy," and picks up a piece of bacon with his fingers.

"Wait," I say.

My father stopped saying grace after my mother died. Not that we ever ate together. But I knew he didn't say it when he was alone either. Before my mother died, he was never alone.

I know when Jesus fed all the people in the desert, he said something before he "brake the loaves." I always loved that — *brake the loaves.* I want to say to Bethie, "Bethie, you brake my heart." But we don't know what Jesus said. All he did was look up to Heaven and give a blessing.

I don't look up to Heaven. I look at my father. I look at Jesus. And I say, "Lord, we thank you for this food you place before us. Edith and Ethel, we thank you for this food you are before us. Amen."

I take a little bite. I kind of close off my nose so I won't taste it. But the feel of the food in my mouth is a good feel. As I chew, I get incredibly hungry. Pretty soon I've got my mouth completely full and I'm chewing away and swallowing like crazy. It's the pigs who are feeding me.

My father and Jesus have bacon hanging off their forks and are just looking at me.

"It's good," I say. "It's really good."

By that time I've opened up my nose. I've opened up *everything.* I'm inhaling our pigs. I feel them coming alive inside me.

Not as pigs. As me.

I realize this is what life on earth is all about. The physical part. Edith and Ethel are Jesus. They are sacrificing their bodies to our survival and our pleasure. *Take ye,* they say to us. *Eat. This is my body.*

So I eat them. I can actually taste the difference between them. They're both delicious. And they're both pigs. But they were different pigs. That's why they don't taste the same. And I can't get enough of them. I thought Jesus had a big appetite until I see myself chowing down the bacon. My father has to get up to fry up some more. He doesn't seem to mind. He's kind of like Jesus making the eggs this morning. He wants us to like what he's cooking. It's like he's coming back from the dead.

Not that I think Edith and Ethel are the same as Jesus. The pigs give what feels like eternal life on earth, because when you eat something really good you feel like you could live forever. You feel like you *should* live forever, because life is so good. Even though you realize that you won't live forever. Not in a place where you can eat bacon and get to put on your thick warm socks on a cold New Hampshire morning.

When you eat Jesus, you realize that you *will* live forever. *Who eats my flesh and drinks my blood has eternal life, and I will raise him up at the last day. He lives in me, and I in him.*

I look over at Jesus, like this really is the Last Supper and he knows it and he knows I'm going to lose him even as I find myself. But he's just eating happily away, grease on his lips and sweat like silver dew in the creases around his gray eyes.

But my father . . . my father has tears in his eyes. Real tears. I don't know if he cried while I was gone to war. But I do know that I haven't seen tears in his eyes since that day he walked in on the pigs and saw that one of them had crushed all her babies. And now here he was crying over losing them all — the babies, the pigs, all the animals he tried to save but lost.

"What's the matter, Dad?"

My father looks at Jesus. His eyes are burning red. His tears are not from sadness but from anger.

"Why *him*?" he says.

"Why me *what*?" I say.

"Why did you bring him here?" my father says. Now I don't know if he's talking to me or Jesus.

"To say goodbye," says Jesus.

"I have no goodbyes left," says my father.

"You have three," says Jesus.

"Three?" My father looks at his fingers.

"Your wife. Your son. Yourself."

"Am I going to die?" says my father.

"Not really," says Jesus.

"Better me than him," my father says.

"Better me than you," says Jesus.

My father points at the hole in Jesus' shirt. "Tell me about your wound."

"Fatal," says Jesus. "You got any more bacon?"

Jesus does the dishes. He insists. I let him. It isn't my house anymore. I have my own house. Or did. Until I went to war. When you go to war, you stop living in the world. You have to leave it behind in order to save it.

My father has turned against the war. He tells this to Jesus while Jesus fills the sink with soap and water.

I can't believe what I'm hearing. "Why?" I ask my father. It's like I fought for nothing.

"Because of you," my father says.

It's the first thing he's said to me since I left him and Jesus alone in the kitchen.

When I enlisted, and told my father, he said, "You have no choice."

I didn't need him to tell me that. But I loved it that he did.

Now he doesn't seem to know the difference between good and evil.

I tell him, "Americans don't try to kill anyone who doesn't try to kill us."

"I'm tired of all the killing," says my father. "Maybe when you get to be a certain age, and you've seen so much fighting, you just want the fighting to stop."

Jesus says, "If the only ones who fight are those who want to fight, the only ones left will be those who want to fight."

"I want to fight," I say.

Jesus hands me a towel. "You dry," he says.

• • •

My father makes coffee. He makes it in an old percolator you sit on the flame on the stove. It's done bubbling and steaming and shaking just around the time Jesus and me finish the dishes including the skillet. My father pours us all a cup. He never gave me coffee before. Maybe he thinks I learned to drink it in the Army. Everyone else drank it in the Army. Not to stay awake. To thin their blood.

"I don't drink this," I say.

"Cream and sugar?" he says.

"Of course not." Now I don't have any choice. I raise the steaming cup to my lips.

"Watch out, darling, it's hot," says my father.

I smell the coffee. Not out of my cup. In the air. Every morning he would get up before my mother and make coffee. She'd come into the kitchen in her slippers and bathrobe. "It smells divine," she would say. He'd pour her a cup, and she would sit down with her hands around it like Bethie does. Then she'd just look at him. Stare at him. He'd smile back at her and tell her to watch out, darling, the coffee was hot.

It really is the most wonderful smell in the world. I haven't smelled it here in years. He probably hasn't made coffee since she died.

I say what my mother used to say. "Don't worry."

Then I take a sip.

I go, "Mmmmm."

My father looks at me like he's not sure who I am.

Jesus understands exactly what's going on. He waits until he finishes his own coffee and then says, "It's time to go see her, Wesley."

"Certainly," says my father. Like he's always been called Wesley.

He goes to get his keys.

"I hate to tell you this," I say to Jesus, "but nobody calls my father Wesley."

"Your mother did," says Jesus.

"When?" I ask.

"None of your business," says Jesus, and I think he actually winks at me.

"Do you have something in your eye?" I say.

"Only you," he says.

It's dark enough outside that my father puts on his headlights and his fog lights. The three of us squeeze into the split bench seat of my father's Ram. He has the three-quarter-ton 2500 because the 3500 Laramie came with leather seating and my father doesn't believe in sitting on animal hide.

Jesus sits between me and my father. He's like a little kid. The truck's a truck no matter it's a heavy. So it bounces a bit. Jesus loves that. He leans forward against his seat belt and swivels his head to take in the countryside and the houses that are swallowing it up.

"Looks like rain," says my father.

"Not yet," says Jesus.

"What're you, a weatherman?" I say.

"Aren't we all," says Jesus.

He's not even from around here but he's right. This kind of early-summer storm comes in slowly. The sky gets darker and darker but sometimes the whole thing passes without a drop. Come August, when the air is all water, black rain falls as soon as the sun goes out.

So when we get to Spring Hill Cemetery, it's nice and appropriate. The weather is sad. But it still can't hide what a mess the place is.

When my mother was buried, in early spring so many years ago, the ground was cold and brown and flat. Now, in early summer, grass and weeds have grown up around the small pale headstones. What leaves were left from the winds of Greenland's winter have decayed and seem to be alive and growing up out of the cracks in fallen stones that make you feel these people died a second death, from being forgotten.

But my mother's plot, her stone, her final mortal resting place are all beautiful. The stone is clean and polished. The grass upon her grave is groomed and emerald green and glowing with a dew that everywhere else has burned away. There are fresh-planted flowers where, if her headstone were an actual head, her throat would be, flowers like a necklace she could smell. My mother always loved the smell of flowers. My father used to bring her flowers every summer night. Not here. At home. When she was alive and he was too.

"It's beautiful, Dad," I say.

"It is," he says.

"Do you come every day?" I ask.

"Never," he says.

"What are you talking about?"

He looks around the place before he says, "I haven't been here in years."

"Years?"

"Since Ethel rolled over on her babies."

"That was Ethel?"

"That time it was Ethel," he says. "Of course."

"So who?" I say.

"Who would do this?" says my father, like my mother has a new boyfriend in the afterlife and he tends to her grave with his care and his tears.

"Don't look at me," says Jesus.

Then I know. I know what's happening.

He's going to raise my mother from the grave. My mother, who's buried beneath a stone that says:

Jesus softly whispered to thee
Come to me, I'll give thee rest

She's been with him this whole time. Now he's going to give her back to us.

There's an old brown woolen Army blanket close by her grave. It's flat against the soil, neat and clean, almost dainty for something lying on the ground in an old forgotten cemetery. I wonder if my mother lies beneath it. Resting there. Risen from the dead. But not yet given back to the world.

"Look." I point to it.

"Lift it up," says Jesus.

I'll do it. I'm not scared. I don't care what she looks like now. I don't care what the grave has done to her. Or death. Or time. I want to see her. I want her to see me.

"Don't," says my father. He puts his hand on my shoulder.

"It's all right." I bend and find I'm strong enough to move out of his grip, though I can feel him holding me as hard as he can.

I pull the blanket back, not slowly, but not all that quickly either. I pull it back the way my mother's beautiful hands would pull the blanket up to my chin, gently, happily.

She isn't there. It's just a hole in the ground. A shallow grave. Half dug. A hole. But a beautiful hole. It's neat on all sides. There's no dirt weeping down. The soil inside is packed as hard as the eternal granite on the beach, to make a Forever Home, like Dippity's. There's none left scattered on the shallow shadowy floor of the grave, and the dirt from the grave itself is spread carefully around the edge, like a dark frame on a sunlit painting.

I always wondered if my father was going to be buried next to her. Now I know.

"Who's done this?" says my father. He's definitely po'ed.

"Don't look at me," Jesus says once more. Which is the way to get everyone to look at you. I know it's Jesus who did this. I just don't know how he did it. Or when.

I don't want my father getting on Jesus so I say, "Don't worry about it, Dad. It's Mom we're here to see."

Jesus must know I'm protecting him, and he better understand that I'm giving him his cue. If he's going to raise my mother, this is when he should do it. We all need her right about now.

"You're right," says Jesus. "We're here to see Dorothy Gookin Pease."

He rubs his long fingers over her name on her headstone as he says it. I kind of expect a cloud of smoke to arise from the stone and my mother to float up out of the smoke. I know it's what a child would think would happen, or a Christian who believes not so much in miracles as in what God told us would be true. That we would all meet in Heaven, that Jesus, when he was lifted up from the earth, would draw all of us to himself. When it comes to Heaven, we all want to be a High-Value Target.

But my mother doesn't rise from the grave. I see her, but she's inside me. In my mind and heart. In front of me, there's only Jesus and my father. But Jesus has hold of my father's hand and he's pressing it against the sunken letters of my mother's name. He says, "Isn't it interesting how your wife's name is an empty name. Her name is all carved out. There's nothing there. All you're feeling is what's missing. Her name is actually in the little grains of stone that were carved out and flew away into the air. Where do you think they are now, Wesley?"

My father pulls his hand away from what I realize is just as Jesus says it is. My mother's name is nothing there. You can see it, but it doesn't exist.

My father looks out into the darkening sky. "How should I know?" he tries to answer Jesus. "They're all blown away. They're just little atoms."

"So are you," says Jesus.

"But I'm here, Ray," says my father. "And she isn't."

"Of course she is," says Jesus.

"Where?" my father wants to know.

"With Warren," says Jesus.

My father turns from Jesus and looks at me. Just looks at me. I don't know if he believes Jesus and he's looking for my mother. But the way he looks at me I realize it's the first time he's really looked at me since before she died. He once came looking *for* me, that terrible day he fetched me from school. But he never looked *at* me. He never saw me once he couldn't see my mother.

My father holds me this time with love. I can feel it. I can't tell if it's love for me or love for my mother. I don't care. We're standing there on my mother's grave and he's got me in his arms. He's not her flesh. But I am. I'm her only child. I'm all that's left of her on earth.

"I'm sorry," he says. "I'm sorry, War."

"You don't have to," I say.

"I miss you so much," he says.

It doesn't matter to me if he's talking to me or to my mother. I only wish I'd been enough for her.

He says, "My son."

I think about my mother calling me her one and only. "Why did you want another child?" I ask. I don't know if I'm talking to my mother or my father.

"You were so good," my father says, "we wanted more. Just like you."

That's when I realize that it wasn't my mother Jesus had raised from the dead. It was my father. He was dead to me, Jesus had told me. It wasn't me, the prodigal son come home. It was my father.

Jesus says, "Your father is alive again."

It gets as dark as night. But it doesn't rain.

I can feel them gone.

I always loved to be alone. I used to think about coming home from the war and visiting my mother's grave all by myself and talking to her face-to-face.

But this is a different kind of being alone. I don't like it. I miss my father. Most of all, I miss Jesus.

I look for him. Forward, back, left, right.

No sign.

"Hey!" I call out.

Nothing.

"Dad? Ray?"

No answer.

"Jesus!" I cry out his name.

I think I must feel like Jesus when he suddenly found himself alone in the desert. It's like my father had just told me, *This is my son, whom I love and am well pleased with.* Then he leaves me all alone.

I fought alone in the desert. That's not what they teach you. They teach you you're part of a unit. They teach you you're one body with many limbs. They teach you what General Patton said: "The Army is a team. It eat, sleeps, fights, dies as a team. This individuality stuff is a bunch of doo-doo." Except he didn't say *doo-doo.* They teach you that if you have a battle buddy by your side, you're twice as strong.

For a sniper, your battle buddy is a spotter. You have the sniper rifle. He has the assault rifle. You have the eye. He has the scope. He's supposed to be the boss, like an E-5 to my E-4 (and I was ranked E-4 and not just E-3 because I was a Specialist). But I believed that the shooter and not the spotter was the boss. Spotters might call us trigger monkeys, but snipers one-upped them by calling them Jackos and the name stuck.

I had spotters in training. You had to. I also spotted in training. You had to. But until the very end I never had a *spotter.* I never had a *buddy.* I never had anyone I couldn't bear to lose. I knew you didn't die as a team, no matter what the generals said. You died alone. And when your buddy died, he left you alone. I didn't want to lose anybody but myself. I didn't think I could bear that. Every spotter I ever had I would think of as Ryan. I would think, *What if he gets killed?* I would push him away before he could. I didn't want to lose anyone else in my life.

At Fort Bliss, you're part of Team Bliss. I liked going to Texas to train, not because it was Texas but because Harl Pease Jr. had gone to Texas to train. He flew, and I walked on tiptoes, but we were both soldiers. The old soldier and the new soldier.

When you land at the El Paso International Airport, the first thing you notice (if you have warrior eyes) is a huge sign: IT'S A GREAT DAY TO BE A SOLDIER. I wondered why they felt they had to tell anyone that. The next thing you notice is the heat. They call Fort Bliss Fort Blister. It's the best place to train for The Mess. That's where they teach what the National Guardians call "the deadly art and science of deliberately stalking and killing the enemy without remorse and from distances that are hard to fathom."

Team Bliss has a kind of prayer:

I BELIEVE

A Soldier is the most important person entering this facility.

A Soldier is a flesh-and-blood human being with hurts and wants like my own.

TAKE CARE OF THE SOLDIER.

Then they have the soldier's creed:

I am an American Soldier.

I am a Warrior and a member of a team.

I will always place the mission first.

I will never accept defeat.

I stand ready to deploy, engage, and destroy the enemies of the United States of America in close combat.

I am a guardian of freedom and the American way of life.

I am an American soldier.

At Fort Benning, the sniper school was in the Harmony Church cantonment area. (So was the ranger school. I snuck in for the drownings and the beatings and the push-up drills that turned your shoulder blades to shields. None of it matched the stress-fire drills we had in sniper school — sorry, ranger dudes.)

Church is where you should always go to learn to shoot straight. They expected us to achieve ninety percent first-round hits at six hundred meters with the M24 Sniper Weapon System. I achieved a hundred percent until I missed on purpose. I missed on purpose not because I was worried about another solider "with hurts and wants like my own." I never thought about any other soldier. If I had, I would have missed every time. I missed on purpose because I wanted to see what it felt like to fail. I didn't like the feeling.

Six hundred meters was nothing. I wanted to break the record of the guy in Afghanistan who used a McMillan TAC-50 to take down an enemy at 2,430 meters. That's nearly a mile and a half. Your bullet has time to say, "Hello, how are you, goodbye," while it's flying toward the enemy's cerebellum.

A lot of snipers went for a center mass hit, so the target would bleed out. But I liked to penetrate the braincase. They used to teach making a target of the medulla oblongata. But why aim for the little brain when you can hit the big one? That's the one that leaves them dancing.

But even the sniper creeds to "close combat," so that's how I ended up in the Jazira desert in western Anbar province near Ubaydi where the Euphrates River crosses from Syria to Iraq. Everything and everybody else crosses too. Foreign fighters and weapons and for all I knew plaster heads of John the Baptist from tourist stands outside the Umayyad Mosque in Damascus. Smuggled in to scare us Christian soldiers. You can look to the west for the Isles of Shoals and you can look to the east for the deserts of Kedar. All you'll find are the false gods of phony soldiers. These people have forsaken the God who brings water to the desert. Even their underground tanks have leaked.

I was wearing the Wiley X Sabers I'd ordered two pairs of from Haz-Mat just so I could get free shipping. Which was ridiculous because who needs two pairs of ballistic shades in the desert when you always wear one on your face or on your lanyard around your neck at night or in the caves? And the other pair gets crushed in your pack? Free shipping got us to buy more than we needed. We hated it and loved it. It's what we called getting killed — *free shipping* — because when you were dead they shipped you home free — free of cost and free of fear.

It was Ramadan. The Holy Month. We knew it was holy because

the new al-Qaeda boss in Iraq, Hamza al-Something, posted an audio clip on the Internet telling his guys to "work hard in this holy month to capture some Christian dogs." Our guys listened to that over and over and learned from our terps' translation when it ended and would bark and laugh and bark and laugh. Not the terps, who all wore masks even in the caves and took phony names. Not me either. I had too much respect for dogs, considering what my father did for a living.

For Christians too. Our side would never tell its people to "capture some Islamic dogs." We killed and captured the kind of people who killed and captured Christians and Jews because they were Christians and Jews. We killed them because of what they did. Not because of what they believed. True holy warriors don't kill for religion. They kill for God.

Iraq is a holy land. The Garden of Eden was in Iraq. The Christians in Iraq pray in the same language Jesus spoke. Now they all got driven to Ain Kawa so they won't get slaughtered in Mosul and Basra and Bartillah and Baghdad. Abraham was born in Ur Kasdim, which we protect with Ali Air Force Base. We're all Abraham's children. Like Paul said, if you belong to Jesus, then you're Abraham's seed. You're the heir according to the promise — the promise of peace and everlasting life. In Abraham and Jesus, all nations are blessed. Even this one.

Ramadan days were still hot as heck, but the nights were very cold. Our infantry battalion was looking for insurgents in the caves in the escarpment. Desert escarpment looks to be formed by eolian erosion. The wind never stops. The dunes are always shifting. Not like those on Cape Cod, where I once went with my parents who said they were taking me to the end of the Earth. That got me all excited. The way it would get any kid. We ended up at a fantastic beach on the tip of the United States where the ocean would come in and move the sand and the wind would fight the ocean. Here, in the desert, the ocean was long gone and the wind was God's eternal breath. No ancient seashells, the way one soldier told me there were in the Najaf Sea, which isn't a sea anyway but a desert outside Najaf. Where this guy had a dummy as his spotter and used it to draw fire from the sniper he killed who shot his dummy but not fatally the guy told me and I believed him. Here, the wind kicked up sand that stung you like you were meant to be one of those flagellators and this was God's way to be sure you stayed awake and alive and purified the way only a warrior can be.

The caves were in cliffs in the dunes, where the sand had hardened into holes. A hole is a nothing. But a cave is a shelter. Except these had been carved through in the dunes so they were cave complexes with tunnels. Some of the tunnels were so complex we thought they might connect the whole Husaybah-Haditha-Haqlaniyah-Barwana areas. A bunch of our services got together with some Iraqis for Operation River Gate. Some Marines had to use thirty rounds from 40-millimeter grenade launchers to take out a dozen enemy in Husaybah, more than two per Desert N——. Our attack helicopters answered an enemy rocket-propelled-grenade attack on Karabilah. We lost nobody. They lost everybody. If only we could rid the whole world of them so easily. Imagine.

In the caves we were always finding weapons caches, and primitive bomb-making matériel like printed circuit boards and faded TV remote controls and washing-machine timers and once a kid's walkie-talkie that smelled sweet from candy breath, and what they must have thought were their scary black uniforms and black ski masks. Actually, these masks are kind of creepy when there isn't anyone inside and you think you're looking into the empty eyes of evil. You see these masks on the guys who are about to cut some poor hostage's head off with scissors and a knife you'd buy on what I heard was called an infomercial. I couldn't watch those tapes. But I did. They say that growing up on a farm prepares you for sex and death. Well, I don't care where you grow up, nothing prepares you for sex. As for death, nothing prepares you for what those people do to other people. I can see killing our soldiers. Soldiers have respect for other soldiers who will die to try to make you die and kill to try to keep from dying. But to take innocent people aside and to frighten them almost to death before you do to them what it was you frightened them almost to death over . . . To snip off their heads chunk by chunk and to saw off their heads shred by shred just to make an impression . . . This isn't politics. This isn't crime. This is something we don't have a word for. You keep hearing people saying *heinous* this and *heinous* that. I know what *heinous* means. For this, it means *nothing.* It's like calling the Crucifixion *heinous.* Killing God is worse than heinous. So is this, because these people kill their own God when they kill the innocent.

Then we kill them.

There are seven things God hates. One of them is hands that shed innocent blood.

These little caves reminded me of where Jesus hid out on the Mount of Temptation in the Jericho desert. I always felt close to Jesus in the war. Not just because I carried him inside me, but because this was close to where he once lived. Sometimes when the sand blew in my face I imagined it was the same grains that blew in his face in the desert when he got tempted by Satan for forty days. Sand is sand. It's what other things turn into. Dust to dust. Sometimes when the sun shined so bright and long and hot I got through the days by thinking that Jesus was a man who suffered not just in the terrible end but in the desert from the sun that made you feel you couldn't hide from it anywhere and you couldn't hide from yourself either. We were both alone and being tested by our God. But he was more alone than I was. And I don't mean because I was always surrounded by troops.

I wondered if the Arabs thought of the caves the way I thought of God. The fort where no one can follow me. The rock where no one can reach me. The shield so no one can kill me.

Ramadan lasts only twenty-nine days. It's always the ninth month of the Islamic calendar. Their whole calendar is based on the moon. You'd think the Muslims would treat their women better with their most important sacred time changing every year according to the moon. The moon belongs to women. Our calendar is based on the sun. The sun is male. Maybe that's why the sun is always a challenge more than a comfort. We were here to turn the sun dark and the moon into blood. Not the blood of women. The blood of the dead. The blood and fire and the vapor of smoke that come on the last days of earth and the last days of war.

One of our Hajji patrol named Abed told us about how in ancient times you weren't allowed to make love for all of Ramadan. Our guys were going on about how they couldn't last that long. Stupid guy talk that you don't want anyone to hear or suspect.

Then Abed read from the Koran about how all of a sudden it was permitted to have sexual intercourse with your wives during each night after each day of fasting. So our guys go, "Wives!" like that's just a great idea to have more than one. I had only one and she wasn't even my wife really and I couldn't bear to think about her so I didn't.

They got less enthusiastic when Abed told them the tradition goes back to Muhammad. He had twelve wives. Abed recited the names of all of them, which sounded very beautiful but you still couldn't tell one foreign name from another until he got to the last one. Mary. A Christian girl. Of course. I asked Abed about it and he told me that our own Mary is mentioned in the Koran. Muhammad calls her the greatest woman who ever lived. Even the story of how she had Jesus is in the Koran. The angel Gabriel came to her and told her she was going to have a son. She told him it was impossible, because she was pure. Gabriel said that her child would be God's child. "All He needs to say is 'Be.' And it is." I loved those words. I made Abed repeat them: "All He needs to say is 'Be.' And it is." Kind of like the birth of Dodie. You know where your child comes from. You also don't have a clue. Except from God. All children are from God and from the God in all people.

Bethie was good having her, she didn't curse, except at me a little bit, which I'd heard from my own father was normal, to blame the guy for the pain because you can't blame the baby you haven't even met yet. My father told me even female animals say bad things in labor about the males who got them pregnant.

But when Abed told us what Mary in the Koran said, I still didn't think about Bethie. I thought about my mother. What Mary in the Koran said was, "If only I had died before this happened to me, and had been forgotten." They were about the saddest words I'd ever heard. But they made me feel better about my mother, dying because she wanted to die. Like Mary.

What gets me about the Muslims is how badly they treat their women by not letting them be who God made them to be, free people. I was probably the only one who heard what Abed read right after he read about having more than one wife, which was this: "They are the keepers of your secrets, and you are the keepers of their secrets." I never missed Bethie as much as when I heard those words. She rose up in my brain.

The Muslims fasted from dawn to dusk. Abed read to me from the Koran, "You may eat and drink until the white thread of morning separates from the dark thread of night." I tried it myself and stayed up with him all that night after we didn't eat all that day. I almost never ate anything. That meant I hardly ever had to sit on a grenade crate for relief. Snipers are all trying to be single threads in the sheet of night. *Covert.* But that night I opened the field-ration MREs, which stands for Meals Ready to Eat. I took the spicy Jamaican chop for myself because the Abeds of this world don't eat pork. He did like the raviolis and the Old World Stew. I got them for him from the chaplain to be sure they were halal. Old World Stew had *dhabiha* beef in it. That meant the cow was slaughtered by someone who believed in their prophets. There's no Humane Slaughter Association for warriors, thank God. But those Muslims are kind of like veterinarians when it comes to animals. They won't electrocute them. They won't even stun them. They spend a lot of time talking about the kindest way to kill. Which to them means slicing open the jugular and then letting the blood drain completely away.

Most people seem to have a soft spot for animals.

And a hard spot for people.

Our guys called MREs Meals Ready to Evacuate or Muslims Ready to Exterminate. I never mentioned any of that to Abed. We had our fill by midnight but we stayed up drinking juice, with him reading from the Koran and me listening. I didn't tell him this either, but we were like the guys who keep watch because you just don't know when the master of the house is going to show up, morning, noon, or night, and you don't want him to catch you sleeping. So Abed and I didn't sleep. We stayed up until I could see for myself how there really is a single moment in time when day unravels from night and it's exactly like there's a thread of pure light that rises out of the fabric of darkness that's been wrapped around us in the desert chill. I had nothing against the Koran. It's not the Bible. But sometimes it's pure poetry. We weren't there to kill religious people. We were there to kill people who use religion to kill people.

Mostly these people kill each other. They blow up each other's mosques and assassinate each other's imams. But eventually they're going to come for us. Most Christians are happy enough to have Jesus for themselves. Muslims want everyone to worship Muhammad.

Jesus, when he was out in his desert, not all that far from here, fasted for all forty days straight. None of that dawn-to-dusk business for him. I read somewhere that forty days is the longest the human body can go without food, if it has fluids. We've got forty days' supply of proteins and minerals and some kind of fatty acids. Jesus must have known that. Even though he said he was not of this world, he was interested even back then in the physical things. The things they call the things of this world. The sacred plants and animals and stones. Not the present world, like Demas forsaked Paul for. The eternal world, that the Earth is but a stone in and the sun a single drop of light.

And Jesus got hungry, just like any other human being would. If I know him, he probably sat there thinking he was hungry enough to eat the little surviving stones you find in the desert. So Satan came over to him when the whole thing was just about over so Satan knew Jesus was good and hungry. Satan said, "If you're the Son of God, tell these stones to turn into bread." That's when Jesus said to him one of his most famous sayings, "Man doesn't live by bread alone." Most people think Jesus meant that we live by spiritual things also, like our feelings of love and the forgiveness Jesus taught us and maybe something like humility. But that's because they stop there with the bread thing and don't read the rest.

The other thing we live on isn't our spiritual feelings. It's the word of God. Every word that comes from the mouth of God.

It was like Mr. Smith said. Words are divine.

The Word was God. God was the Word.

The Word was a sword. It was the sword of the Spirit. It was the two-edged sword that came out of Jesus' mouth. It was the sharp sword that *was* Jesus' mouth.

Then there was the sword that Jesus said you should sell your coat to buy. He wasn't talking about the Word then. He was talking about a sword. A real sword. The kind he said he came to bring. The kind you kill with.

Us soldiers didn't have swords anymore. We had knives. Mine I had from home, the little four-inch Olsen hunting piece I wore against my leg in a leather sheath that was as much part of my skin as my skin was part of my body. Most guys went for bigger knives, wouldn't you know it. Stratofighters. Or Horrigans, which I would have chosen next because they were made of Damascus steel by a guy who came from Maine of all places, just over there. Or Ka-Bars with seven-inch blades. Some of them even got sent from home by their parents or wives that embarrassing Ka-Bar Iraqi Freedom Commemorative. Aka Preemies. Most everyone used an Arkansas Ouachita touchup stone. But I went with my sliver of razor grit whetstone from the village of Pike, New Hampshire.

So my knife was nice and sharp that morning when Abed taught me how day gets unthreaded from night. Light from dark. Sadness from happiness. Swarms of flies like they were born from the rising of the sun.

As the little strand of sunlight grew and rose up out of the horizon and absorbed the night right into it, we could see, from the cliff our cave was on, coming out of the darkness in the distance, a man. He seemed to be floating on the air, moving steadily toward us. His feet weren't touching the ground.

Only when he got closer did we see he was riding a bicycle. At first he wasn't on the road. That wasn't unusual. This was the time of year the Euphrates was lowest, and sometimes the sand around it stayed hard with old moisture and people walked and rode on it the way they couldn't on sand. But eventually this guy on the bike found the road and rode it slowly toward us, like he didn't have a care in the world.

One thing I learned in war is that people who look like they don't have a care in the world soon won't.

We didn't have an official TCP there, which is a Traffic Control Point. But I took off down the cliff. Abed took off after me.

We raced each other to the road and got there at the same time. The guy on the bike wasn't there yet. We watched him come toward us. He looked like any other guy out for a bicycle ride in the desert.

I held up my hand. He glided up to me slowly and put his feet down on the ground to stop.

"No brakes?" I said.

He looked at Abed.

Abed said something to him in Arabic.

The man shook his head. No brakes.

He pointed to his feet. Brakes.

We all laughed.

"Fred Flintstone?" I said to him.

He didn't get it.

Abed did. He put his finger against his own chest and said, "Barney Rubble."

Very funny. You get so suspicious at war I wondered if this was some kind of code between the two of them. Then I remembered it was me that started it with the Flintstone thing. Abed knew. But this guy didn't have a clue.

"You Muj?" I said to him.

That he understood. He shook his head.

He had a kind of fat face. But a very skinny neck.

"Open up your jacket," I said.

He looked at Abed.

Abed said something to him in Arabic.

The man went for his jacket at the same time I went for my knife. His finger was between the buttons over his chest when I cut that finger off. It fell to the ground and bounced off the big toe that stuck out over the edge of his right sandal. The way he watched his finger saved our lives.

"*Wahhabi?*" said Abed, which is what the city guys called Sunni suicide bombers, and which our guys got confused with that green Japanese flavor-upper the city guys sometimes put in prisoners' eyes to make them talk fast.

"I'll bet," I said.

Abed held the man's arms behind his back. Blood dripped down onto Abed's fatigues. I could tell he was holding his nose from the inside. I was tempted to talk to him funny.

I unbuttoned the man's jacket myself. I thought I'd find a bunch of water pipes filled with TNT. But this idiot had a frag jacket with copper tubes sewn into the lining. In the tubes I hoped wasn't TATP. Which is known as Mother of Satan because it can go off at a moment's notice. It's lucky for Abed and me the guy didn't blow up when his bike rode over a stone in the road.

"You're an idiot," I said to him.

I was zip-tying his wrists when he screamed, *"Allahu Akbar!"* and pulled one arm free and went for the trigger wire with what turned out to be his missing finger.

Old habits die hard.

I had to draw out my old hunting knife again. This time I signed my name in his flesh. He was my painting. My still life. My *nature morte,* which is what Mr. Smith taught us in homeschool is what the French call them — still lifes, I mean.

He was a deadweight in Abed's arms. This didn't keep Abed from trying to reach down to get the dead man's finger off the ground.

"What are you doing?" I said.

"He must be returned whole to his family," said Abed.

"He wouldn't have been whole if his bomb had gone off," I said.

Abed thought about that for a moment. "I agree," he said and kicked the man's finger into the desert sand.

"How did you realize?" Abed asked.

"His neck's too skinny," I said, referring to how the rest of him down below was too bulky. "And he started to unbutton from the middle. Nobody does that unless they got a wire under there." To demonstrate, I started to unbutton my shirt, top button first.

"You hold him," said Abed.

He pushed the guy into my arms. I think he didn't feel it would be right to let the guy just fall down there on the ground. And maybe blow all of us up.

Then Abed picked up the guy's bike and got on it and started on a joyride down the road laughing and waving back at me. *That's one happy Arab,* I thought to myself.

He wasn't so far away from me that the dead man in my arms didn't save my life when the bicycle seat exploded.

I was on my back watching pieces of Abed rain down through the gathering black flies on the dry desert sand.

The man in my arms was pocked with shrapnel from the bomb. His pants were ripped. I could see he had a name and phone number tattooed on his leg, which they did here so they might not get thrown into a common grave. If he hadn't killed Abed, Abed probably would have called his family for him.

I put him down gently on his back because that's what Abed would have done. I went over to where Abed was no more. I said to the stain of him on the road and on the sand, and to his soul I couldn't bear to look up to see because I knew the sun would hide it, "May Allah be pleased with you."

Then I sat down there with my face in my hands. The guys from our rifle company were rushing down from the bomb going off. Our techie figured out it had been detonated using an FRS radio. We called those things an AITF (All In The Family). The Iraqis loved their cell phones and wannabes. Even when their prepaid minutes ran out, they carried the things around talking to nobody. A family radio handheld doesn't have much range in open terrain. But we never did find who remoted Abed.

I'm on my knees holding on to my mother's stone when the clouds peel back and the sun shoots back out of the sky. I've got her stone in my arms. Tears are pooled in my eyes. The sunlight refracts my tears and stabs me in the eyeballs. All I feel is pain inside and out. I'm blinking like a crazy man. My lashes dry my tears. But nothing drains my sadness.

When I can finally see, I see a man. He's coming toward me. He kind of glows in the light, which I figure must be from some drop hanging off my eyelash. He looks like he's stepping on the fallen gravestones. He's got a rainbow in one hand and a sword in the other.

I push myself up off my mother's stone and go for my knife. My sheath is there on my leg, but the knife isn't. Only my sunglasses, hanging off by one earpiece the way some pseudocool soldiers used to hang them off the top of their T's until they realized they got all smeared from the sweat dripping off their chins.

I think it must be the guy who killed Abed. All I can think of is

Abed flying in pieces into the sky and never coming down. He wasn't even my friend, just an IA guy I got too close to to get over losing.

"That's enough," I say.

What I think I mean by that is, *Stop walking—don't come any closer.* But when the words come out of me, I feel like what I've said is, *I've had enough.*

I don't know what that means. But it makes me feel better. It makes me feel like I could kill this guy with my bare hands. It makes me feel like if that's the last thing I ever do, I can leave this world in peace.

Well, he must have thought I meant the first thing. Because he stops walking. The sun is behind him and lights him up like a candle on a foggy night. I can see he's as tall as I am. His face is lost in shadow, but what hair he's got is short like mine though neither one of us is ever going bald. We've got the same hard slope to our shoulders, because I got sort of cut up there from having guns true-crossed over my chest while we scrambled from one defilade to another and I was the only one who didn't crouch against the imaginary hostile fire that're never the rounds that get you. And he's dressed like me and Jesus (and every other guy around here who doesn't wear those silly baggy hip-hop shorts on a summer's day) except he's wearing black hi-tops, which I envy him and the way his jeans are tucked behind the tongue.

It's kind of like looking into a mirror. He's me and not me. Just the way you're never the person you're looking at even when it's you. Sometimes I think you spend your whole life trying to bring peace to your own war with who you are.

Only Jesus can do that.

But this man isn't Jesus.

He isn't me either.

I've had a sword in one hand, so to speak. But never a rainbow.

"Who are you?" I say.

"War?" He kind of asks me my name.

He's still hiding in the sun. But I know that voice.

"Ryan!"

When I went off to war, I asked Ryan to look after Bethie and Dodie. He never did end up getting homeschooled by Mr. Smith. But Bethie and me went to his graduation anyway, where he looked tall like a giant with that weird hat on his head. And he came to Exeter Hospital to be with me on the cold day between Christmas and New Year's when Bethie had Dodie. Not into the delivery room. But he was waiting for me in the waiting room. Right where I'd left him.

"It's a girl!" I said to him.

"You knew that before," he said. He meant from the photos they take that once they learned to take them should have made the whole world pro-life right then and there. I saw the photos taken by sound inside Bethie. Not all miracles are Jesus'. (But only Jesus is miraculous.)

"Yeah," I said. "But I wanted to say it."

"Congratulations." He held out his hand because one thing we agreed on without ever discussing it was we would never high-five. "How old is she?"

I laughed and didn't take his hand. Instead, I opened my arms like he was the one who'd had the baby. I didn't know why, but at that moment I felt more alone than I had before I had a child, like I was suddenly cut off from my life. I felt like I did when I tried to find my mother somewhere, inside myself or in the air or in the dead gray space of my father's eyes. I needed someone to hang on to for a minute. Ryan seemed to know that. He let me hold him for a lot longer than guys generally do.

"Come on," I said. "You gotta see her."

"What's her name?" Ryan asked.

"Bethie," I said, and dragged him down the hall and past the nurse's station to Bethie's room.

Bethie herself was kind of half reclining in bed up against about twenty pillows with the baby up against her chest. The baby was about the size of a loaf of bread, but she was sucking away and trembling while she did it. It was the good trembling. She couldn't believe her luck in being alive.

"Hungry," said Bethie.

"Look at her go," I said.

"Me," said Bethie. "*I'm* hungry."

"Here," said Ryan. He had a flower in the pocket of his parka. He handed it to Bethie.

"What, am I supposed to *eat* this?" Bethie said in that way of hers. But tears came to her eyes.

"You're so hungry you're crying?" I said.

"I'm so *touched*." She put the flower against her skin next to the baby's little head.

"Thanks," I said to Ryan.

"I got one for you too." He took another flower out of his parka and handed it to me.

That's when I knew he would always look out for us.

Ryan does the same thing now. He hands the rainbow to me.

Flowers. A whole bunch of them this time. Flowers like the flowers on my mother's beautiful grave. It's the only grave here that's alive. The only one anyone's ever tended. The others are disappearing into the earth. Like the bodies beneath them are ashamed and are pulling their markers down down down.

"You?" I don't take the flowers.

He nods and keeps the flowers between us like in the pictures of the antiwar fools keeping flowers between themselves and the guns of the soldiers. Every good person's antiwar until some bad person isn't.

"How come?"

"Somebody had to," he says.

"The whole time?"

"This is where we met," he says. "You and me."

So maybe this is sacred ground to him. This is where he walked all the way to be with me the day my mother came to be here always.

This is where I lied when I told him it wasn't *that* tough to lose her and bury her and miss her for the rest of my life. This is where he and I started being friends.

He's a very beautiful man. It's like being with Bethie has completely transformed him. Except he looks tired. Being with Bethie can do that too. And working all night like Ryan did. At the pharmacy.

"Actually," I tell him, "we met at school. You never told me what they had you in Principal Strone's office for that day."

"Smiling," he says, and puts the flowers behind him like a guy going to the prom.

"Who were you smiling at?"

"Mrs. Cross."

"Oh, man, she was mean."

"She said she was going to wipe that smile right off my face. Then she tried to do it with the eraser from the blackboard."

"So *that's* why you looked like you were eating chalk. I always meant to ask you about that. So why were you smiling at her in the first place?"

"Because she was mean," says Ryan.

How could I hate him?

"We need to talk about Bethie," I say.

"Yeah, she told me she saw you. I didn't believe her. She said you called me Jody. I kind of like that name."

"It's only a saying." I wondered why we had to give names to whole groups of people who angered or frightened us. The Sunnis used to call Kurds *Jwan* and the Iraqi Christians *Margaret*. I had no idea why. They hated the Shiites too much to give them any name a human being might have given himself. The Shiites called the Sunnis *Omar*.

"You can call me Jody if you want," says Ryan. "I never liked the name Ryan. I'm not even Irish."

"What about Bethie?" I say.

Ryan shakes his head. "Not a good name for me."

"Ryan!"

"She's warm," he says. "Bethie. She's always warm to the touch.

Always. Even in the middle of winter. Warm to the touch. Why do *you* think that is, War?"

Is he here to take her away from me or give her back? I can feel her now. I didn't feel her when I saw her on Bittersweet Lane this morning. She was there, and I was there, but there was a great gap between us. What us soldiers call a defile. A skinny deep abyss that screws with lateral troop movement. Another word for the rape of the innocent. September Eleventh — *that's* the word for what it was. Not *heinous*. They *defiled* us.

"You should never ask why a woman is the way she is," I tell Ryan.

"You think?" he says like I'm the expert.

"She's always warm," I say. "Why in the world would you want to know why?" No more than I'd want to know why Jesus is merciful and wants to spend the day with me.

"She got that way from you," he said.

"Oh, yeah, like every time you and me hugged you noticed how warm I was."

Ryan laughs. He knows we never once hugged until Dodie was born. Why would we?

"She's the one who told me that," he says. "I would tell her, 'You're always warm.' And she would say, 'It's War you're feeling.' "

"Hey, man," I tell him. "It's the oldest story in the book. I ask you to take care of my girl when I'm away. And you end up taking my girl."

"Which book is that?" says Ryan.

"Very funny." He wants me to start quoting the Bible. He wants me to find him and me in the Bible. "I didn't say it was the oldest book. I said it was the oldest story in the book."

"We were trying to keep you alive," he says. "The only way we could connect to you was to be with each other."

"Did you have to sleep with her?" I can't stop myself from asking.

"If only," he says.

"What's that supposed to mean?"

"If only," he says again. "Aren't you the one who told me that just because you sleep in the same room as a girl you don't have to sleep with the girl? Except Bethie doesn't sleep. I don't think she ever sleeps. She just lies there."

"She used to sleep," I say.

"That was until you went away."

"How do you know?"

"She told me. I was worried about her. She told me."

"And how do you know she's so warm to the touch?"

Finally he walks all the way to me, right up to me, and he puts the flowers in my hand and when he does it he puts his hand around my hand around the flowers. We're holding them together and we're kind of holding hands. He keeps the sword in his other hand. I can see it's a shovel.

"See," he says, "you can touch somebody without sleeping with them."

He keeps his hand around mine while we lower the flowers to my mother's grave. It's warm, his hand.

"So am I warm?" I ask.

"You will be soon."

"From you?"

"From the sun," he says.

We look up at it.

I go for my knife with my free hand.

He's blind from the sun.

So out of the sheath that held my deadly sharp Olsen I pluck my ultracool Wiley X Sabers. I put them on his eyes like I'm an eye doctor. Like I'm fitting on a new part of his face and one mistake and he'll be distorted forever. I slide the earpieces in just above his ears and then lower them slowly. He looks like a soldier with his new short hair.

"What are you doing?" Ryan says.

"Giving these to you."

He smiles. "How do I look?"

"All the chicks are gonna love you."

"All *what* chicks?"

"Bethie's the only one I'm not sure about."

"She's going to laugh at me, right?"

"You know her too well," I say.

"Neither one of us does," he says.

He takes off the glasses. Not to give them back to me. Just to look at them. Admire them. I like someone who can take a gift right unto themselves, as the Bible would say. Most people act like they're losing something when you give them something. Jesus knows that acceptance is a form of charity.

"These are really great," Ryan says.

"I ordered them special. The Army gives you giant ugly BCGs."

"What're those?"

"Basic Combat Glasses,'" I tell him.

"Not as cool as these?" he says, just what I want, like he can read my mind.

"Aka Birth Control Glasses," I get to tell him. "BCGs."

"Oh, War," he says, because he misses me.

"Not something I could tell Jesus," I say.

"Not something you'd want to," says Ryan, not understanding.

"Tell him what?"

Jesus shows up out of nowhere. Just the way my father did the day we buried my mother right here. But Jesus probably had actually been in my mother's grave.

"Who're you?" Ryan asks him, even though Jesus just kind of told him.

"I'm Ray," Jesus says. He holds out his hand to Ryan. "Nice to meet you, Ryan."

"Do I know you?" asks Ryan.

"Who else could you be?" says Jesus.

Ryan smiles. He likes to be known as my one and only friend.

I look around. It's just the three of us. "Where's my father?"

Jesus points to my mother's grave.

"I thought it was you who came out of there," I tell him.

"Your father's spirit's in there," Jesus says. "The rest of him went home."

"Why?"

"He must have wanted to be alone. You and your father are —"

"I didn't mean why did he go home," I say to Jesus. " I meant why is his spirit in *there.*" I point to my mother's grave.

"He begged her forgiveness," says Jesus.

"For what?"

"Do you know how she died?" he asks me.

"She took her own life," I say. It's what I'd been saying all my own life since then.

"How?" Jesus asks.

"By her own hand," I say. They were words I'd heard whispered since then. In my own head.

"How?" Jesus raises his voice like I'm not used to and the word sounds like he's howling.

"No idea," I say. My father never told me. I never asked my mother.

"Your father's gun," he says.

When Paul greeted Jesus with his own hand, he told Jesus that all the other brothers greeted him too. With a holy kiss. And that any man who didn't love Jesus was cursed.

God himself used his own hand to root out nations and crush people. Through God we batter our foes and trample our adversaries. It isn't our sword that brings us victory over our enemies and shames those who hate us. It's God through our sword.

When we can't avenge ourselves with our own hand, against

those who seek harm to our lives, God strikes down our enemies the way he struck down Nabal. It's kind of like the Martha story, except this time it's Nabal who isn't generous and his wife, Abigail, who is. So God kills Nabal and David marries Abigail.

I think of how Bethie said she's going to marry Ryan. That all they have to do is pick a time and a place.

I wonder if I brought this all upon myself.

With my own hand.

Jesus takes the shovel from Ryan's hand and gives it to me.

"I can't," I say.

"Can't what?" says Jesus.

"Dig her up."

"She is up," says Jesus.

"But she killed herself," I say. How could she be in Heaven?

"The longer I live," says Jesus, "the more I understand how hard it is."

"How hard what is?" I ask him.

"To live," says Jesus. "Now dig." He points to the other half-dug grave.

"Hey, that's my job," says Ryan.

"But he's my father," I say.

"But this is your grave," says Ryan.

Now I understand.

If I'm ever going to find my mother, I have to dig. I have to dig as close to her as I can. I have to put myself next to her the way two people who are buried next to each other become one person after a very long time.

So I start to dig. I throw dirt up out of the grave. It lands at the feet of Jesus and Ryan. It covers their shoes. They just stand there looking down at me. The sun is off just behind their heads. It's like another person watching me. Its eye is bright with wonder.

I think while I'm digging in the earth that maybe we're all buried here. Not beneath the ground but on the Earth itself. This is the land of our inheritance. Even if we don't get to live to a hundred and ten. This is where we come to live before we dig inside ourselves and find our final resting place.

It's still a hot day but getting later. I sweat a lot but can feel an evening breeze arising even in the grave when I get to my height. If you buried me now standing up, all you'd see would be my short hair growing like grass on the surface of the Earth. I'm six feet under.

I put my hand against the side of the grave where my mother lies. The dirt has been cool but here it's warm. I say, "Mom?"

"War?" she says like Ryan did but not to ask my name. She says it in wonder.

"Mom?" I say again.

"How are you, War?" she asks.

"Great," I say.

"Me too," she says.

"Really?"

"Of course," she says.

"Where are you?" I ask.

"Where do you think I am?" She's almost laughing.

"In Heaven?"

"I'm right here next to you," she says.

"Can I see you?"

"I don't know," she says. "Can you? I can see *you*."

"Really?" My heart leaps. Is it possible? *Woman, behold your son.*

But I must sound like I don't believe it, because she says, "Whose shirt is that?"

"Mine," I say. "I mean, it's mine now. I traded for it."

"It doesn't fit quite right," she says.

"You don't like it?"

"I didn't say that. Stand up straight, War."

Of course, I do. I'm standing in a grave and I stand up straight because my mother tells me to.

"That's better," she says. "Now it fits more or less."

"Mine had a hole in it," I say.

"I would have sewn it for you," she says.

"It wasn't on the seam," I say.

"I know."

I realize she's seen my shirt because she's seen Jesus.

"I got shot," I say.

"He told me."

"Who?" I ask, because I want to hear her tell me.

"Your friend."

"Ray?" I ask, to see if he told her who he really is or am I the only one who knows.

"Of course," she says, like could I possibly have some other friend who would visit her in the grave.

"What else did he tell you?" I ask, but I think I know: that he would always be with her.

"He told me what I've been waiting to hear."

"I knew it!" I say.

"Yes," says my mother. "He told me we would be together forever."

"Thank goodness," I say. Because I had been afraid Jesus would abandon her because of how she died. "He'll never leave you."

"Not your friend, War," she says with a little laugh I remember from when she would correct me but wanted to be sure I knew she wasn't criticizing me. *"You."*

"He said *that*?"

"He did."

"And you believed him?"

"There's something about him," she says. I know exactly what she means.

"Could you see him too?" I ask.

"Not really," she says. "It was kind of dark. Mostly just your white shirt."

"Oh," I say. "Well, could he see you?"

"I don't think so," she says.

That's a strange relief to me. Maybe Jesus doesn't want me to see her. Maybe I'm supposed to see her the way she was when she was alive. The way she'll look in Heaven and not in the grave.

"Can *you*?" she asks me.

I look at the side of the grave again. I put my hand on it again. This time I feel her hand against mine, her fingers on my fingers through the earth. Her hand is warm. It's not like the warmth of the summer air, that surrounds you. It's the warmth of life, that fills you.

"Can you feel that?" I ask.

"Can *you*?" she says again.

"Yes," I say this time.

"Then I can too."

"This is amazing," I say.

"Not really," she says.

"It is to me," I say.

"I know," she says.

"I still can't see you," I say.

"Of course you can," she says.

"Where?"

"Inside you," she says.

Then she disappears. I know she disappears, even though I can't see her. Because I realize that what we call seeing is feeling. I felt her there. Now I feel her gone.

I look up out of the grave at Jesus.

"What happened?" I ask him.

"You tell me," he says.

"I talked with my mother."

"It's about time," he says.

"I heard her voice," I tell him, so he'll be sure to know what I mean — that for the first time, *she* talked to *me*.

"I heard it too," says Jesus.

"All I could hear was you," Ryan says to me.

"My mother's inside me," I say.

"Yes," says Jesus.

Jesus helps me up out of the grave. All he does is reach down with his hand. But to me it's like he's bringing up my soul. Keeping me alive. Out of the pit. I remember hearing about the twenty people the Iraqi police found buried in the sands of the Nahrawan desert before I started my tour. I thought about them the whole time I was in the other desert, to the west of Baghdad.

When you're at war, you don't know if you're fighting for the dead or for the living. Then one day you realize you fight to keep the dead alive as much as to keep the living from becoming dead. The same as Jesus.

He redeems my soul from the power of the grave. There's no great earthquake as he pulls me up. Just his fingers around my wrist and the gentle scattering of sand off the toes off my Wellcos as I climb up out of the heart of the Earth.

Ryan reaches down for the shovel. I grab that too. The two of them grab hands and back away together as I rise up until I'm back among the living. And there we are, the three of us, all connected, standing on the ground around my mother's grave.

For the first time since she died, I'm comforted. By her. By him. As a mother comforts her child, he's comforted me.

"It's time to get you home," says Jesus.

Three

How I Got Here

RYAN'S CAR is so old it's got a front bench seat. It's also huge.

"What kind of car is this?" I ask him. It's missing all insignia.

"American," Ryan says.

It's got fins. Like the whale Jonah spent three days and nights in just like Jesus did in the heart of the Earth.

I peer into the backseat. There's a child seat back there.

"Let's all sit in front," I say.

"I'll drive," says Jesus.

He opens the driver-side door.

"Why not." Ryan throws him the keys and opens the passenger-side door. He tosses the shovel into the backseat. Seeds of dirt land on the baby seat.

"You get in the middle," Jesus says to me.

"No way," I say. "You told me you never learned to drive."

"What!" says Ryan.

"I told you I was never *taught* to drive," says Jesus. "Get in."

So there I am sitting between the two of them while Jesus has got one of his strong hands wrapped around the big skinny shiny steering wheel with its finger holds all the way around. His other arm is up on the door. His fingers are playing with the silvery latch on the triangular vent window. He's got it turned inward at an angle so the breeze blows right on my face and cools me off from my digging. Jesus drives very fast and I close my eyes and drink the wind.

Jesus gets pulled over on Post Road by a cop who's waiting in the Congregational Church lot by Hobbs Road. We're nearly all the way to Sylvan Road by the time he catches us. The cop never gets on the siren, but he has his lights all on. It's like being chased by a rainbow.

I think of the flowers Ryan brought that we put on my mother's grave, trailing after us in the wake of the wind off the fins of the car. The cop does put his mic on and is telling us, "Pull over, please. Pull over." His voice sounds like it's made of metal.

We sit there on the side of the road. Ryan's car is too old to have flashers, but it does have a turn signal. Jesus hasn't turned it on. So I reach across Jesus and pull up on the skinny stalk myself. It makes a funny clicking sound. Like a tiny old clock. It doesn't sound modern.

The cop's car is dancing there behind us in its colored lights. And we're sitting here with our little blinker going. Cars go by us, and the people in them look in at us. Three guys crammed into the front seat. You don't see that much except in Texas. Otherwise it's quiet. You can hear the birds. Little ones and the occasional gull who's wandered over from the ocean looking for a dumpster.

"Now what?" says Jesus.

"*Now* what!" says Ryan.

I know what Jesus means. It's like being suspended in limbo. You're sitting there waiting in great peace while your heart's pounding. Nothing is happening. Two cars on the side of the road, one sitting in judgment of the other.

"He's just checking us out," I tell Jesus.

"Admiring the car," Jesus says.

"More like looking it up on his computer," says Ryan.

"I would think this is one-of-a-kind," says Jesus.

"Hey, Ray," says Ryan, "he doesn't want to *buy* one. He wants to find out if this one's stolen."

"Don't look at me," says Jesus.

He makes me laugh. "Get ready to show the man your license," I say to him.

"Lucky we had those beers so long ago." Jesus remembers exactly what he said to me in the restaurant at Pease. *Show the man your license.*

"Beers!" says Ryan.

"Beers?" says the cop.

There he is, standing right next to Jesus at the window. He's like a belt buckle and a gun with a deep voice.

"Officer," says Jesus.

"License and registration, sir." The cop bends over to look right at us. I can't see any judgment in his eyes. His mouth looks like he hasn't smiled since middle school.

Jesus holds out his hand toward me and Ryan.

Ryan goes into the giant old glove box for the registration.

I take Jesus' wallet out of my back pocket.

Jesus hands the registration to the cop.

"Whose car is this?" asks the cop.

"Mine," says Ryan.

Then the cop says to Jesus, "And you, sir?"

"I don't own a car," says Jesus.

"I'd make you out for a truck," says the cop.

"That's very kind of you," says Jesus.

"If you like trucks," says the cop. "Your license in there?" He points to the wallet in Jesus' hand.

Jesus hands him the wallet. "Please remove the license from . . . What's this made out of?" the cop asks.

"Camel," says Jesus.

"Camel," says the cop in a way you couldn't tell if he believed it or didn't. "Where's it from?"

"A camel," says Jesus.

The cop doesn't smile but not because he doesn't want to. "Whose camel?" he asks.

"Not mine," says Jesus.

"You have a camel?" says the cop.

"I used to," says Jesus.

"What happened to him?"

"Her," says Jesus.

"Lady camels?" says the cop.

"Isn't it something," says Jesus.

"Sure is," says the cop. "License?"

Jesus slides it out of the wallet.

Before he gives it to the cop, he runs his finger over it the way he did in the restaurant. For all I know, the cop will get a shiver and he's going to look down at a picture of himself.

"Raphael Santi?" he says.

"Ray," says Jesus.

"Italian?" says the cop.

"Part," says Jesus.

"Ever eat at Ronaldo's?"

"Is it good?" says Jesus.

"Huge portions," says the cop. "Huge."

"Then who cares if it's good," says Jesus.

"Right here in North Hampton." The cop looks at the license and then looks up at Jesus and then at me.

"You two brothers?" he asks.

"We only just met," says Jesus.

"Long-lost," says the cop.

"Could be," says Jesus.

I bump him in the leg with my knee. No one wants to be called "lost" by Jesus.

"It's that you look so much alike," says the cop. "Except he's a lot younger. Just when did you have this picture taken, Raphael?"

"Don't they take it when you get your license?" says Jesus.

"They do," says the cop.

"Then then," says Jesus.

The cop looks back down at the license. "I wish I photographed that young."

"Don't we all," says Jesus.

"Amen to that," says the cop, and I wonder just how much he knows. "And what's your hurry?" he asks.

"Wedding," says Jesus.

"Yours?" asks the cop.

"No," says Jesus.

"Then I'm gonna have to give you a ticket. I only let off people who are speeding to their own weddings. You know how fast you were going?"

"The speed of light?" says Jesus.

The cop shakes his head. "If that was true, I never would have seen you."

"I hadn't thought of that," says Jesus.

"The limit here is forty," says the cop.

"I'll remember that," says Jesus.

"I bet you will." The cop takes out a book of tickets and opens it up and starts to write on the top sheet. "So what's this about beers? You boys been drinking?"

"Warren here and I had a beer each at lunch," says Jesus.

"At lunch." The cop looks at his watch. "It's almost dinner."

"Wine," says Jesus.

"*What's* that?" says the cop.

"At dinner we switch to wine," says Jesus.

"I bet you do," says the cop.

He hands the ticket to Jesus. "What's that in your shirt?" he asks.

"Bullet hole," Jesus says.

"Thought so," says the cop. "I hope you weren't wearing it."

"He was," says Jesus.

The cop looks at me.

"It's true," I say, like I need to defend Jesus.

"You're lucky to be alive," says the cop.

"I never thought of it that way," I say.

"You should," says the cop. He pounds his hand on the door of the car. "Now drive slow."

"Thank you," says Jesus.

The cop was walking away but now he turns around. "Why do people always say that? When I just wrote them up?"

"For saving our lives?" says Jesus.

The cop shakes his head. "For finally getting the hell out of here," he says.

"Also," says Jesus.

"The painter," says the cop.

"Right," says Jesus.

"You got the same name as that Italian painter. Santi. Raphael Santi."

"Glad you like it," says Jesus, like he chose it himself. Which of course he did.

"I didn't say I did," says the cop, "but I do."

"And yours?" says Jesus.

"You can read it on the ticket." The cop tries not to smile for the first time and disappears completely into the dancing lights of his car.

"Ray *Santi*?" I say to Jesus.

"You got it," says Jesus.

"You should name yourself after another painter, Ray," I tell him.

"Like who?"

"Leonardo da Vinci," I tell him. He's about the only painter whose name I know.

"Why him?" asks Jesus.

"He was a sniper," I say.

"A sniper?" he says.

I'm glad to be telling Jesus something he doesn't know. "He fought against the Romans. He designed his rifle himself. He also invented a machine gun with eight barrels. But with his rifle he took out the enemy at two hundred seventy-five meters."

"Is that a lot?" asks Jesus.

"It was a lot for Leonardo da Vinci," I tell him.

Jesus gives me a big smile and starts the car.

He takes the back roads like he likes and ends up speeding past Car Barn Pond on Timber Swamp Road. Since he's not from around here and doesn't listen to Ryan and me and is going too fast to listen anyway he gets trapped to the south by Drakes River and the Nudas Canal and Hampton River itself. So he ends up on 88 eventually via Old Stage Road. Then he has to turn around on Parsonage Road to make his way to Lafayette Road.

That's US Route 1. It's famous for going from Maine to Florida and was once the most famous road in America. Now I hear it's a two-thousand-mile mostly strip mall. I'm glad Jesus doesn't head south on it, because I'm sure he'd want to stop in all our fireworks shops, especially with the Fourth of July coming up. Us soldiers get nervous around fireworks.

He doesn't seem to mind driving Route 1. A brief part of it is so marshy it's unbuilt. Jesus sticks his mouth out his window and breathes the commercial-free sea air. He points toward the other window. Ryan's car is too old to have a passenger-side mirror. So while I'm sitting there out of force of habit trying to peer over the dashboard for debris that might hide roadside IEDs, Ryan is sitting with his whole head out the window looking backward for more cops, since Jesus just keeps speeding right along. At the speed of light, I guess, because no cops seem to be able to see us.

Jesus says while he's pointing, "The estuary lies over there. The salt water mixes with the fresh. You wouldn't want to drink it but it's where the sea and the river make peace. There used to be eelgrass beds there but they got wiped out by slime mold."

Ryan brings his head back into the car. He licks his lips like he's cleaning them. "Slime mold!" he says. He's still just a kid.

"Wasting disease," says Jesus.

I think of the poor doe my father killed with his captive bolt gun. I wonder how many wasting diseases there are. I think there are reasons to be grateful for the quick death. The kind I brought to my enemies. Me. Mercy.

"Killed all the eelgrass," says Jesus. "That's why the rainbow smelt are gone and the killifish. And the Canada geese and the black ducks don't stop here now. People eat eelgrass too. And they use it to smoke deer."

"I had a killifish once," says Ryan.

I remember the tree that grew out of the stones in his front walk. I always thought of it as his pet tree. I never saw his fish. I didn't know he had fish. Or a fish. I feel bad that I didn't.

"You had a fish?" I say.

"Once," he says, like once was enough because of course it must have died.

"What happened to it?" I ask.

"It died," he says.

Jesus steps on it.

Ryan smiles and sticks his head back out the window.

When we pull up to the little house on Bittersweet Lane and Jesus parks on the seagrass-gray dirt driveway, Bethie comes out to greet us. Not like this morning, when she hid in the house and the ghost of her face lit up the window in the final dark of the early day. Now there she is almost jumping down the three weathered wooden steps to the sparse grass the ocean sand allows to sprout in the dry salted ground. The desert had also once been underwater. There were shells in the sand of the Najaf Desert. I took this on faith. I never got to see them. Here, seashells are used to bed the driveway. They sparkle white and silver in the gray earth.

For me, seeing Bethie, the whole earth is reclaimed, like life when it's gone and returns in the spirit that still tastes the salt in the wind.

I know it's stupid of me, but I wonder, when I see her running toward us, *Who is she going to hug first?*

It's Ryan.

But it's me she talks to first.

"You're here," she says with one arm around Ryan. Like she can't quite believe it. Though it's better than what she said to me this morning: *You can't be here.*

"Thank you," she says to Ryan.

I realize the reason she hugged him first is because she's grateful to him because she thinks it's Ryan who brought me back to her.

"Ray drove," I tell her.

"I got a ticket," says Jesus.

"Am I supposed to be impressed," Bethie kind of asks him.

"With how fast we got here," Jesus tries to explain. Which is not something you should do with Bethie.

"You hurt that car and I'll give you a lot worse than a ticket," she says to Jesus.

"It's a beautiful car," says Jesus. "It's the first car I've ever driven. I couldn't resist."

Bethie shakes her head. "You telling me you never drove before?"

"Trucks," says Jesus.

"You?" says Bethie in that sarcastic way of hers, like she would never make him out for a truck.

"Drove a deuce," says Jesus.

"A deuce!" says Bethie sarcastically.

"I was just being modest," says Jesus. "Five-ton."

Bethie scoffs. "Size doesn't count."

I want to laugh and to put my hand over her mouth at the same time.

"Six-by," says Jesus.

Bethie seems to realize he's kidding her and maybe testing her at the same time. "A six-by's the same as a deuce, *Ray*." She says his name like it's a pseudonym for Idiot. "A six is less than half a five."

"I knew that," says Jesus.

"Yeah, right," says Bethie. "You're a real mathematician. It's lucky you got here alive."

"Lucky Warren did," says Jesus.

Bethie stares at him halfway between awe and anger.

"Go see your child," Bethie says to me. Like she's taking over from Jesus.

I look at him, because he's the one who kept telling me before it wasn't time.

"Don't look at me," he says. Which of course is impossible.

When I left, Dodie was still sort of a baby. I didn't know her very well. I guess because she didn't talk a lot. She was more like a little animal. I loved animals. I was brought up around animals. My father took better care of animals than he did of human beings. Than he did of me.

But Dodie didn't talk much then. She was someone you played with. You held her against you. You petted her. You said things to her you would never say to anyone else. Maybe because you thought she didn't understand and couldn't talk back. It was safe to tell her you loved her. You always knew she could be taken away from you. But you always knew she would never leave you.

Now she's somebody I don't know even more than I didn't know her then. I went off to war and came back to this *life.*

I expect to find her in a crib, because that's how I left her. Instead she's sitting at the kitchen table in a regular chair on a couple of Amazon.com boxes. It's like a little Bethie is sitting there. Except Dodie's hair is a lot longer than Bethie's is now. And when she looks at me right into my face I see my mother and my father and me in there mixing with Bethie and Mr. Smith and maybe even the Mrs. Smith I never met to make up Dodie.

I think if I look hard enough I'll see Ryan too. And Jesus. And all of humanity. Or at least everyone I've ever met and looked at. Like poor Abed. We all come from One. The whole world is in the face of one child. Any child. Once in Iraq I looked into the face of a dead Shiite kid who got shot by a Sunni on the Day of Ashura, which the Shiites take a lot more seriously than the Sunnis so the Sunnis don't mind killing other Muslims who are sitting ducks on a day they get distracted by going around beating their chests with flails and slicing them open with zanjeer zanis and carving up their scalps with razors. This kid was shot in the heart. I couldn't look at him without seeing Dodie. I prayed for him like he was my own.

Dodie looks up like she knew I was there.

"Hello," she says.

I don't know what to say to her. Just don't.

"Who?" she says.

"Who do you think I am?" I say.

"I don't," she says.

"Don't think I'm anyone?"

"I don't *know*," she says, and I'm hearing Bethie.

"Daddy," I say. "I'm Daddy."

"Oh." She turns sideways on the boxes and lowers her feet to the floor and comes over to me and wraps her arms around my legs.

I put my hand on the top of her head. "Who told you to do that?" I say.

"Me," she answers.

She takes my hand and leads me over to the table. I pick her up under the arms and put her on the boxes. I can feel they're filled with something heavy. Like books. I figure either poetry or auto repair. Definitely not Ryan's old weights.

I take a seat next to Dodie and put my chin in my hand and stare into her face.

She covers her face with one hand and points at the refrigerator with the other.

"If you will excuse me," I say, like she's someone I just met and want to impress.

The refrigerator's not empty like this morning. There's a bottle of what looks like champagne, except I know enough French to know it's Spanish. Which is all the French I know except for *nature morte*. And trays of things on crackers like meat and cheese, covered in plastic wrap. There's no room for anything else.

"A glass of champagne?" I say to Dodie.

She points at the open door.

I see yogurt. Lots of yogurt. It's all plain yogurt. When she was little, I mean tiny, she used to eat fruit yogurt. I'd stir it up from the bottom and try to get a piece of fruit on the tiny yellow plastic spoon I'd put on her bottom lip because that made her open her mouth. Now it's all plain yogurt. Like she's grown up and has put aside childish things.

I get a spoon and bring the yogurt to the table and take off the top. I'm about to pull off the plastic covering when she reaches out and puts her hand over mine.

"Oh," I say and hand the container to her.

She takes the extra edge of the plastic between her thumb and finger and gives it a big pull. It comes right off with that zippy sound and that feel of releasing a vacuum. I'd enjoy it more if it weren't like the sucking emptiness before a bomb goes off.

Dodie gives a little chuckle and looks right into my face to be sure I get it.

"Hey," I say, "that's my favorite part too!"

She pushes the yogurt toward me.

"Eat it," she says.

"It's yours," I say.

"Eat it, Daddy!" She bangs the spoon on the back of my hand.

"Let's share," I say.

"Eat," she says.

So I take a spoonful. I make a face. I mean, I don't make a face; a face makes itself on my face. "Oooow," I say. "Sour!"

Dodie laughs. Then she opens her mouth. I spoon some yogurt in. She swallows it and smiles.

"Sour?" I say.

"Nuh-uh," she says.

"Not sour?" I say.

"It's good," she says. "Eat, please."

So we share the yogurt one spoon at a time. One for me and one for her. I know it's only yogurt. Plain yogurt at that. But it's like we're sharing each other. It's like we're feeding each other part of ourselves.

When we're done, Dodie gets off her boxes and her chair and clears the spoon and the yogurt container from the table. I watch her walk toward the sink and put the spoon in it and the yogurt container in the trash. I wonder if Bethie trained her because she knew when I came home I'd be no better at clearing the table than when I left.

But I used to do the dishes! Sometimes. Usually. Often. Now and then.

I once did the dishes. I once made the bed. I once brushed her hair. Bethie's, I mean.

I like the word *once.* It can mean *one time.* Or it can mean *many times,* but *long ago.*

I like contradictions. If we didn't have contradictions, how could we want to kill people and save people at the same time? How could God be God?

Mr. Smith once told us about another American poet whose name I forget but who said that life consisted of answering two questions: How to Live. What to Do.

I decided that most of marriage except for the love part consisted of two questions: *Who Does This? Who Does That?*

Like I said, we never figured that out. Bethie even put up a chore chart on the kitchen wall. I either forgot to write down what chores I'd done or didn't write down what chores I was supposed to do or didn't do the chores I wrote down I was supposed to do.

Bethie was right. I was always going away. Every day I went away. Every night I went to the d—— beach.

I was looking for my mother. What I found was Jesus. Who led me to my mother. Who was inside me the whole time.

The chore chart is still there. The same nail holds it on the same narrow splintery beam. The nail head is rusty. When you live near the ocean, rust travels on the sea breeze. The paper is brown and curls in on itself like a fist with a secret.

I flatten out the paper. I'm afraid my name will be crossed out and Ryan's written in. But my name is still there. Under it is CHANGE DODIE'S DIAPER/CLEAN UP AFTERWARD and a space for me to check off I'd done it. The space is blank.

I look back at Dodie. She's standing at the sink with her hands on her hips. Like she's waiting for me to do something.

She wears a summer dress. It's this more than anything that makes her seem a girl, not a baby. Her feet are bare. Her dress stops high enough for me to see her legs are strong. The dress is blue and has short sleeves for summer but little puffs at the shoulders, a sort of gathering of fabric that looks on her like flowers growing from her long hair. Around her waist is a sash that's tied so you can see her waist almost like a grown woman's, this tiny girl so real she fills and breaks my heart at the same time. I walk behind her and look at the dress below her waist.

"Are you toilet trained?" I ask. I feel all grown up saying it.

"What!" she says, like she either doesn't understand or thinks I'm butting in . . . no pun intended. Like I'm impertinent.

"Are you wearing a diaper?"

"No," she says.

"Do you ever? Wear a diaper?"

"When I was a baby," she says.

"What are you now?"

"Toilet trained!" she says, and shows me her underpants.

I want to do something for the chore chart. I want to change her diaper. But she doesn't wear a diaper. I want to be part of this life again and not leave just a blank space under my name.

It was much easier in the Army. Who does this. Who does that.

My job was to kill people. I was good at my job.

A sniper's like a god. Not *the*. Just *a*.

You get someone in your sight and decide their fate.

Up until that moment, they were free. I'm not one of those God's will people. I believe in Jesus. Who believes in us. *We* do what *we* do. Then God takes us home.

I headed home by way of the Euphrates river towns along the insurgent rat line. It was mostly a Marine operation. To purify the Damascus / Baghdad rat road. Nine battalions. Infantry, artillery, supply, intelligence, logistics, chaplain, and Navy corpsmen. I was in an Army specialty platoon. We kind of went along for the ride. Except we were usually the tip of the spear. The advanced echelon. In. Out. And away. Leave the cleanup for the Fobbits.

Those Forward Operating Base wusses had a riddle:

> *Q: What's the only sponge that gets cleaned?*
>
> *A: A Marine.*

Ha ha. Marines were known as Bullet Sponges. Read the weekly casualty reports.

They didn't like Army. But I liked them.

The town of Rawa gave the rigid digit salute, aka the finger, to the Euphrates. Maybe in more peaceful times it was just a tickler. You came around a bend, there the mud-walled town sat between the river and the cliffs on a digit of land that went scratching for water for its date palms and its cotton fields.

In Rawa we linked up with and backed up the Iraqi Security Forces by giving them new Strykers to ride in and snipers to watch their a——. Our Strykers were wheeled, not tracked. But you wouldn't much know the difference, because you could deflate the tires from the inside if you hit some mud. There wasn't mud in the desert. Except around the wadis in the time of the spring rains. But sometimes there seemed like enough massacre blood soaking the sand to slow you down. Or maybe it was just tears.

You could get eleven soldiers in a Stryker. They didn't build it for an even dozen to remind us that a soldier was always missing. The

Stryker got its name from two guys named Stryker who both got the Congressional Medal of Honor and who were both KIA, one in World War II and one in Vietnam. They weren't even as related as Harl Pease and me. They weren't related by blood at all, except for the blood they spilled for their country.

I had barely arrived in Rawa when I was compelled to ground my gear and take out a sniper who was keeping the IA jundi from a dump-lot where we found a pathetic cache of one AK-47, four grenades, and PKM machine-gun rounds in a Marlboro carton. The blood from the guy I killed splattered what him or someone else had written on the wall behind him: JOIN THE JIHAD. After our guy had translated that for me, I came up with my own slogan: I HAVE COME TO BRING THE SWORD. Jesus said that of course. I wrote it on the wall in the guy's blood. In American English.

In the center of Rawa the severed head of an Iraqi police lieutenant was sitting in a fruit basket on the front steps of the mosque. We located the IP's family and gave them the head. I peeked inside his house, because I always got a feeling of comfort from seeing furniture and teakettles. His kids cried of course. The saddest thing was how they all three opened their arms like they wanted to hug him. But the rest of his body was a just a phantom. They moved their arms like little birds.

One of our own guys was a bird-watcher. He got killed in the cotton fields on the riverbank in Rawa. The last thing he saw, aside from my face, was a black francolin. I know this because he told me. I thought he was telling me one of our black guys had been the one to shoot him. I said, "Who?!" He whispered, *"Francolinus francolinus."* That's when I realized he was talking about a bird. Because my father was a vet and sometimes he spoke Latin like that. Every kid loves those funny names that are the same first and last. We bird-watched the bird that got our guy killed. His last words were Latin, so maybe God let him in as a good Catholic. We shot his killer bird and ate it ourselves. It was very good even if all we got was about a bite apiece.

Turned out it was a kind of pheasant. God meant it to be eaten. That wasn't the bird's fate. It could have died of old age. But it got our guy killed and then we came along.

My dad and I used to go pheasant hunting every year before my mother died. He said it was good sport for a little sport like me. One year when I was eight we went two weekends in a row and then one of those following Mondays my father even took off from work. So we got the season limit of ten in the quickest way possible. The daily bag limit being two. Not like human war, where there is no daily bag limit thank God. Our family gorged on pheasant that October. They were ring-necked and the color of the brush they dashed into like shrubs with legs. Me and my father didn't use dogs so we really had to be fast. Even more we had to keep our eyes open. I learned more about the deadly art of sniping from pheasant than I did from deer. Even though the snipers I took aim at barely moved, only their chests breathing and their veins throbbing like guitar strings. We usually hunted pheasant where they were stocked on private land. Post Road in Greenland and the beautiful Connor Farm in Exeter. But the one and only time my father took me pheasant hunting after my mother died he took me to the Mascoma River Wildlife Management Area in Canaan. I didn't know why anybody would name their town Canaan. I knew from Bible-study group about the curse of Canaan. It's in the very first book of the Bible. I wondered if my father took me there because he felt naked like Noah when my mother died. All his sadness was written on his body. And he knew I'd seen it.

"Can I see your room?" I ask Dodie.

She doesn't say anything. But she comes around to me and takes my hand and leads me back there.

"Woom," she says.

"Rrrrroom," I correct her.

"Woom," she says.

It's tiny. I always liked how tiny it was. Tiny rooms are safer. Danger comes outside the walls. You'd never want to leave yourself if you didn't have to.

Her tiny room still smells like a baby. Maybe even better. Now that she's toilet trained.

"Nice crib," I say.

"Bed," she says. Maybe she calls it that because she doesn't want to say *cwib.*

I put my hands on the rails. The dropside is down. This is her freedom. To have the dropside down. But it's still a crib. It still has bars.

"Wait here," I say.

I go back into the kitchen. I find a pencil in a drawer. It's the same pencil I wrote with when I left here over a year and a half ago. I know that because it's got my teeth marks in it near the tip.

I flatten out the chore chart. Then I write in the next blank space: BUILD BED FOR DODIE.

When I turn to go back to her, she's there.

"Are you following me?" I ask.

"Bed," she says, and turns around so it's me who has to follow her.

She leads me into my old bedroom. Mine and Bethie's. She closes the door behind her. I don't know why a little girl would close a door. But it makes me feel good she did.

This room doesn't smell the way it always did. Like Bethie and me. I don't know if there's anything of Ryan in the air. But there's nothing left of me.

Our old bed is made the way Bethie always made it. Even the spare red blanket folded at the foot of the bed. Everything neat except the pillows aren't under the bedspread. Bethie didn't like to put the pillows under the bedspread because she said she liked to see them waiting for us.

My pillows are missing. There's only one stack of two pillows.

Then I see where Ryan sleeps. There's an airbed on the floor on the other side of our old bed. That's where my pillows are.

Dodie climbs up on our old bed. From there, she looks over at me looking down at Ryan's bed on the floor.

"You," she says to me. "Daddy."

She makes room for me beside herself on the bed.

Only when I lie down next to her does she lie down next to me. More than next to me. She cuddles up against me. Her head is on my shoulder. My tears light up her hair like diamonds.

We headed up river from Rawa to Haditha. Haditha's desert from the west where we came from. Except for Buhayrat al Qadisiyyah, northwest, an eerie dead lake made from Euphrates water by the Haditha Dam. Marines guarded the dam so the insurgents wouldn't blow it and take away the last electricity in the whole dark Corridor of Death between Syria and Baghdad.

On the other side of the Euphrates, water and the blood in the water turn the land green and lush. This was where Marines get dropped off by Apaches among the palm trees. Back in the desert, where we came from, we followed through the checkpoints of the axis of advance and moved in with amtracs, LAVs, and tanks.

The insurgents severed heads here too. In Rawa they liked to hide the torso. Boo! In Haditha they laid the body out flat on its stomach and then put the sawed-off head eyes-up on the dead guy's back looking northeast toward Baghdad.

The kids around here never had to wonder where the rest of their daddies was. They could watch the whole thing, if they wanted. Pretty much every day at dawn on the Haqlaniyah bridge. Or if they weren't up for that, they could buy a DVD of the whole thing by afternoon.

It always amazed me how these people had cell phones and DVD players. And they ate dust for dinner.

Except around the time we got there the insurgents shut down the cell-phone network because they didn't want women talking on them. Women were always seen as dangerous by men who could never get them out of their minds.

The bad guys still had their walkie-talkies. I guess they used them to talk about killing us and defiling the women they honored by taking away their freedom.

It was a girl named Iman who led the Marines into their Haditha massacre one November. She was nine. There was some confusion between her name and the imam who got killed after he fired on some of the 25th Marines with an AK-47. I got no sympathy with killing unarmed civilians. Not on September Eleventh. Not on November 19.

Of course that's easy for a sniper to say. And a Christian.

War doesn't test your faith in Jesus. It tests your faith in yourself. All you got left sometimes is Jesus.

We came into Haditha in the sweep-up after Operation Matador and Operation New Market.

I got all excited hearing about the old Operation New Market. There's a Newmarket, New Hampshire, and I'd tell everybody about it. Hunting wild turkey there. On the Lamprey River, named for a guy whose name means *by the river where peace is found*. So we started to call the Euphrates the Lamprey and laugh our heads off. And how guys from my high school before I started homeschooling with Mr. Smith always talked about how they wanted to go to the Master Bartenders School in Newmarket. *Master,* they'd say, like it was a Dartmouth for Drunks. Operation New Market was called Souk Jadeed in Arabic. *Souk* means *market*. Every town here has a souk. *Jadeed* is really *Jadid*. But we spelled it *Jadeed* because we knew everybody would pronounce it *ja did,* like in *I did*. It didn't seem like much of a secret operation if it was named *I did*.

I got a lot of mileage out of Newmarket, New Hampshire, until some guy from Chicago told everyone about a belly dancer from there named Sonya who had a website called Sonya's Souk. Soldiers went online to see her. After that, all they could talk about was the tattoo between her t—s. I wouldn't watch it. And when I said, "What's it a tattoo *of*?" nobody could answer me.

In the meantime, the Naval Criminal Investigative Service was doing its dirty work to try to find out which Marines had killed the fifteen civilians in little Iman's house. Morale was down all around. Most of what we were doing was searching buildings to try to flush out insurgents and their weapons and ammunition. The idea was to kill them there, like birds out of the bush, or push them toward the checkpoints we'd established on the perimeters of Haditha, particularly on the road to Hit. To kill them before they got to Baghdad. To get to Baghdad before they did.

I want to fall asleep but can't. I know that if I fall asleep I won't ever wake up. Soldiers believe that. It may not be true. But you don't want to test it. Insomnia isn't a way of life. Insomnia *is* life.

It's like not eating. If you don't eat, there's less of you to kill.

So I'm laying there next to my child. I don't sleep. But I dream.

I dream I'm laying there and everyone comes into the room to look at me. Bethie. Ryan. My father. Mr. Smith.

They all have tears in their eyes.

But my own tears are gone. Over. They've risen from Dodie's hair to become small glistening stars in the darkening sky I can see through the tiny window out my tiny house to the universe beyond.

Dodie climbs onto my chest. Facedown with her head in that curve between my neck and my shoulder you think could only have been made by God so that small children could find peace in resting there.

In my dream, Bethie lays down on one side of me.

Ryan lays down on the other.

I put my arms around the two of them.

They turn toward me and each puts an arm over me and Dodie.

I take Bethie's hand. Then I take Ryan's hand. I put their hands together over me and Dodie. I lock Bethie's fingers into Ryan's. Ryan's fingers into Bethie's.

That's how I give them my blessing. Now we can be a family for all eternity.

Convoying out of Haditha near the Haqlaniyah bridge we came upon the burning wrecks of two fired-up Zeal troop carriers. Courtesy of JAM. JAM is what we called the Mahdi Army. The Mahdi Army got named for the promised Mahdi who was going to come to Earth with Jesus and save us, if only the Mahdi could be so lucky. JAM stood for their Arab name, Jaish al-Mahdi. But when we captured any of them we told them their name was really Jews Are Masters. Oh they didn't like hearing that! Of course there was only one Jew who was actually The Master. Aka the Nazarene, the Galilean, the Redeemer, the Savior, Emmanuel, the Messiah, the Son of God. They didn't like it when I told them that either. They didn't like hearing that Jesus was going to be coming by himself.

JAM had hit the Zeals with RPG-7s. Guns by way of the Mujahideen (unholy warriors) in Afghanistan who got them from the Russians. Weapons sold to kill your enemy kill you just as dead. What Marines weren't killed by the grenades were mowed down by truck-mounted PKMs. Also Russian. Updated Kalashnikovs on tripods. Which couldn't take the spastic ammo of a long-barreled Dragunov. Still, what was it like to crawl out of a Zeal with your back on fire only to be greeted by the oldest bullet in the book that had learned to come at your chest at 10.8 rounds per second?

Our Marines were charred, shredded, or both.

We took off like h—— not from but toward the enemy. We pushed the deer on the road to Hit. We no more found them than they found us.

Hit laid between FOB Camp Cupcake and the Navea Training

Center. Camp Cupcake was once an Iraqi air force base under the late Saddam Hussein. Now it was our biggest base west of Baghdad. Our guys wanted to stop off for a stuffed crust at the base Pizza Hut or fried dumplings at Tsao Lo Wo's. But I had orders to go on past Hit to Navea. Anyway, I promised myself I would never eat at a Pizza Hut again until I could eat at the one on Portsmouth Avenue with Ryan. And I preferred my MREs in the field to wontons in DFACs.

You could go on past Hit, but you couldn't pass Hit. Not without Hit hurting you. It smelled of death and screamed with fire. Its air was made of smoke and sand. Its name rhymed with Bittersweet. Anyone who went in went in on short-term deployment. You died or got pulled out when death started clinging to the Velcro of your Advanced Combat Uniform military spec all-terrain digital camouflage cargoes. Which if death won left you dead for all the world to see in your silly brown camo polypropylene skivvies.

Like Desert Camouflage Uniform poly undies were going to fool anyone.

My Minsticky job at Navea Training Center was to train the jundi in the so-called latest weaponry. The thing about the latest weaponry was that by the time you got it in your hands there was someone outmoding it in lethality. Thank God for that.

But I had an Army Achievement Medal in special weapons. And the Iraqi Civil Defense Corps, police recruits, and army regulars needed to learn how to kill people. So we could stop killing people and go home. So America could win the war not by defeating a country but by giving it back to its people. In one piece.

The men I trained (no women in that army) had completed a month learning marching, drilling, and first aid. So they could go on what the Department of Defense called "Transition to Security Self-Reliance." And grunts called "Transition to Certain Self-Destruction."

They'd also qualified in an eleven-obstacle confidence course. That was run by a Latino US Marine drill sergeant named Felipe, who called himself Dr. Feel. He wasn't much of a talker. More of a screamer. The confidence he taught was not in yourself facing life. It was in yourself facing death. Dr. Feel would yell at recruits who didn't have the strength to hold on and fell the thirty feet from the Slide for Life, "Fly the f—— back up!" Some of them died. Dr. Feel didn't care. He had the live ones carry the dead ones downrange doing what he called the kay-dance, while they chanted in lousy English, "I used to date a beauty queen, now I h—— my M-16."

Those jundi who survived had also qualified on the rifle range from twenty-five meters. They were shooting with old M-16s. Some of the weaker ones with M-4s. But all their guns got jammed with the silver moon dust we called dirt here. Dirt that even got through the condoms we tried to teach them to put over their muzzles after their weapons' takedown, but they wanted no truck with condoms for whatever. Dirt ground so fine by war after war century after century that it wasn't just in the air but was the air. Like after September Eleventh. When you breathed, you breathed in people. Like Jesus, except their souls were long gone.

Even the Friendlies who'd never fired a shot in anger knew that the 5.56mm round had trouble penetrating a cinder-block target (like their houses) or even a torso (like their torsos). Some of them even told me the bullets couldn't make their way through the paper targets. Before I got there they were shooting at Terrorist Targets of O (Say Can You) Sama that the Marines got off Amazon. And Masked Thugs who were supposed to look like the enemy hiding inside their keffiyeh. Except the Masked Thugs came in huge packages from Big Daddy's Guns in Carrollton, Texas, not all that far from my old Fort Bliss in Texas terms.

What I got them trained with were Barrett XM109s.

And targets made of flesh and blood.

I was testing the gun for Barrett. It was one step up from the M82 that the Army redesignated the M107. What Barrett wanted, and had, was a One-Hit Objective Sniper Weapon. One Hit = Instant Kill. It fired twenty-five-millimeter shells originally intended for a grenade launcher. It misted anyone it hit. Or would have. The problem being, the recoil was, as they say, "beyond human limitations." Not mine. I learned to fire the thing and stay mostly in place and take the pain. Most guys though got thrown back by the gun almost as far as the enemy would have been by the kill shot.

So they kept the M107 in munitions inventory as a kind of mini-lightweight .50-caliber bolt-action sniper rifle. And developed the XM109.

The first time I held it in my hands was at the range at Navea. Its barrel was nearly twelve inches shorter than the 107's, but the gun weighed fourteen pounds more. Twenty-five millimeter versus fifty millimeter. It was like holding a tiny crucifix that felt like the True Cross in your arms.

I used to think there was no greater feeling in the world than holding a fine gun in your arms. Then, when I had a child, I realized that there was no greater feeling than holding your child in your arms. Better than a gun. But without guns, we wouldn't be able to hold our children in our arms. Not alive.

The XM109's twenty-five-millimeter round was designed out of the thirty-millimeter AH-64 Apache's dual-purpose high explosive. Dual Purpose = Armor *and* Personnel. You could take down SCUD launchers with it *and* the people doing the SCUD launching.

It was meant to fire at long range. So we had to open up the range at Navea. The BORS computerized sight was compensated for at least a thousand meters. But its armor-piercing lethality was listed at two thousand meters.

Of course what I wanted was to break the record of the guy who took down that Taliban fighter at a mile and a half.

So first we put out our paper targets a thousand meters away. Between us and them there was enough space they were invisible. Osama. The Masked Thugs. Couldn't see them. And only a couple of my guys could hit them. Me and them. Working all of us off a spiked bipod that steadied the gun but didn't necessarily reduce what was still a heavy recoil.

One guy named Mansoor got knocked out by the gun but hit his target anyway and when he woke up and I showed him the tiny pieces of paper he kissed the gun that had pushed him over on his a——. Another guy after my own heart.

I figured the paper targets left the guys uninspired, so I asked for volunteers to go over to Hit to get some real people to shoot.

"Real people?" someone said.

"That's right," I said.

"I go!" said a big guy named Faatih. "Take prisoners. Shoot the s—— out of them."

"Not that real," I said. "We don't shoot prisoners. I want bodies. Enemy bodies. Volunteers?"

Mansoor wanted to go but his shoulder was wrecked.

But I got my little squad of four. Jawwaad. Munajj. Shaheed. Mubashir.

It wasn't an authorized mission. But it was a CAP. Combined Action Patrol. Combined meaning me and a bunch of Iraqis. Jundis. Not quite a Combined Action Platoon, like in Vietnam. But close enough to make me the goodwill ambassador from the Nation Of Triage. Which is NOT. As in, Not Yet. Not Now. Not Ever.

We had to grab a beat-up old Humvee with Hajji armor welded to the sides. The truck looked like a Christmas present wrapped by a married man. The only weapon on it, aside from what we carried, was an M-16 mounted but not bolted to the back that by the time anyone could swing it around to fire would be fired upon. It was considered a dead man's post. No one would take it so I did.

I also made myself the occasional point man, so I'd get out of the truck now and then to check for roadside IEDs, mines, and unexploded mortars. My Arabs didn't want to ride in the Humvee in the first place. They considered it an OV. OV = Occupier Vehicle. It might be safer than their tiny old rusty Luvs and Mighty Maxes and Starlets. But if they died in our Humvees, they didn't get to Heaven. Like God cares what car you drive.

The road was a road only because it was a road. No one built it. It was made of desert sand, compacted by truck tires and feet and hooves. Sometimes it felt like the beach at home with the tide far out and the blazing sun gone into the pocket of the Earth that turns to turn away sometimes from its creatures' pain.

For white light I used the little Princeton Tec Eclipse LED I kept hooked onto my belt loop. I'd been tempted by the new Impulse, because you could clip it to your hat. But the first guy I knew who ordered the Impulse and put it on the brim of his Boonie got shot through the brain. Not to mention nearly post-mort guillotined by the Boonie's chin cord. So I kept on going with my old Eclipse. I figured you could live without a groin. But not without a brain. Most everyone else in my unit believed the opposite.

We went at night, of course, because that's the best time to travel safely and to find the day's bodies for the next day's target practice. It was nice walking alongside the truck looking for hidden explosives. Very peaceful. I turned on my night-vision goggles. Iraq became as green as New Hampshire. I pretended I was headed out for the beach. Trees then sand. Just like here like there. What they called *dar al-harb*. The House of War.

I also moved the rear sight aperture on my M-16 to the large setting so I could pretend to be able to shoot in the dark at someone who would by that time have shot me so many times, or once, that the only aperture that would matter to me would be the opening to my vision of paradise. Not the Muslim paradise. My own. If we meet up in Heaven with our loved ones from earth, that means we make Heaven here and take it there. It's not a separate place. It's a better here there.

The road to Hit was a used-car lot. Not exactly like Portsmouth Avenue, because here all the cars and trucks had been used up.

They were like what hulls of ships must be at the bottom of the sea. Opened up to let the screams out. The ground around most of them was yellow and black. Which I always thought of as the colors from Stryper's first album *Yellow and Black Attack*, though most guys liked to comment it was the color of p—— and s——. The stain of explosives. Each one left the mark of a human being opened up to let the screams out.

But the air didn't smell of human waste or blood. It smelled of dog. Not the dogs of a veterinary, no matter how sick they were. The dogs of Iraq smelled of fruit. Fruit that had rotted but was still sweet. Wet old fruit that grew out of the sand and was a kind of miracle until you touched it and it turned to red puke. The dogs ate it and became it. They could be told apart from the desert wolves only by their songs. The wolves sang from far away the low moans of frightened men.

The first dog I actually saw, not just smelled, was nipping at a corpse by the side of the road. I had Shaheed stop the truck and took a look at the dog with my Eclipse. The dog took advantage of my light and went for what was left of the dead man's liver. Must have been something wrong with the dog's nose if he needed my LED. Whoever the dead man was, there wasn't enough of him left to shoot at. He was bulletproof.

I got back on the truck. I asked my guys, who ought to know, "How do you tell a Sunni from a Shiite?"

They all laughed at me. I could even hear Shaheed, who was driving the truck, laughing.

"You follow these people to worship," said Jawwaad. "Sunnis go to mosques. Shiites go to Husseineyyahs. You wait until the Sunnis are in their mosques, then you blow them up. And shoot them when they run away."

Mubashir shook his head. "Animal!" he snarled at Jawwaad. Then he told me, "The way you tell one of them from one of us is you ask him when the moon was born."

"When was the moon born?" I ask him.

"At the beginning of time," said Mubashir. "The god of the moon was called Hubal. He was also the Lord of the Kabah. And do you know who *else* was the Lord of the Kabah? Allah himself! So you see, Specialist Pease, the One God and the Moon God were one."

"Until Muhammad came along," said Jawwaad.

"True." Mubashir made peace with Jawwaad.

Shaheed braked the truck. He stuck his head out the window.

I tried to swivel the M-16 toward whatever had caused him to suddenly stop. "What's up?" I said.

Turned out Shaheed just wanted to tell us something. "The way you tell Shias from Sunnis is Shias believe in the resurrection of al Mahdi. And Sunnis don't! One day the Twelfth Imam will return to earth. And the earth will be filled with peace and justice." The very thought of that seemed to fill Shaheed with joy. He smiled up to Heaven and stepped hard on the gas like he wanted to catapult us all the way there.

"Like Jesus!" I screamed. Because it was true.

"Give us a break!" said Jawwaad. He was the only one dressed like me — cover for action. Raiding party jeans. Black T-shirt. Shoulder holster. No desert camouflage uniform. No body armor. No Velcroed SSI US flag reversed. "The way you tell a Sunni from a Shiite is their name. Remember the fourteen Omars. I shot half of them myself. Omar! And if they change their name, you listen to them talk. How you all like my southern Shia accent, Speshlist Pease?" he said. "And now *you* answer *this*. How do you tell a Presbyterian from an Episcopalian?"

"You don't," I said. "How do you know about these things, Jawwaad?" I asked him.

Jawwaad moved off his bench and came right over to me where I stood in my gun position. "Someday we come to your country the way you came to our country. To save you," he said, and burst out laughing.

It was like his apostasy brought destruction. Out of his laughter came a single blast of what sounded like a Dragunov.

From where I stood at the back I could see blood so red it lit up the black air as it flew out the window of the truck. Shaheed's head followed its own blood but got stopped by the door sill and just hung there while Shaheed kept on driving the truck pretty straight on the road to Hit.

"He's dead," I said.

"May Allah be pleased with him," said Munajj.

"I hope Allah doesn't know he died in an OV," I said.

Mubashir pointed to Shaheed's lolling head. "He died outside it."

"Don't worry about Shaheed, Specialist Pease," said Jawwaad. "He's fulfilled the destiny of his name."

"How?"

"His name means *martyr.*"

"Better it means *driver,*" said Munajj.

The dead Shaheed had lost control of the truck. We started to leave the compacted sand for the soft deadly desert sand. Munajj catapulted over the side of the Humvee and opened the door of the cab and let himself in on top of Shaheed.

He sat that way, driving on a dead man's lap, until we came to the Pink House at the river, close by the water treatment plant. It was lit up enough I had to cancel my night vision so I wouldn't be blinded by the lights.

This was Combat Outpost 3, manned by the US Army Task Force 1-36. They'd taken over from the 22nd Marines who'd taken over from the 1st Marines who'd taken over from the 2nd Marines who'd taken over from the 25th Marines who'd taken over from the 23rd Marines who'd taken over from the 1st Marines who'd started it all. No one lasted in Hit. So they brought in the Army.

Task Force 1-36 was known as The Spartans. I always loved the Spartans. They were the greatest warriors of all. They were the "with your shield or on it" kind of soldiers.

The guys at the perimeter security checkpoint were as big as

American trees and fitted out in Kevlar and ceramic-plate body-armor vests. They didn't like the looks of us, one dead brown man, three live ones, and me.

I didn't want them lighting up our Humvee before we got a chance to explain ourselves, so I said, "Let me do the talking."

So naturally Jawwaad said to the lieutenant who was shining his light into Shaheed's dead eyes, "Good evening, Lieutenant. We trade one dead body for a dozen." Then he turned to me and said, "Mercy, how many in a dozen?"

The lieutenant put his weapon on fire and pointed it at Jawwaad's face.

I said to the lieutenant, "Before Helen was Helen of Troy, she was Helen of Sparta."

The lieutenant kept his gun on Jawwaad but smiled at me. "That's right, son. But that ain't the password."

"What is?" I never expected him to Alpha Zulu us.

"Twelve," said the lieutenant.

"That's the password?"

"No," said the lieutenant. "We don't employ passwords. No time for passwords in this town, son. That there's the answer to this gentleman's question."

"Yes!" said Jawwaad. "I remember. Twelve to a dozen. We need twelve dead, sir."

"For what?"

"Target practice," said Jawwaad.

"Check the morgue," said the lieutenant. "And while you're at it, drop this fella off there. Save us the trip. Sniper?"

"Juba," said Mubashir.

"Not Juba," I said. "Boom boom. No silencer."

"Juba's in Baghdad," said the lieutenant.

"Me too soon," I said.

"Lucky you," said the lieutenant. He didn't safe his weapon, but he waved us through.

. . .

The Spartans reminded me how much I liked *The Odyssey* that got started by Helen with the Trojan War. And how Mr. Smith taught me that in the Bible there's a story almost the same. Mr. Smith said the Bible is an adventure story and that all great adventure stories are about journeys and that all great journeys are about finding paradise. In that story Paul got in a shipwreck and went from one island to another. He ended up in one place where a few of the barbarous people showed him kindness. *Like here,* I thought. *Just like here.* Then Paul got betrayed by Demas, who left him because Demas loved what he called *the present world.* In war, you fight to save the present world. You don't love it. You can't completely. But you don't want to leave it.

As we drove to the Hit city morgue, I told my guys the same thing Paul said in the shipwreck. "Be of good cheer."

Paul learned that from Jesus.

So did I.

Jesus knocks on the bedroom door. I know it's Jesus from the way he knocks. I don't know how to describe it. It's just a knock knock. But it's Jesus and no one else.

So Bethie walks in.

No!

I made that up. I want it to be Bethie. But it's Jesus.

He closes the door behind him too.

"How come you closed the door?" I say.

"How come *you* closed the door?" he says to Dodie.

"I was wondering that myself," I say.

"Want to be alone," she says.

"Like your daddy," says Jesus. He knows me too well.

"*With* my daddy," says Dodie.

"Me too," Jesus says to her.

"Who?" she asks him.

Jesus sits down on the bed where Dodie and I are laying. She's between him and me. "I'm Ray," he says to her.

"Way," she calls him.

"Rrrray," Jesus says.

"Ray," Dodie says.

I give him a look.

"Fast learner," he says.

The Hit city morgue was between the 1-36 Firm Base 1 at the Hit Teacher's College and Firm Base 2 at the Hit Youth Center. Both closed until further notice. The rooms were left sandbagged. Someone had written GOD DOESN'T LIVE HERE on a wall of Base 1. Whoever wrote that didn't know God. God loves war because it gives men the chance to make right what other men have made wrong.

Of course the morgue was open. There were more morgues being built in The Mess than schools or mosques. Or anything except graveyards.

Electricity was spotty like everywhere else. So the refrigeration units were keeping the bodies at near room temperature. Room temperature in Iraq in late spring was like summer in New Hampshire, except for the smell. New Hampshire always smelled like home. This smelled like h——.

There were bodies everywhere. Only a couple of them had been washed. Muslims are supposed to be washed with scented water before they're buried. They call it *ghusl*. They're also supposed to perform *ghusl* after they have sex. I could never figure that one out.

Even the washed bodies hadn't been wrapped up in white cloth. No time, I guess. We liked it when we found bodies in white cloth, because then we could separate them from the bodies that were going to get buried in the clothes they died in. Their martyrs got buried in the clothes they died in. That's how we got to know who our real enemies were. Or had been.

Though it was the middle of the night, a couple of men were delivering new bodies off an old truck. The morgue attendant pointed to where he wanted them stacked. He wore two pairs of surgical gloves. One over the other. Different colors. And a stubby old SKS AK-47 strapped over his back.

"Speak English?" I asked him.

"No," he said.

"That's English," I said.

"Yes," he said.

"We're here to make your job easier," I said.

He shook his head.

"Tell him what I said," I told Jawwaad.

Jawwaad said something in Arabic.

The man laughed.

"Why is he laughing?" I asked Jawwaad.

Jawwaad said something else to the man.

The man said something back to Jawwaad.

Jawwaad said to me, "He said the only way to make his job easier is to kill him."

"Go ahead," I said.

"Kill him?" said Jawwaad.

"Sure," I said.

Jawwaad got that look that only Jawwaad could get. He took his pistol from his shoulder holster and put it to the head of the morgue attendant.

The morgue attendant shook his head against the barrel of the gun like it was a mosquito. "Was kidding," he said.

"Speaks English!" said Jawwaad.

"No kidding," I said.

"No kidding," said the morgue attendant.

"I kill him for lying," said Jawwaad.

I put my hand on Jawwaad's pistol. "First see if he can answer this question."

So I said to the morgue attendant, "How do you tell a dead Sunni from a dead Shiite?"

"Look at his a——." The guy didn't even have to think about it.

"That's sick," I said.

"No," said Jawwaad. He pulled his pistol off the morgue attendant's forehead. "He's correct."

I looked at our other guys. Mubashir and Munajj both nodded.

Jawwaad said, "The minute a Sunni gets to Jahannam, the angels whip him on his a——. Then they take away his soul."

"What's Jahannam?" I said.

"Hell," said the morgue attendant. He moved a finger all around the room. The blue glove underneath showed through the white one on top. "Help youself," he said.

Jesus says to Dodie, "Your daddy has a present for you."

Dodie sits up in bed and turns from him to me.

"I do?" I say.

"In your pocket," says Jesus.

"Oh, that," I say. "It's only a . . ." I reach into my pocket and take it out. "Stone," I say. "It's only a stone." I wish I had something a little girl would love. A doll or something. A tiny stove with teacups.

"Open your hand," says Jesus.

I open it and there's the little piece of granite with the vein of quartz trapped in the middle.

"Tell her," Jesus says to me.

"Tell her what?"

"Tell her what it is."

"A rock," I say.

"A *rock*?" Jesus shakes his head at me.

Dodie reaches out a little finger and touches it.

"Where did it come from?" Jesus asks me.

"The beach?"

"And where did the beach get it?"

"Oh," I say, because I think I'm finally getting him. "The Earth. It's a piece of the Earth."

"It *is* the Earth," says Jesus.

"Not the whole thing," I say.

"The whole thing," says Jesus.

Dodie puts her hand out flat on the stone and wraps her fingers around it as far as they'll go.

We took exactly a dozen bodies. With Shaheed's that made a lucky thirteen. The bodies we took were the most unmarked we could find. All with arms and legs, fingers and toes, noses and ears and eyes. No visible chemical burns. Not even sniper perfs. They must have died of shock. Concussion. Internal bleeding. Fear. Despair. Hunger. Relief.

When we got back to Navea, over the berms and beyond the concertina wire, it was dawning. The air was cool. "More drag on the bullets," I told my guys.

To be a great shooter, you needed to be a weatherman. You needed to know which way the wind blew, et cetera.

We tied the twelve bodies up on posts. They looked like from those old photographs from World War II. Like the Gypsies, brown-skinned and dead. We pulled string around their heads just under their noses, so they would look proud and see what was coming. Not that they could see us. We went too far away for them to see us. And they were too far away for us to see them.

We trucked Shaheed's body down the range with us. I wanted him for one last target practice. I laid him down with my guys. They were in the prone. Shaheed was on his back, looking out to where his soul had flown. Despite the many hours since he had died, his body didn't smell. I asked why. I got told it was because he had fulfilled his name. He was a shaheed, accepted by Allah.

I started a little fire so we could read the wind from the smoke. I gave everyone my specific lecture about taking slow shots at the target's center mass and not using the mag well for support, and my general lecture about gravity. Gravity and the flight of the bullet.

You feel like God when you talk about gravity. It's not like the wind or the humidity. It's an unseen unfelt force. But if you don't pay it attention, you cannot hit your target.

You can dial in your distance all you want, on your optical ranging sighting system. You can even wait for them to make a laser-guided rangefinder for your gun. You still need to know the air and feel the force of God on your body and your bullet.

Besides, human bodies don't reflect laser light. That's why if you're going to learn how to shoot them, you have to use them to learn to shoot *at* them.

They shot at them all morning. The air got warmer and the bullets got faster and the mosquitoes got nastier. More and more of the IA jundi showed up. Word must have spread. I thought it was because the Iraqis were learning to handle the recoil of the XM109. And because they finally got embarrassed by the way they'd S&P, which was Spray and Pray, which was to take a hundred shots when one would do. But it turned out it was only because of our targets.

Half the guys wanted to shoot at them because they were human. And half the guys didn't want to shoot at them for the same reason.

Faatih was the most enthusiastic. That made him just about the worst shot. He excused his poor aim by saying they were dead to begin with.

"Faatih," I told him, "you have to shoot between heartbeats."

"*What* heartbeats?" he said. "They're all dead."

"Between your *own* heartbeats," I said.

I had them start at about a thousand meters, give or take, and stayed there. The bodies were assigned to individual shooters. I put spotters downrange but enough off target so even the worst shots were unlikely to hit them. They reported back by walkie-talkie. As the morning went on, more and more of the twenty-five-millimeter rounds were finding their targets. By noon, we got a call that there was nothing left to shoot at.

We walked there. Everyone was tired. Shooting drains you. Even when you're not getting shot back at. Your body gets pounded. And your mind gets smaller the more it concentrates, until there's nothing left of it and you have one moment of peace and then you lose your mind.

Except me. I wasn't tired. I hadn't taken a single shot.

When we got to the posts, they were just posts. Human posts. Covered with hair and blood and little flags of clothing and tiny shreds of the rope we'd used to tie the bodies on that looked like what birds bring back to make nests for their babies.

"Good work, men," I said.

"This isn't right," said an IP recruit named Madoo.

"These were people," said a timid guy named Aadil.

I was glad to hear him talk for once.

"Help me out here, Jawwaad," I said.

Jawwaad looked like he wanted to barf.

"These were bodies," I said. "Not people."

They couldn't look at me. And they couldn't look at the posts. Their eyes were dead to the truth.

This wasn't desecration. Desecration was what happened on September 11, 2001. Desecration was killing the innocent. Causing them to jump out of a building so high that when they landed there was nothing left of them but a stain. It was what was done to their *minds* in the time between when they jumped from the building and when they landed in the building's ephemeral shadow. It was making them scream in prayer.

Great warriors always made trophies of their enemies' bodies. When I was little I used to hide from my father and read books about the war that took my cousin once removed by death, Harl Pease Jr. I read how a man named Sledgehammer Sledge said he prayed to Jesus and watched his comrades use their knives to knock the gold teeth out of the Japs they'd killed. They didn't sell the teeth. They wore them. I also read about a sniper in Vietnam named Dave Nelson. He tied himself to the branch of the tree he sniped from so if he got wounded he'd be sure to stay there killing until killed.

I remembered something Abed had told me in the caves. There were Muslim holy warriors called Sulus. Before a Sulu attacked a Christian, the Sulu said, "There is no god but Allah." Every Christian a Sulu killed became his slave in Heaven. When a Sulu who died in battle got to Heaven he found beautiful young women whose eyes were like pearls inside shells.

When Abed said that, it was the first time I saw Bethie. The first time I let myself see Bethie. I saw her eyes, like pearls, pale blue pearls, looking at me. I was in Heaven, and she was looking at me.

"Our bodies are shells," I told my men. "Our souls are the pearls inside them."

Dodie puts the rock up to her mouth. She licks it a few times. She kind of kisses it. When it's good and wet she rubs it against her cheek.

Then she gives it back to me.

"What?" I ask her.

"Play," she says.

I roll the rock around in my hand. She watches it in a way that I want someone to look at me. She watches it like there's nothing else on earth.

When I close my hand over the rock, it disappears. Dodie can't believe it. She looks away from my hand into my face. I smile at her. I can't help it. I give everything away.

She holds out her hand. I put the rock back in it.

"Good," she says.

This is how you play with a child. You hand things back and forth. This is how I should have played with Bethie. I didn't give her enough.

Of me. I must have learned that from my father.

Dodie hands the rock to Jesus.

Jesus looks at the rock. He holds it out toward Dodie. Not close enough for her to take it. Just so she can see it.

"Look how beautiful this is," he says. "This isn't your New Hampshire smoky quartz. This is milky quartz. People look for this when they're looking for gold. Lacy gold grows out of quartz like this. And *feel* it!" Jesus moves the stone between Dodie and me. He takes her hand and moves it to my hand and puts both of our hands together on the rock. "Touch the quartz with your finger," Jesus says. His strong hand takes my index finger and Dodie's index finger and moves them both along the side of the rock, where the quartz forms a rim. "It's cool," he says. "The granite isn't. The granite is warm from our hands and from the air. But the quartz is cool. I know you can feel it. This was made many miles below the surface of the Earth. This is called a crack-seal vein. Here, where the quartz has formed. And this little hole — see, this little hole? There were once quartz crystals here too but they eroded away. This little hole is called a *vug*. That's one of my favorite words. Vug. Can you say *vug*?"

"Vug," says Dodie.

"Warren?" says Jesus.

"Vug," I say, I have no idea why.

"Vug vug vug vug vug," says Dodie. Then she laughs like I've never heard her laugh. She throws her head back so far her long hair brushes the bed. And she just laughs.

Jesus looks at her. He looks at her like he's her father. He looks at her like he loves and admires her more than anyone else on earth.

"That's very funny," he says to her.

This makes her laugh even more.

"What's so funny?" I ask.

"Vug vug vug vug vug," says Dodie.

"Vug vug vug vug vug," says Jesus.

That night, I used Shaheed's body for target practice. I tied it to one of the poles and I went away twenty-five hundred meters. That was seventy meters more than the world record. Set in Afghanistan three years before by a sniper with the Princess Patricia's Canadian Light Infantry. Way back in Vietnam, my hero Dave Nelson had a best range of eleven hundred meters. He also had seventy-two kills. I was shy of that but gaining.

My XM109 had a five-round magazine. But I allowed myself one shot. Like Juba. The old Fort Benning One Shot/One Kill. None of the IA death blossom spray and pray. Snipers saved money. In Vietnam it took an infantryman an average of fifty thousand rounds to kill one enemy. It took a sniper 1.3 rounds. Dave Nelson saved taxpayers $22,999.83 per kill.

Snipers are the purest warriors of all. They kill only other warriors. No one should get killed in a war who isn't trying to kill in a war. No children. Not yet.

I used a twenty-two-millimeter sniper round. In another weapon I could have used a 7.62 x 51 NATO cartridge, better known to us New Hampshire boys as the good old .308 Remington. The 7.62 x 51 is maximum ranged at 3,725 meters, which is almost two and a half miles. No one's ever hit anyone at that distance. Not on purpose. I wouldn't have wanted to either. At that distance, the bullet would have too much time to tell the target to better start praying.

I used a sandbag for stability. It was still warm from the sun or from the arms of other men who had laid upon it with a gun between their hands like a spear pointed into the lethal distance. A sandbag is a pillow filled with nightmares. You don't want to hug it.

What I didn't use was a night-vision sight. My Raptor 6X was rated up to 2,425 meters for a human target, so it might have helped. But I didn't want that help. I wanted to shoot in the dark. I was the guy who walks in darkness and has no light so he trusts in the Lord. Story of my life.

The night air was cool. It wrapped around my brain and kept it calm. I thought of nothing but the kill.

When you shoot at a target you can't see, you use science and prayer. No one from the ACLU's going to care or mind.

I loved shooting in the darkness. It was kind of like living, only faster and louder.

The muzzle flash flowered in the black air.

I drove to Shaheed in the same old Humvee he died in the same driver seat of. His dried blood on the steering wheel flaked off under my fingers and floated into my lap.

My shot had found him. Not his head. I wanted to hit his head. But I missed it. Not on purpose but still because of something I did. I missed it because I couldn't bring myself to hit it. I wanted to hit it because that's my job. And because I wanted to obliterate the wound from the Dragunov that had killed him. I'd zeroed my scope, hand-temperatured my barrel, measured the wind, checked my altimeter when I as much as moved my butt a centimeter, determined the air temp the way my father had always taught me, by feeling the sides of my nose. But I dropped my shot a tiny bit too much. Maybe three millimeters out of the fifty-one meters I'd calc'ed it would drop. I missed his head.

Not his heart. In the dark, fired blindly, my shot had found his heart.

I had the world record at a distance that was hard to fathom. But no one knew it. No witnesses. I was like the guy who runs a hundred meters in nine seconds when no one's there to see it and in ten before a crowd. I didn't care. It wasn't a live target anyway. I didn't have to compensate for movement. Movement is the sniper's greatest enemy. Movement is the prey's greatest strength. Movement is freedom. You don't always survive it. But it's the only thing that might save you.

I took Shaheed's body down from the post. Dead bodies usually weigh more than they weigh. Not Shaheed's. It weighed almost nothing. It weighed almost as little as his vanished, sacred soul.

Jesus says, "It's a sandwich."

Dodie shakes her head. "Rock," she says. Now she's got it between her dirty pink feet in the middle of the bed. I'm on one side of her. Jesus is on the other.

"The granite is the bread. The quartz is the . . . what do you like in your sandwich, Dodie?"

"Quarts," she says.

"Quartz?" says Jesus.

Dodie nods. "Quarts," she says.

Jesus says, "So it's a quarts sandwich."

"Yes," says Dodie.

She picks it up. She licks it again a few more times. She puts her lips around it and starts to take a bite.

"Watch your little teeth," I say.

She smiles like she got me good and hands the rock over.

"You," she says.

So I put it partway into my mouth and pretend to take a bite too. This gets her. She laughs as much as she laughed when Jesus made her laugh. I don't know why this makes me feel so good. I can't believe I'm in competition with Jesus. I only know he's got me and my kid pretending to eat a rock. The rock is not just the Earth. It's her and me. It's what brings us and holds us together.

Jesus tells Dodie, "Now *I* have a present for your *daddy*."

She grabs back the rock with one hand and holds out her other hand to Jesus. "What?" she says.

"Quartz," says Jesus.

"Quartz," says Dodie. The way she looks at Jesus tells him she's learned how to say the word and he better know she has.

"That's right," says Jesus. "More quartz." He says it like *qwwwartz*.

Dodie shakes her hand at him.

Jesus reaches into the pocket of his jeans and takes out a stone. It's shaped like an old Burnside cartridge from the Civil War. But those were brass. This looks like glass. Glass within glass.

Jesus puts it into Dodie's open hand. She knows it's not for her.

But I can tell she wants to touch it before I do. She wants to be the one who gives it to me.

I hold out my hand. Dodie pushes my fingers out flat so she can stand the stone on my palm.

She stares at it there. I can't tell if it's because of how beautiful it is or if she's waiting for it to fall over. Or me to grab it and make it disappear.

"Do you like it?" Jesus asks.

It was like when he wanted to know how Bethie and me liked the eggs he made.

I say the same thing I said this morning. "Fantastic."

Jesus reaches out and puts his finger on the stone. He traces it, not the rock but the rock inside the rock.

"Look," he says. "That's clear quartz inside. It's a crystal that stopped growing for a while. And when it wasn't growing, microcrystals grew on the outside of it. Sometimes the microcrystals are the same mineral and sometimes they're different. These were smoky quartz. So when the clear crystal started to grow again, it captured the smoky quartz and grew around it. Now it's like a crystal inside a crystal. You can see through the smoky surface to the clear crystal inside. The clear crystal's transparent. But you can still see it. Isn't it amazing?"

Jesus lets go of it by turning it over into my palm and then moving my fingers so I would hold it.

"What's it called?" I hear the word *galena* in my mind. In my father's voice, like it came through the static from far away on the breath of God.

"Phantom," Jesus says. "It's called a phantom crystal."

Jesus puts a blanket over Dodie and me. It's the same red blanket I used to lie under with Bethie when we used to lie down sometimes in the middle of the day. Or just, like now, at twilight, when she'd try to hold me back from going to the beach and looking for whatever I was looking for. My mother. My self. My life that I never knew was either drifting toward me or drifting away from me on the ocean swells.

I know I'll never lie under this blanket with Bethie again. But when it's over me and Dodie, and I can feel Jesus' hand straightening it out over the two of us, I feel like the blanket will protect not the love I had and lost but the love I never knew I had and found. My little girl is life itself. Our children are what we disappear into before we disappear into God.

Jesus says, "It's almost dark. We have to leave soon. You two should rest."

"Don't wanna sleep," says Dodie.

"Who said *sleep*?" says Jesus. "Just some quiet time together."

"Who taught you about quiet time?" I said. "You sound like a teacher."

"Student," says Jesus. "I'm a student."

"You seem to know everything," I say.

Jesus shakes his head. "You learn something new every day."

"That's pretty trite, Ray," I say. "So what about today? What did you learn today?"

"You," says Jesus. "I learned you."

"I thought you knew me before."

"Nope," he says.

"I thought you said we went to school together."

"I said I was in your class. I didn't say I knew you. I said you knew me."

"From way back." I'm happy I remember what he told me. I want him to know I've been listening to him.

"Way back," he says. "But I didn't really know you until today."

"So how well do you think you know me after just one day?" I ask him.

"Completely," he says.

"Fast learner," I tell him.

He gives me a friendly punch in the arm.

"Ouch," I say.

"That didn't hurt," he says.

"How do you know?"

"That's how well I know you now," he says.

I do what Jesus says. Who wouldn't? I lie there under the red blanket with Dodie in my arms. I don't sleep, but I drift away to where there's only Dodie and Jesus and me. Like here. Except it's not here.

I know what Jesus is doing. It's not that I can read his mind the way he can read mine. I guess if you spend a whole day with Jesus, you get to know him. Or should I say, if Jesus spends a whole day with you.

He's telling me to hold on to Dodie while I can on Earth. Because it's going to be a long time until I get to hold her in Heaven. I'll be waiting a long time until I hold her again. She will live a long time on this, the only world there is.

That makes me very joyous.

We got waylaid on the way to Baghdad in a place called Yusifiya. It's about fifteen clicks south of Bad Dad. Which I was itching to get to because I heard it was the New York City of The Mess. And I always wanted to go to New York City. I never even went to Boston. I was a country boy with the world inside me. Busting to get out. I wanted to kill everyone in Baghdad who wanted to kill me. So everyone else who wanted to go to Baghdad could go there and never have to look up for anybody but God.

We came into Yusifiya in our Strykers. I was in a nine-man ICV, which is an Infantry Carrier Vehicle. Ahead of us were two RVs. Which of course we called Recreational Vehicles because they didn't have our firepower. But they were really Reconnaissance Vehicles. I was upstairs cradling my own rifle next to the MK-19 that was operated out of the Remote Weapon Station in the belly of our beast.

Our onboard computers could tell our own guys from the enemy by the blue circles moving over the map of the town like bubbly creatures from some ancient video game. Or so they told me, my not being a gamer. This way we didn't take out our own vehicles. Which was not something a sniper ever had to worry about. A sniper's fire was never friendly.

A few of us were singing along to the boombox blasting a song that everybody knew but not the same lyrics to. "Rockin' in the Free World." We're not rocking *in* it. We're rocking to *bring* it in. Freedom.

They sang the song the way it was. But I sang, "I am the *lamb*."

The lamb with the rifle.

There were eight thousand of us in all, counting the jundi. We were looking for two of our soldiers who got kidnapped from a Euphrates River checkpoint where a canal laps the land with what looks like blood but smells like some meat the sun has fouled. Sure enough they showed up DAD near the power station. One bomb among the many IEDs emplaced there in a drainage culvert went off. It killed an IP but not our guys. Our two soldiers already had their throats slit. Their eyes looked up to God off the broken hinges of their necks. Two young privates. My age. Not for long.

We couldn't move their bodies because they were booby-trapped. I watched them get unwired. There was a bomb between the legs of one of them. No one joked about it for once. I kept waiting for an explosion. Our defuser engineer from the Explosive Ordinance Disposal Mobile Unit turned out to be a woman in the huge bomb-disposal suit. When she unpeeled and her blast plates shuddered to the asphalt, I thought she was a tiny angel stepping out into the dried blood of Hell. I took my hands off my ears so I could applaud.

The whole town was wired. Yusifiya was a preschool for terror. Suicide bombers put on their vests here and got exfiled up north to the big city. They always sat in the backseat with one guy on either side. The bombers prayed with smiles on their faces. The other guys wore different smiles. They knew enough not to let the bomber drive a car. Not yet.

Our two dead soldiers had their throats slit as an act of mercy. Or impatience. Long before that, in their time but not in Earth time, someone had tortured them. We didn't know who until the Mujahideen Shura Council put it on their website. A new boss named Mujahir who took the place of the dead old boss named Zarqawi used his own knife. It said right there on the computer screen that he was "graced by God Almighty with the implementation of the sentence."

That's one reason I didn't use computers. Too easy to take the name of God in vain.

We cuddled our dead and geared up and spread out over Yusifiya. If it was like they said — the tip of the Triangle of Death — we folded it under. Most of the battalion went looking for weapons. They found sniper rifles with night vision, which worried everybody but me.

I went out on my own, like snipers will. But they made me take a spotter named Malik. He looked like he had a pair of giant binoculars permanently glued to his dark eyes. His nickname was Science Fiction. Like mine was Mercy.

I told Malik I wanted only fat guys.

So Malik felt useless.

Anyone could see the fat guys. I'd aim through the unseasonable clothes. If the vest was TNT and not C4 the fat guy would explode and shrapnel would twist in the air like black snow on the beach at home in a blizzard in the dark of night. That dead man was a dust devil, spinning straight to Hell.

Malik was good at finding insurgent snipers through those eyes he wore, though. To make him feel better, I let him guide me to a peephole and I put a bullet right into it and out of it gushed brain poo and out of the gash below came the barrel of a gun, inch by useless inch.

. . .

I come back from where I've been in my mind with Dodie and it's totally dark. The little bedroom that once was mine. The air outside the window. I can't see Jesus but I know he's there. I can feel him. Not the way you can always feel him inside yourself if you let yourself. I can feel him in the room. I know he's there. I know it more than I've known it all day, from the first moment I saw him walking toward me off the Isles of Shoals and across the ocean sand. More than when he touched me and walked beside me and fed me. I could see him then. Now I can't see him. But I know he's here even more than I know I'm here. Without him, I would fail to be.

I say to him, "What's going on, Ray?"

"Time to go," he says without a moment's hesitation.

"Where?" I say.

"Follow me," says Jesus.

I have to laugh.

"Where?" Not that I care. I would follow him anywhere.

"The beach," he says.

I think about how he said the same thing on the beach of the sea of Galilee. Which isn't a sea. It's just a lake. *Follow me,* he said. The fishermen did. That's probably why Jesus likes the Isles of Shoals. Other people had excuses. *I have to bury my father.* Which I always knew didn't have to do with burying anybody in the ground. It had to do with taking your father into yourself and throwing your father out of yourself. *I have to say goodbye to my family.* Oh, no, said Jesus — *don't look back! Whether you're going to Heaven or you're going to war — don't look back.*

But the beach is back. For me. Back to where we started. He's going to say goodbye to me. I don't want him to. But I say, "I'll go wherever you go."

"Can you recommend a cheap hotel?" he says.

I laugh. I haven't laughed this hard in years. Maybe ever. I laugh so hard Dodie at first jumps away from me like I'd exploded. Then she starts to laugh too. She rocks on her little bottom on the bed. I can't see her but I can feel her.

Jesus says, "Everything filled this time of year? It doesn't have to be on the beach, Warren."

"You just need a place to lay your head?" I say.

"I wouldn't mind a shower too," he says. "But, yeah, a place to lay my head. That sounds good."

"I'll bet it does," I say.

It's so Jesus. Everything comes together. The mud whelk snail and the petrel bird and the frogs and the mice and the ocean birds that cried out in the darkness of this morning when he found me on the beach. This is the man who said, "The foxes have holes. The birds have nests. But the Son of Man has nowhere to lay his head."

And I always thought I was alone.

We pulled into Baghdad blasting and singing about pulling into Nazareth to find a place to lay our heads.

It was dawn. And this was the most beautiful city I'd ever seen. Not that I'd ever seen a real city. But this place was golden-red in the rising sun. The streets were wide enough for tanks to dance on. Along their sides were date palms exploding bright green in the air like the end of an Independence Day fireworks display on Seabrook Beach, New Hampshire. Mixed in with the round date palms were skinny poplar trees that went up bare forever until at the very top tiny leaves shook and whistled in the warm morning breezes and from the passage of our Strykers and our Bradleys and our Humvees. I was surprised to see date palms. On the airport road, Route Irish, aka St. Mary's, they'd all been cut down so insurgent snipers couldn't use them as hides. Here they were too beautiful to go. And what they hid was some of the white brick rubble of fallen walls and concrete blast barriers and dead electrical wiring severed and frayed by explosives. Off in the distance was the dome of a mosque that when the sun hit it became soft blue like an advent candle. Like the sky had come down to earth.

This city is where the Garden of Eden might have been. Someone said that Baghdad meant Garden of God. The Mongols were here before us. But we weren't the Mongols. The Mongols stayed and now they were killing each other off. And us too.

I was there on a MOUT, which for our Army is a Military Op in Urban Terrain, though for once the Brits had it nailed better as what they called a FISH, which is Fighting In Someone's House.

It was called Operation Together Forward. Or Forward Together. Nobody seemed to know which. Maybe because everybody knew that no matter how much forward we went, we were never really together with the Iraqi Security Forces. Because too many of them were traitors to us and killers of their own people. I don't mean their own enemy soldiers. I mean their own people. The whole place was a slaughterhouse run by the animals.

Somebody taught me what they called the operation in Arabic. *Amaliya Ma'an ila Al-Amam*. It sounded like poetry to me. So that's what I called it to myself. I thought of Mr. Smith when I said it in my mind. *Amaliya Ma'an ila Al-Amam*. Poetry is sometimes just the music of words. Mr. Smith taught me how to hear the world.

Here the world was loud. People tossed thermite grenades they'd made using the aluminum kerosene stoves they cooked lamb on where there used to be sidewalks. Kids threw or slingshot rocks against our Humvees. They set off firecrackers to eclipse the snap of sniper rounds. Generators roared even over diesel whine. Mosques had loudspeakers that were either calling people to prayer or blasting the actual prayers five times a day. Or the mosque voices were insulting Americans or insulting even louder the people they called Puppets, which were their own people who either helped us or pretended to help us and then tried to kill us.

Men screamed at each other even when they were just playing dominoes on a creaky table in front of a gutted store that still had glass shards in what used to be windows. Women didn't play dominoes. But they screamed louder than the men. One woman was going through the streets holding a frayed pajama leg screaming,

"My son! My son!" The hand that wasn't holding the pajama leg was pounding her own face. Not just on the forehead.

One day I came on a funeral procession heading toward the Ghazali Cemetery up Bor Said Street from Tahrir Square. That was the center of the city. The funeral tied up traffic. I'd split from my platoon. I hadn't come to Baghdad to go dabbing. I didn't need my platoon leader's permission to take the shot. I never briefed back my plans. I was my own QRF, which is a Quick Reaction Force. I spent almost all my time outside the wire. Which meant that I almost never went to base and slept where I could find a place to lay my head and ate when people we'd been sent to protect and save gave me food. Or from kebab stands. I had a favorite kebab stand in Shorja Market that I would have died at if I'd been snacking there the day someone detonated a bomb right inside it and twenty-seven people got killed and thirty-five wounded, some with kebab screwers in their eyelids like our soldiers had with the Fraser fir needles from our Christmas tree.

Just about every car in the funeral procession had a coffin trussed to the roof with rope and butcher string and bungee cords. Some cars had two or three coffins, but those were smaller, probably with kids inside them. There were tiny round bouquets of flowers around some of the coffins. There were flowers all over the place in this city. I didn't know how they stayed alive.

Alongside the cars, people walked. The men waved pistols around with one hand and carried candles or burning incense with the other. They waved the pistols to get people out of the way. They didn't shoot their guns the way they did when they were happy about something.

The women were dressed in black abayas, the way they always were. The black wasn't for the dead but for the living. They could be shot for wearing black for the dead, which was blasphemy. The abayas came up only to their necks. I was always wanting to see their faces, but they wore niqabs over everything but their eyes. Their eyes were full of tears.

The women also carried candles in one hand. With their other hand they beat their chests. I could hear the sound through all the other sounds. Even though it was hollow.

The whole thing went slow enough so I could walk alongside it. I wasn't there to be nosy. I was there to protect them. Though they didn't know it.

A lot of people got killed at cemeteries. People got killed wherever people got together in groups. When people pitched their funeral tents at home, those got bombed too. I always wondered about suicide bombers whose charge went off and they were the only ones killed. I wondered if they got to the heaven they thought they were going to and they learned the only person they killed was themselves, if that made them feel like committing suicide. I figured it would. They tried to kill as many people as possible. It didn't matter who. My job was to kill one person at a time. Of course, it was also to kill as many people as possible. But I got to choose the people. One at a time.

People who set off bombs in public places were not people. We didn't have a word for them in any language. If any language had a word for them, that word would kill the language. It could never be spoken again by anyone. It would be a dead language. Murdered by the murderers without a name.

When we got into Ghazali Cemetery I couldn't believe how big it was. My mother was buried in a cemetery so small I could picture her whispering to everyone else there at night telling them about her son who was fighting somewhere they'd never heard of for reasons they'd never dreamed. Here, it was a city of the dead, with streets and white-brick houses filled with the dead and half-built tombs open to the air with ghosts of the future floating in and out of them. There were trees here and there that looked like the life had been sucked out of their roots by dead people trying just to breathe in the grainy ground. More ladies in black sat next to some of the tombstones crying through their niqabs that covered their entire faces so their eyes were tears that glowed fiercely in the sun and then rolled down their black flat faces into the dirt. I thought the tears might explode and took my gun off safe.

The cars all started up one alley. When a family reached its plot, it would turn off and people would get out of the cars before they'd stopped and would reach up with open arms to untie the coffins like they were reaching into the sky and asking for help.

I stayed with the procession as it moved on and kept my eyes on as many coffins as I could. There was one family that had about nine flimsy coffins on maybe five cars. They all had that Mercedes peace symbol on the hood. But three of the cars were huge old American sedans. And two of them were tiny Seats. At first I'd called them *Seats*, like chairs. Then somebody told me they're called like *see-otts*, which I had no trouble remembering because in New Hampshire we pronounced the word *art* like *ott*, so whenever I saw a Seat car, which was from Spain, I thought *see art*, like in a museum.

You could buy those Mercedes peace symbols in the street markets, where they had stalls that sold everything. Like henna lamps, that had shades dyed from the same kind of henna some men put into their beards and you could smell them from a mile away. The men, not the lamps. And a drink called Orange Fanta that was everywhere and had a small green leaf on the label that looked like the leaves high on those poplar trees.

One guy in our platoon bought a Mercedes symbol and welded it on the turret of his Bradley by the smoke grenade launchers. When his vehicle suffered a mobility kill from an RPG he claimed it was the peace sign that had saved his life. He took it off the Bradley and started to wear it around his neck.

The family with the five phony Mercedeses all pulled over together. Their plot had nine new holes dug in the ground. At least thirty people got out of the cars. They stood around in a kind of circle looking back at the coffins on their cars like they couldn't believe where they were and what they were there for. They were a giant family but they shrank from all their dead.

I was looking at their coffins too when I saw one of them start to move. It shook a little bit at first and then it bounced against the roof of the Seat. I could hear the sound you imagine you would hear when somebody's been buried alive and is trying to get out. Not the scratching, which you would never be able to hear. But the pounding. And then the sound of nails creaking when the wood started to release them.

It was one of the small coffins that kids were buried in. I couldn't believe they'd use a child as a bomber. Unless it was a small woman. Or a man bent double over his suicide belt that when it exploded would straighten him out real quick.

What the bomber didn't know was that they hadn't untied his coffin yet. This one was bungeed on beyond the little nails. As the coffin bounced against the cords, the cords moved like the thick strings on an electric bass and I thought I could hear them playing the soft beginning of a song.

I raised my rifle to shoot him through the side of his coffin. A woman saw me and saw what I was aiming at and screamed. I didn't know what she screamed. I didn't know if she was screaming at me or at the coffin. Or at all her relatives, to tell them to cover up.

She grabbed my arm. She grabbed me so fast her own arms flew out from under her abaya. Her arms were pale and thin and didn't have any hair on them. I couldn't believe it. Not that she was so strong she pulled me off my aim. That her arms were so smooth. And so beautiful out from under her abaya.

"He's going to blow you all up," I said.

"Please," she said. Or that's what I thought she said. It could have been an Arabic word. Or somebody's name.

"Mashood!" I heard people shout. "Mashood!"

The men went to the car and cut the bungees with box cutters and knives. They slid their knife blades under the lid of the coffin. They pried it open. Some of their knife blades broke off.

The women rushed to the car with their arms raised. Like they were exposing their bodies to the full force of the blast.

The only woman who didn't go to the car was the one holding my arm. She wasn't gripping it so hard now. She was holding on to it like if she let go she would fall to the ground.

If I took my arm away to shoot, she'd fall. I couldn't let her go. I couldn't take aim. So I put my other arm around her. I wasn't wearing my Kevlar. I couldn't really protect her. But I thought I could. I thought that when my body disappeared, hers would be left.

A hand came out of the coffin. A small white hand. Then it fell back in. I thought it was a signal. A signal to itself. I thought it was going for the wire connected to the trigger of the bomb.

"Now," I said. And like the men heard me but didn't understand what I'd meant, they altogether tried to reach into the coffin. The ones who could came out with a boy. He was wrapped in a clean white kafan. He had long black hair that came down over a blood-caked bandage on a head wound.

"Mashood!" they cried again.

The boy opened his eyes and smiled.

The men brought him to the woman I was holding.

She let me go and put her arms around him.

I put my arms around Dodie and lift her from the bed. She's still asleep. I follow Jesus and carry Dodie from the bedroom. If I didn't have her to hold on to, I wouldn't be able to leave this room. It's not Jesus but Dodie who ties me to the earth. Jesus, I realize, is for another world.

There are lights on in the kitchen. I cover Dodie's eyes. Bethie never did used to turn off lights. I'd bug her about it. But I always also liked having a light on in the house when I'd come home in the dark from the beach. Bethie was the real light in my life. I've realized this too late.

"Where is everybody?" I ask.

"At the beach," says Jesus.

"What for?" I ask.

"The wedding," says Jesus.

He opens the refrigerator.

It's pretty much empty again. Except for the bottle of champagne. Jesus takes it out. He hands it to me. "Carry this," he says.

"I've got Dodie," I say.

"Carry this," says Jesus.

He puts the bottle in my hand that's under Dodie's bottom. The bottle's so light, I realize it's empty. But the cork is still in it. And the wire is still around the top.

"There's nothing in it," I say.

"Sometimes it just fizzes away," says Jesus.

"So I'm taking an empty bottle to my wedding," I say.

"I didn't say it was empty," says Jesus.

"Or that it was my wedding," I say.

"Or that," says Jesus.

He holds open the screen door. Moths are plastered to it.

"Don't let them in," I tell him.

"Maybe to them it's out," he says.

"So to us this is in?" I ask as I take the first wooden step down.

"Sure," says Jesus. "In or out — what's the difference? You go where the light is."

"But it's dark out," I say. Because it is. You can't see a thing.

"It's dark *in*," says Jesus. He laughs.

I don't know if it's his laugh or the sizzling of the moths that wakes up Dodie.

She stares at the moths on the screen. "Singing and dancing," she says. She moves her arms and legs against my body.

"I know who told you that," I say.

"Ryan," she says.

A huge moth leaves the others and flies into the house.

"Bye-bye," says Dodie.

"Where did the moth go?" I ask her.

"Out," she says.

. . .

Baghdad had eleven bridges across the Tigris. It was like a river of soy sauce with dumplings floating in it. We ran missions from the east bank to the west bank to the east bank and back again. From conflict zone to conflict zone. You'd come on beautiful houses and green parks and small clear ponds and pools of sewage and sandbags and blast walls and razor wire and National Police checkpoints and bombed-out cars and trucks (but not Humvees — we cleared them out) and headless bodies floating in the Tigris and bodiless heads on soccer fields.

Everybody played soccer, kids and grown-ups, in the streets and on the fields. Two bombs went off in a soccer field in A'amil, which was Shiite, right after two mortars landed in a soccer field in Abu Dsher, which was Sunni. They were killing each other off in their playgrounds.

In Firdos Square, where they once took down the statue of Saddam Hussein, somebody blew himself up in the same place the statue had stood, in the middle of a group of people who had come to see where the statue had stood. The bomber didn't know if those people were there to cheer or to weep. When I saw all the blood and body parts, I thought how lucky the statue had been. One of our forensic guys who said his job was to collect hands, only hands, told me that Firdos Square translated as Paradise Square. That should have been enough to keep any Muslim away. He found somebody's hand in the lobby of the Sheraton Hotel. That led one of our other guys to make a joke that got repeated over and over: "Any luggage, sir?" I didn't laugh. It was a woman's hand anyway.

On Haifa Street, the Sunday after Saddam Hussein became the late Saddam Hussein, Sunnis put nooses on blindfolded Shiites and hung them from the lampposts. Not fast enough to break their necks. Slow enough to choke them.

At the Mutanabi Street book market a bomb exploded. It destroyed twenty-six people and so many books that their pages blown into the air shut out the sun and then when they fell to earth burst into such flames that people thought the sun had fallen out of the sky in despair and revenge. Someone told me they had lots of books in English there, old books. I imagined one was the body of Emily Dickinson and it exploded with a *pop*. It was Mr. Smith who taught me that a book was the body of the person who had written it. Like Jesus being bread and wine.

The Tigris got the color it was, they said, from the blood of the bodies in it starting with the time of the Mongols and from the ink of all the books that had been slaughtered.

On Abu Nawas Street on the east bank Iraqi workers wearing orange jumpsuits were planting trees and shrubs. They were completely alone, except for armed guards, because all the shops and fish restaurants were boarded up. And us Americans had shut off the street months before. There was still fish garbage in the street. The bags had decayed but the *masgouf* were still there sworded on their sticks. It was like someone put them out fresh every night. They didn't smell. They were like eternal dead animals floating on the top of an ocean of unbreathable air. Even the heat ignored them.

We expedited cordons-and-searches in other rich neighborhoods. In Karrada four kids got blown up going through garbage. The bomb was meant for us. Not for little scavengers from Sadr City. So we shut the place down block by block into no-goes and went from house to house. It wasn't sniping, but I liked it because I got to meet people. I didn't mind meeting people I would never see again. The people I tried to avoid were the people I knew I'd meet again and then one day they'd be dead and I'd try to find them in the empty hole where the last time I'd seen them they'd been alive. Sometimes the air was the shape of my mother but there was nothing inside it. Even when I closed my eyes the empty shape came inside them.

Of course the people didn't really like to meet us. We couldn't take a chance knocking so we had to beat down their doors. They were always home, because it was too dangerous to go out. Though of course people did go out. Like to the Sadriyah market. Three car bombs went off there. One to the east. One to the west. One to the heart. The streets were so narrow that emergency vehicles got backed up all the way to the Wethbeh traffic circle. No one could get through. Though some of the living got out with some of the dead in their arms. It was mostly a food market, so it was hard to tell the fruit from the flesh. Except for the hindquarters of lambs, which had twisted through the smoke like boomerangs. One stall sold black cloth for abayas. Some of the cloth had been blown into the air and came down on the living and the wounded and the dead. The cloth didn't care. And soap from the soap stand blew apart and smelled like lemon as it actually foamed up in the hot blood running through the streets.

It was a Sunni attack on a Shiite market. The day before, Shiite soldiers had attacked Sunnis just a few blocks away in al-Fadhil.

Being in Baghdad was like being in a house with a family that was so ashamed of itself it wanted the house to be empty forever of human beings.

One house we busted into in Mansour was the most beautiful house I'd ever seen. There were red and blue rugs on the floors and clean deep white couches and chairs and tables made of dark wood that looked like it came from an ancient ship and lamps with parchment shades and a kitchen with a stone island bigger than my whole kitchen on Bittersweet Lane and a TV with a screen so big we could see all of us reflected in it and we looked like soldiers in a movie you wouldn't want to mess with.

One reason we all fit in the screen is that we'd been ordered out of our shoulder armor. Because when we wore it we looked too frightening to the people we were there to protect. Us strapping American boys. Young men in vests webbed or clipped or stuffed with flash-bang grenades, stunners, half a dozen thirty-round magazines of this or that, glowing GPSs, fearsome Horrigan knives of those Damascus steel blades with a desert-sand pattern, Surefire flashlights for blinding and bezeling both, disposable double flex cuffs, and, last but not least, tourniquets, in case someone got cut shaving years off lives. Giants in a land where people were small because shrapnel filled the air.

Another new regulation come down from the unit command sergeant major had us snipers going around in groups of twelve. Dirty Dozens, they called it. I called us Twelvers. Useless for stealth. Fine for firefights. Except we didn't engage in firefights. A good sniper fired once. Then no one could find him. Not the dead man. Not the dead man's friends. Take one shot and none came back. Take two shots and four came back. Sniper math. Juba knew what he was doing. But after four Marine snipers got killed together in Ramadi and six got killed together in Haditha, the solution was to send us out in groups so big we couldn't have snuck up on a dead camel.

If you have the shot, take the shot. The sniper's creed. Also the hunter's. Also everyone's. *If you have the shot, take the shot.*

Then they changed the rules of engagement to forbid firing upon a target unless it had been PID'd (Positively Identified) as displaying hostile intent. Like we could read minds. Only Jesus could read minds.

So we busted into houses. I thought the pretty one was empty until I found a woman in the last of the bedrooms. It was at the end of the house and huge. She was sitting on the edge of the bed facing the door, like she was waiting for us. "Clear!" I called out, because she displayed no hostile intent. And because I wanted to be alone with her. She wasn't scared either. She didn't cower the way so many did who didn't know we were there to save them. I hoped I didn't have to shoot her.

She had on a pretty dress like the kind my mother used to wear in the summer. Flowers on a white background. Cloth I used to think was floating above her skin in soft folds that held cool air. Just to look at this woman made me feel better. She wore open shoes with straps that went around her ankles. Her hair was short and dark.

Her eyes were green. I could see them grow as they looked at me. Not just open wider but grow. She seemed shocked to see me there. Not just an American soldier in her house. *Me.*

I motioned with the barrel of my gun for her to stand up. When she hesitated I wondered if she was booby-trapped.

"Hal tatahaddath ingiliziya?" I said. It was the only Arabic I knew except for things like *Allahu Akbar.* We all got taught to say *hal tatahaddath ingiliziya*, so we could ask people if they spoke English, but almost none of us learned to say it right. And a surprising number of Iraqis did know how to speak English. Which was a good sign and a bad sign.

"Of course," she said.

"Stand up, please," I said.

"Who are you?" she asked.

"Specialist Warren Pease, United States Army."

"You look like my son," she said.

"Where is he?" I caught myself looking around. The hairs on the back of my neck would have stood up if I had hairs on the back of my neck. It felt so strange, I took off my helmet.

I wore the old K-Pot, because the new ACH, which is the Advanced Combat Helmet, came up too far in the back for a war where the other side attacked you from behind with sniper fire and IEDs that went off just as your momentum took you past them. Heads that got blown off got blown off *forward.* Into the traffic.

But I didn't like helmets. A lot of the time the only helmet I wore was the helmet of salvation. In war, you just belonged to the day. Any day could be your last. On Earth.

The best weapon was always the sword of the spirit. The Word of God. Like Mr. Smith said, words are divine. They can heal. And they can kill.

The woman gasped when she saw me bareheaded. "There he is," she said.

She was looking right at me.

"I'm not your son," I said.

"May I show you his picture?"

"Where is it?" I said.

She pointed to a chest of drawers. I didn't see any picture. Only some women's things, like perfume and powder, and a small vase with a beautiful flower in it.

"No you may not," I said.

"He looks like you," she said. "So much."

"I'll have to take your word for it."

"No you won't." She got up. She didn't seem to care about my gun.

She went to the chest of drawers and started to open the top one.

"No!" I yelled.

"But it's true," she said.

Before I could shoot her, she came out with a picture in a picture frame. Of course, I could have shot her. But I figured I'd still have time if she came out with a gun.

"Why do you keep it in a drawer?" I asked.

"Look," she said.

He did look like me. Maybe because he had short hair too. And we were the same age about. And he was a handsome devil.

Just kidding. But he did look like me. And like her.

"I know why you keep it in a drawer," I said.

Her son was the enemy. He was one of those young guys who went around in a checkered yasmak with only his eyes showing. An Islamic warrior. I didn't care if he looked like me. I'd kill him if I saw him.

"Because he's dead," she said. "I cannot bear to see him. And yet . . ."

She reached up and touched my face.

I backed away.

"How did he die?" I said.

"He was executed," she said.

"We don't execute people," I said.

"The butcher did it," she said.

"Saddam?"

"And then he sent me the bill." She went back to the drawer. She took out a little plastic bag. In it was a piece of paper and what looked like small gold rocks. She zipped open the baggie and handed me the piece of paper.

"I can't read this," I said.

"It's the bill," she said.

"For what?"

"For these."

She took my hand and turned it palm up and emptied the baggie into it. The small gold rocks were bullets.

"Twenty-five dinars," she said. "I had to pay the government for the bullets they used to kill my son. We called it the death tax."

"Who called it that?"

"All the mothers," she said.

She started to cry. She made no sounds. Her face didn't even look sad. But tears fell from her eyes. They streamed. They fell on her pretty dress and disappeared into the flowers.

I used to think the saddest thing in the world was when your mother died. But as I looked at this woman, I thought the saddest thing might be when your child died. I wondered if my mother died because she didn't want to be alive when her child died. And not because she couldn't have another child. I wonder if she knew what was going to happen to me. Who would want another child when children died?

I put down my gun. I said, "I wish I was your son." I opened my arms.

"I wish I were your mother," she said, and came right up to me. She put her face against my shoulder. Her tears beaded on my ACU. There was no camouflage that could hide them there.

I put my arms all the way around her. She disappeared inside them and almost inside me. I could feel her fists tapping lightly against the hardness of my tactical vest. I wished I was wearing my Twaron vest, which was softer. I could feel her hands more than I would have felt a bullet hitting me.

I said, "I'm sorry."

"For what?"

"My armor," I said.

"I feel nothing but your soul," she said.

She stepped back and looked into my face. Her tears were gone. To me. She even smiled a bit. She took my hand that was closed over the bullets. She opened it and looked at them.

"My tears," she said. "My golden tears. For you." She closed my hand back over the bullets. "May they protect you forever."

"I am protected forever," I said. "What I need is to be protected for the rest of my tour."

"Your tour?" she said. Like I was saying I was a tourist.

"My time in your country. Fighting. For you."

She nodded. "You even sound like him. You say the same things he would have said."

"Then he's protected forever too," I said.

"Yes," she said. "But far away. Too far away."

"And he can't see you?" I said.

"I fear not," she said.

"And you said you can't bear to see him."

She looked at his photograph and then at me. "I can," she said. "Thank you."

She handed me my gun and took my arm and walked me out of the bedroom to the front door. She didn't seem to notice, or at least to care, that it was splintered and hanging off one hinge.

"Goodbye, Specialist Pease," she said. *"Assalamu alaykum."*

"What does that mean?" I asked.

"Peace be with you," she said.

I thought of Jesus when he said the same thing in his language. When he had risen from the dead. *Peace be with you.*

"And you must say, *Walaykum assalam,*" she told me.

I said it. Or I tried. Then I said, "Peace be with *you.*"

"Wa rahmatullahi," she said.

I shook my head.

"And mercy," she explained.

"And mercy." I stepped through the open doorway and out. I felt her watch me as I disappeared into the heat and smoke.

We walk down Bittersweet Lane toward the beach. It's totally dark. I can hear the ocean but I can't see the sky. Dodie walks between Jesus and me. She holds our hands. I can actually feel Jesus through her. I don't mean his hand. Or even his hand in her hand. I can feel a new kind of life. It's Dodie's life. Not Jesus'. But it's a life he's giving to her. Jesus is flowing through her into me. He's filling her with love. Not love for me. That I've got to earn. But love that's Dodie. Love that equals who she is. Love that is all she is. Love that I feel for her because she's the bone of my bones and the flesh of my flesh.

As we walk, light slides before us and upon us. I can see it move down Jesus, from his short hair, over his face, and down his body to his feet. It looks like he's rising out of the earth.

"How did you do that?" I say.

"What?"

"Get covered with light."

"So are you," he says.

"So are I," says Dodie.

I've been concentrating so much on Jesus I didn't see that we'd risen with him.

"The moon," says Jesus.

I look up. Clouds have passed before the quarter moon. The light flows from their skirts in soft gold flames.

"Moonlight," I say.

"Sunlight," says Jesus.

"I see the *moon,*" says Dodie.

"It's the light of the sun that's bouncing off the moon," says Jesus.

Dodie laughs. "The moon is not a *ball.*"

"No, it's not," says Jesus.

Dodie starts to sing:

"I see the moon.
The moon sees me.
God bless the moon.
And God bless me."

"I know who taught you that song," I say.

"Who?"

"Mommy."

She shakes her head. "Ryan did."

"Is that true?" I say. Which I realize is idiotic the second I say it.

Dodie says, "Ryan did. He said for you."

"For me?"

She sings again.

"I see Daddy.
Daddy sees me.
God bless Daddy.
And God bless Ryan."

I laugh like a maniac. I say, "I want to send that guy to the dark side of that moon."

"There is no dark side of the moon," says Jesus.

"I was kidding," I said. "I love Ryan."

"I know you do," says Jesus. "But there is no dark side of the moon."

"Pink *Floyd?*" I say to him.

"What?"

"Not *what* — *who*."

"Someone's named Pink?" Jesus says.

"Yeah, a girl singer. But this is four guys."

"All named Pink?" he says.

"Where have you *been,* Ray?"

"Where haven't I been?" Jesus says.

I wonder if he ever finds a place to lay his head. I wonder if he ever sleeps. Maybe the cheap hotel he's looking for is wherever he is. And it isn't Hotel California because he *can't* check in and he is *always* leaving. And always coming back. For us.

"But as I was saying, Warren," he says with that kind of teacher-energy he gets, "there is no dark side of the moon. Only the far side."

"I don't get it," I say.

"The light from the sun shines on all the moon," says Jesus.

"Then how come we don't see it?" I ask.

"Because the Earth has taught the moon to spin to match its revolution around the Earth. Exactly. We can never see the far side from here."

"How did it teach it?" I ask.

"Gravity!" says Jesus.

"Gwavity!" says Dodie.

"You sound like Porky Pig," says Jesus.

"Ray!" says Dodie.

Me and Jesus swing her between us.

I think about gravity and the beautiful flight of a bullet.

The next bullet I took came from Juba.

We got sent into Sadr City. Which used to be Saddam City. Now it was the late Saddam City. It got named Sadr City by the head of the Mahdi Army, aka JAM. Muqtada al-Sadr. He named it for his father. Who got killed by the late Saddam Hussein.

We came out of an old cigarette factory they turned into the joint security station head shed and put a clampdown on Sadr City. Everywhere we went there were murals of the dead father, Mohammed Sadeq al-Sadr. I'd pretend it was my father. And my city. Not here. My American city. But one thing I liked about America was that we didn't have pictures of the faces of powerful people up all over the place. There should be no gods before God. And Jesus was the only God incarnate. The rest of us should keep our pictures in our wallets.

Our job in Sadr City was to protect the mosques. The JAM were occupying them one after the other. Qudus. Abrar. Shaheed. Badriya, which was in the mixed Talbiya neighborhood where the imam said, "There is no difference between us," so some stun grenades got thrown over the compound wall and killed a Sunni and the next day a guy who hadn't got killed at the mosque got killed at the first guy's funeral. The only funeral it was safe to go to was your own.

Too bad we didn't get there in time to save the Baratha Mosque. That one got blown up by Sunni vesticides after they found the tortured remains of forty-five of their own buried out back of the mosque. But the reason to save Baratha had nothing to do with preventing these people from killing one another to the end of time. It was because this is where Jesus was born! Or so the Koran said. That Jesus was born where this mosque was built. And that Mary and Jesus came to Baghdad. That Mary reached out with her pure hand and dipped it into the water that ran here. Which was why the Baratha Mosque was the only mosque with holy water. Mary's Spring it was called. Now it's a well filled with mud and blood. Christians used to come to Baratha to worship alongside Muslims. Now we came to kill the ones who killed the ones who we promised we would keep from being killed.

So there we were running all over Sadr City taking care of their churches. That's what all this was about anyway. If you don't take care of your churches, you lose everything. I don't mean just the buildings. I mean the people. Every man is his own church.

Except no one ran much around Sadr City. The streets were full of sewage. So what if their toilets didn't work. We had enough grenade crates for the entire population, if only they'd asked.

They didn't. So the sewage ran black and lumpy like puke and flew off our tires and got stowed in the treads of our boots. It ran through the markets and turned the tomatoes black. The eggs too. The yolks even, except for the blood you found in every one. That stayed red. Street goats would take baths in it. When they got slaughtered their meat was as black as what they licked off their skinny legs. When a watermelon stand got blown up by a suicide honey wagon, the watermelon meat was black too. The seeds took out people's eyes and stuck in other people's skin like guitar picks. They were black too. As usual. But it made you wonder.

Honey wagons were what they called the trucks that were supposed to pick up garbage and vacuum the sewage. When the honey wagons got detonated, it added insult to injury. The corpses looked like they'd been burned, when all they were was blown apart and painted wet with the other people's waste.

The sewage tended to run down the sides of the streets. So in the middle they put scrap metal and furniture and air conditioners they had no electricity to run and generators they had nothing to run with and bags of rocks that sometimes held a head instead of rocks and axles of all sizes that rolled around and kids played on like logs in a river of human waste.

It was that same c—— they spooned onto crumbled pavement camouflaging bombs, like chocolate frosting on pear crumble, except they thought we had no taste for it and they were right, so some of our people got outhoused.

All this slowed us down so we could be targeted with small-arms fire and pipe bombs and RPGs and rocks from slingshots. Ordinary streets were kill zones. Fortunately, we still did most of the killing. But not all. It was hard, because the triggermen hid in crowds of civilians. They dressed like them and not in their usual Mahdi black and black, like the Devil's color could scare us. Besides, if they wanted to dress like the Devil they should wear yellow, which would be pretty funny and make them stand out in a crowd. Yellow being the color of sulfur. Sulfur being the wallpaper of Hell.

The insurgents pretended to talk to these civilians, even if it was only prayers they were muttering. Prayers asking God to help them kill us. They didn't even carry their weapons, as tempting as it was for them to go around armed all the time so they could swagger and scare the women and impress the kids. They concealed their guns in car trunks and on the other side of windowsills and grabbed them to fire at us, one shot only, and then put them back and found a seam back within the heart of the crowd.

No sniper liked firing into crowds. We were there to save these people. Not to kill them. But their own snipers had us at a disadvantage. They knew the streets. And they knew our vulnerabilities. So they aimed for our necks and our armpits, where those who wore armor had gaps. To a good shot, an armpit was a road to the heart. When someone got hit there, we said he lost his deodorant.

The Marines had rules:

> MAKE YOURSELF HARD TO KILL.
> KEEP YOUR EYES OUT AND RIFLES READY.

Us soldiers made fun of Marine rules. But we followed them. Kind of like a person without religion who prays.

One day our turret gunner got hit. He was surrounded up there by armor shields. But his stupid head stuck out. They always did. He took a bullet in the skull.

We picked up every MAM in sight. That's Military Age Males. Like us. Except not us. That made them PUCs. Persons Under Control. We swabbed their hands for gunpowder residue. Two guys had some. We had our terp tell them, "One of you killed their soldier. One of you didn't." Spit flew out of the mouth-hole in the terp's mask. "Who was it?"

We expected each guy to scream, "He did it! He did it!"

Instead, each guy screamed, "I did it! I did it!"

We zip-tied them to each other. Strange, they suddenly didn't seem to get along now.

The other PUCs we gave over to the IP. Who did with them what they did with them, depending on what kind of Muslim some were and the others were.

The Mahdi Army was Shiite. The Omar Brigade was Sunni. They killed each other. They killed their children. Their own children — because when they killed their enemies, their enemies killed their children. The whole place was a vengeance factory.

We each got given a picture of Muqtada al-Sadr. He was an HVT, High-Value Target. "If you see him, kill him," we got told. Fat chance of that — the guy lived in Najaf. We called him Muqtada al-Najaf.

In the meantime, me and a spotter got sent off to the Musab bin Umair Mosque. It was in the Talibiya neighborhood, on the southwestern outskirts of Sadr City. The Mahdi Army was moving west. They were gradually crossing the river from Shiite east to Sunni west, leaving behind beheaded bodies with drill holes where there once were eyes. We got told Talibiya was a JAM stronghold. Like that was a warning. I took it as a good sign. A sniper delights in the multiplicity of his targets, the way God does in the multiplication of His children.

They didn't force us out in Dirty Dozens here. Sadr City was too big. And the rules of engagement got reduced to hostile intent being in the eyes of the observer. It wasn't minds we were supposed to read. It was desire — theirs to kill us and ours to survive. Soldiers weren't martyrs and never could be. Soldiers were killers. The only martyrs were the innocent who died. The other side didn't understand this. They made martyrs of their soldiers. That made them murderers.

I got paired up with a guy named Seth. He was new to our unit. He took the place of Malik. Malik got blinded by a grenade he never saw. Not a flash bang but a frag, so he ended up with ball bearings where his eyes had been. They were stainless steel and glowed against the blackness of his skin. The last thing Malik saw was my shot hitting my target in the throat. Malik was between me and the grenade. The last thing Malik said to me was, "Beautiful!"

Seth was from Florida.

"You can't get much farther from New Hampshire than that," I said.

"Sure you can," said Seth. "California is a lot farther."

"I wasn't talking geography, Seth," I said.

"Neither was I," said Seth.

"Weather?" I said.

"Metaphor," said Seth.

It was like Mr. Smith had gotten hold of Seth. Every other guy in our unit would have told you a metaphor was something you held to your mouth to make your voice louder.

"What's your favorite metaphor?" I asked him. Just to be sure.

"War is a picnic," he said.

Now I was sure.

"And picnics are fun," I said.

"Killing the insects," said Seth.

I held out my hand. One thing Seth and I agreed on right then and there was we would never high-five.

He was just a kid. That's not a metaphor. He was just a kid.

My age. But he'd just got here.

The other guys called him Pretty Boy. The Florida sun must have dyed his hair blond. Or his mother must have patted his head before he left for war.

He said to me, "I heard you don't like spotters."

"I do my own spotting," I said.

"I can see that," he said.

"How so?"

"You step outside yourself," he answered.

It was like he understood me without knowing me. That was a gift. I mean, he had a gift. And he gave it to me.

"But who covers your back door?" he said.

"You do now," I said.

"Let's go kill us some insects," said Seth.

. . .

When we get near the beach, the moon's behind a cloud again. I can see a bonfire in the distance. But it's the stars that light our way. They dance off the smooth ocean.

Jesus lifts up Dodie's little hand and uncurls one of her fingers and points it into the sky just over the ocean where the Isles of Shoals float in the darkness.

"See the bird up there?" he says.

Dodie squints into the sky. She shakes her head.

"Not a real bird," says Jesus. "It's made out of stars. See. There's the tail at the top. And there's the beak at the bottom."

"What's it?" says Dodie.

"Do you see it?" says Jesus.

"A bird!" says Dodie.

"A swan," says Jesus. "Cygnus. A constellation."

"It doesn't look like a swan to me," I say.

Jesus takes my hand that's holding Dodie's other hand. He raises our two hands as high as Dodie's will go. It's high enough. The stars are low in the sky.

He traces the stars with our fingers. Mine long pressed against Dodie's short. Like I'm protecting her. And Jesus is showing us both the way.

He makes the sign of the cross with our fingers.

I feel him flowing into my body. I feel him taking possession of me.

"It's also called the Northern Cross," he explains.

I tilt my head and see the cross there in the sky. Dodie imitates me and tilts her head too. "Birdie," she says.

Jesus moves our hands straight up. "At Christmastime," he says, "the Northern Cross sits straight up and down right over there." He points us to the north-northwest horizon.

I can see it there. In my mind. A cross. Standing in the water. Its lights shining all over the Earth.

"If you look behind the swan," says Jesus, "you can see some dust.

The dust is the Milky Way. It has hundreds of billions of stars. They have billions of planets. Even five of the stars in the swan have planets. The brightest star is blue. It's that one there. At the top of the cross. On the tail of the swan. A little to the northeast is the North American nebula. It's shaped just like this continent."

"Is this the only one?" I ask him, just like I did when we were in the bog.

"Continent?"

"You know what I mean," I say.

"Yes, it's the only one," he reassures me.

"It's like you," I say to Dodie.

"What?" she asks.

"My only one," I say to her. "My one and only."

"I'm your children," she says.

"Yes," I say.

We walk down onto the beach toward the bonfire.

"What's the name of that blue star?" I ask Jesus.

"Deneb," he says.

"What does that mean?"

"Tail of the swan." Jesus laughs, like it's so obvious. Then he adds, "In Arabic, of course."

Seth was the only guy who learned any of the Arab stuff like me. We both did it because we liked the stories. Not because it helped us kill the enemy. Or understand the enemy.

Just because, like Mr. Smith said, adventure stories are about journeys and journeys are about finding paradise.

I didn't know this about Seth until we'd inserted on the third floor of an abandoned building on the eastern side of the Musab bin Umair Mosque.

I went up the stairs ahead of Seth.

"Where'd you get that limp?" he said.

"Don't remember."

"Did it hurt?"

"Yeah!"

The hide we chose was a room with bloodstains on the floor and walls. There was human hair in the creases where the walls met the floor. Crumbs of old bread crackled under our feet. In with the crumbs were little pieces of teeth. I wondered if the teeth got blown out when they were chewing the bread or if they just got gnawed down and spit out from boredom or fear. We ground the bread down into dust just settling into the hide. But the pieces of teeth got stuck in the wooden floor like tiny chips of quartz crystal you'd find in New Hampshire granite. I had Seth touch the little pieces with his fingertip. He was amazed for a boy from Florida with how they were the only cool thing there in that stinking oven of a room. Tiny headstones of ice in the fire of war. When sunlight reflected off the mosque came in through the windows, the teeth sparkled.

The Musab bin Umair Mosque was not one of the pretty ones. It was made out of drab stone the color of unsewaged mud. The dome was brown. It didn't have any decorations. Only a loudspeaker on the top. And little windows all around the base of the dome. Sniper windows, so Juba could move around the dome in a circle and fire when the sun was behind him and the moon was before him. He had picked off US and Iraqi soldiers and police all around the mosque. Juba didn't use a spotter. He probably didn't even use a wide-angle spotter scope with range lines. He just seemed to have an eye for his enemy.

Like me. I'd never yet killed an innocent. Like I said, snipers are the purest soldiers of them all. In a good war, the only dead would be those who came to kill.

"Lucky there are no minarets," I said to Seth.

"You ever seen a lighthouse?" he asked.

"Of course," I said. "I'm from New England. You got them in Florida?"

"St. Augustine Light," he said. "Beautiful — if you like bees."

"Why'd you ask?"

"Minarets are lighthouses," he said.

"Yeah, well where are the ships?"

"Lights for people," he said.

"I wish I could see some lights in those dome windows. Just a muzzle flash would do. I could kill him if he'd just make some light."

"He won't," said Seth.

"We won't either," I said.

The thing about sniping was the waiting. You could wait hours or even days. For that one moment when you got your shot. It's what the old Army people from Harl Pease Jr.'s time called Hurry Up and Wait. We always had more patience than the enemy. When they were out in the open we could call in our gunships. Those we didn't angel ran into buildings. So our guys or Marines on SITs would radio in laser-guided artillery or F-18s. The enemy'd run into Allah's Waiting Room. AWR we called it, which for us stood for Alpha Whiskey Romeo. But for the enemy was Allah's Waiting Room. They never waited. They didn't have our patience. They either died there with Allah or ran back out into the Hellfires and fifty-caliber M296 rounds off the Kiowa Warriors, who were naturally enough the allies of the Apaches because in war what goes around just keeps going around.

But sniping from a hide was like waiting for the consolation of Israel. Our enemy was the hidden thing of darkness. Our job was to light him up.

It was so hot in that shoot house I stripped down to my T-shirt and put on the pair of old jeans I always carried in my assault pack. Seth, who didn't seem to sweat at all, kept on his camos and didn't even bother removing the gas mask from his belt. To pass the time, we whispered stories. I told Seth about Ulysses. He liked the part about Cyclops. Who didn't? It's like David and Goliath. Ancient sci-fi.

Seth told me about Musab bin Umair. The guy the mosque was named for. Seth told me: Musab was this rich kid from Mecca. He was really good looking. He wore really nice clothes. Everybody always said how good he smelled. But nobody made fun of him. Everybody loved the guy. His parents gave him everything he wanted. Nobody was jealous though. It wasn't like he was spoiled. It was like he was some kind of god. People saw him and they felt better. About themselves. About everything. Except Musab was the one person who couldn't see Musab. I mean, he couldn't step outside of himself and he couldn't go inside of himself. He was just like everybody else looking for themselves. Except Musab didn't have anybody to make him feel better the way he made everybody else feel better. So instead of looking for himself he looked for God. Musab became a Muslim. So his parents kicked him out of the house. All his friends stopped talking to him. He got thrown into prison. Then he got sent into exile. When he came back home to Mecca, he looked like a derelict. His hair was matted. He had dirt all over him. He went around in a blanket with holes in it. Nobody could figure out why he did it. Except the prophet Muhammad. Muhammad took one look at Musab and he said, "This is what everyone in the world should do. This boy gave up everything for God." Muhammad took Musab into battle with him. He made Musab the Muslim standard-bearer in a battle called the battle of Uhud. Musab carried the Muslim flag in one hand and his sword in the other. When Muhammad's archers disobeyed his orders and withdrew, the Muslims were overrun by the enemy. Musab saw the enemy cavalry coming down so he jumped up and started to wave the Muslim flag and his sword. He ran toward the enemy. Everyone else ran away. Musab was trying to protect Muhammad by making the enemy pay attention to himself. It worked. Musab got attacked by a knight on horseback who sliced off Musab's left hand. The one that held the flag. So Musab screamed, "Muhammad is only a messenger, and messengers have died before him!" Then Musab picked up the flag with his right hand. The knight sliced that hand off too. So Musab screamed, "Muhammad is only a messenger, and messengers have died before him!" Then Musab picked up the flag with his forearms and held it against his chest and attacked the enemy with his body. The knight threw down his sword and picked up his spear and threw it into Musab's chest. The spear went all the way through Musab's body and came out the other side. Musab fell on the Muslim flag and died. The knight who killed him screamed, "I killed Muhammad!" because Musab looked just like Muhammad. But Muhammad was alive. When the battle was over, Muhammad found Musab's body. It was partly covered by Musab's blanket. Muhammad's eyes filled with tears. He said, "The first time I met you, you wore beautiful clothes and you were the handsomest young man in Mecca. Now your body is in pieces and your blanket doesn't even cover you." So Muhammad had Musab buried with his blanket over his head and lemongrass over his feet. Muhammad threw three handfuls of earth into the grave and said, "We created you from it, and return you into it, and from it we will raise you a second time." Then he turned to the people. "O people, visit this grave and salute the man inside it. Salute him, and he will salute you back. Peace be with you, O martyr. Peace and the blessings of God be upon you."

From Musab the mosque we didn't hear such comforting words. When the loudspeaker wasn't calling people to prayer five times a day, it was broadcasting to us. I don't mean to Seth and me. I mean to the Americans. In English.

"God is great," it said. It always started with that. Like we needed reminding. "You infidels continue to occupy our holy lands. You kill our people. You torture them with dogs and water. You insult our women. You destroy our beautiful city. We say to you cross worshippers, prepare for devastation and defeat. We are for victory, martyrdom, triumph, power, and Caliphate. We will break the cross and spill your blood. Justice will be served. God is great."

Over and over this recording would play. The voice of the guy reading the words didn't have the usual Arab accent. He sounded like somebody from England. Seth said they must have used him because they thought Americans were still afraid the English were going to invade the US and try and take their country back.

"Too bad it's not live," Seth said. "I'd like to be able to ask that guy what's the difference between victory and triumph. It drives me crazy to hear that."

"There is a difference," I said.

"No way! What?"

"A victory is to win," I said. "A triumph is to vanquish."

Our third morning there, while we were eating our MRE egg patties and osmotic raisins and hoping to get a predawn glimpse of Juba cleaning his Dragunov in the perfect first rays of sunlight, I said, "Hey, I can hear you chew."

"You don't chew these raisins," said Seth. "You grind them down."

"Just stop moving your mouth," I said.

"I can talk without moving my mouth," said Seth.

"How?" I said.

He didn't answer. He didn't have to. That was the point. I knew what he was going to say. That's how he talked without moving his mouth.

"How did you do that?" I said.

"What?"

"Enter my mind?"

"I didn't," he said. "You just let me in."

"What's the difference?"

"You tell me," he said.

"Listen," I said.

"For what?"

"For nothing."

I tapped on my Timex. Seth got it right away.

It was dawn. If we both weren't awake by dawn, we got woken up by the morning call to prayer. But this morning we were both awake. And there was total silence. No morning call to prayer.

"You know what that means," I said.

"Something's going down."

The only time there was silence in this city was when all the sound had been saved up and sucked up for an explosion. When the Devil held his breath, people burst into flame.

No call to prayer meant there was going to be an attack.

Seth flipped up the bipod of his M249. He stood straight up. Right in front of the window.

"Down!" I begged.

I expected Juba's shot to freeze Seth's smile.

"The only down I'm goin' is there." Seth pointed to the mosque plaza. "Cover me," he said.

"Are you nuts!" I said.

"That was a joke, Mercy," he said as he arranged his ammunition. "I don't need your cover. I'm going to take them out down there. You pick them off from up here."

"We're here for Juba," I said. Juba was my HVT, the way I figured I was his.

"We're here to protect the mosque," said Seth.

He slung his ammunition belt over his shoulder. I could see he had seven four-ball M855 Penetrators for every one-tracer M856 Penetrator Tracer. We got trained to a four-and-one mix. But I figured Seth liked the way this looked more, with the seven green tips in a row and then the one orange. It might cut down on the target-kill capability using TOT, which was Tracer-On-Target. But it looked better, the way green is the color of nature and orange is the color of warning.

Seth looked like an angel. I know that's a strange thing for one guy to say about another. But he looked like someone who got protected by how he looked. You couldn't believe anything that beautiful would ever get destroyed. Or that God would ever let it leave the Earth. Of course, everything did. Flowers and people. Everything and everyone but Jesus.

Seth's hair was the last thing out the door. He didn't like helmets any more than I did.

Seth was like his hero Musab. He was going to die like him too.

They both had my cousin Harl's "complete contempt for personal danger." I wondered if I did, and if I did, I wondered if anyone would ever know.

I had to admit I was glad to glimpse Seth come out from the shadow of our safe house and hit the plaza. He walked right up into the middle of it. He was just like the Earth itself at that moment, half in dark and half in light. He was completely alone. He'd zeed off his radio. No strikes to bring in and no one except himself to bring them in on. When the enemy came, he'd be outnumbered. Had to protect his codes. He and I had eye-to-eye. And I was prepared to lay down suppressive fire.

He wasn't in full battle rattle. Seth never was. Not that I'd known him that long. This was our first mission. This was the first guy I really let spot me. I didn't know why I did it. Maybe I thought I could save him.

All he had was his gun and ammunition and that stupid gas mask he always kept hooked to his belt. He must have thought his pretty face wasn't scary enough and if he put on his gas mask he'd be taken seriously. Yeah, as a space alien. They weren't gassing us the way the late Saddam Hussein did the Kurds. The way some of us died, gas might have seemed merciful. At least if all it did was put you to sleep.

Oh, and Seth wore his vest. But without shoving ceramic plates into the pockets. And no ballistic groin cup because guys on sniper watch found them inconvenient for nature calls. Seth didn't have many of Mommy's Comforts down there by the mosque. He was like Musab, with his sword and his blanket.

I watched Seth the whole time. I stood to the side of the window so Juba wouldn't be able to see me. But that meant I wouldn't be able to see Juba either. Not that I ever had. But I had to figure that Juba was looking for me. Because he'd never seen me either.

And Seth just stood there. Waiting for the attack. He turned every once in a while to scan the plaza and the streets beyond. I could see him listening through that hair of his that the dissolving moon in the gray sky made look almost white. I could feel his feet feel the asphalt for the rumbling of whatever light trucks and cars might be approaching. Not that there was ever much rumbling from what the insurgents drove and blew themselves up in. A lot of them were Arizonas. Cars that got stolen in the States and shipped over here. If the VINs survived, one day someone back home got a strange call from his insurance company.

I was just as glad Seth wasn't overrun, because as high a volume of fire as he could get with his M249, he'd just that quick run out of ammunition. Your gun is your body. Seth could end up standing down there like Musab with both his hands gone and his only weapons left his courage and his love of flag.

He pointed toward the sky. Not with his gun but with his finger. And not at the sky but at the dome of the mosque. He pointed to the dome of the mosque. But he looked at me behind the window. He smiled. Then he flew away.

I watched his body leave the ground. I watched him the whole time. Fly backward off his feet. For a moment he was parallel to the ground. He was floating off the ground completely still. He was standing at attention in a world turned on its side. While blood flew out his forehead like paint that covered the sun. And the whole world went dark.

For both of us. I knew he'd wanted me to look at the mosque. I knew what he'd seen. Juba's gun. But I never saw it. All I saw was Seth get hit. Then darkness.

I didn't know if it was my darkness. Or his.

All I'd done was close my eyes. Once I opened them, I grabbed my gun and left the hide. I took off down the stairs. I busted out the door and ran across the plaza. No one else had come. I was the only one there. An American soldier in his white T-shirt and jeans and Wellcos and gun running to his buddy.

I went down on my knees beside him. His eyes were closed. There was more blood flowing from the corners of his mouth than from the wound in his head. I put my hand over the wound to stop the blood. I could feel the hole with my palm. His skin was cold and his blood was warm. A soldier's blood is not like anyone else's. A soldier's blood is sacred. A soldier's blood is the closest blood to Jesus'. A soldier's blood is always the blood of sacrifice. Like his.

"QuikClot," I said. I patted Seth's cargo pockets for it.

Seth opened his eyes. He shook his head. He looked up at the dome of the mosque.

At that moment, the loudspeakers hissed with static. I expected to hear the call to prayer. But all I heard was the static, getting louder and louder, like it was angry. It wasn't the sound of God breathing in the universe. It was the sound of God with his throat on fire.

"This whole thing was a trap," I said.

Seth nodded.

"Was it his?" I asked. "Or yours?"

Seth nodded again.

"Both," I said.

He wasn't looking at me. He was still looking at the mosque. I followed his eyes. There, in a little window near the sky, was Juba.

"Why didn't you kill him?" Seth whispered.

"I was looking out for you," I said.

"I'm gone," he said and closed his eyes.

I could hear his breath disappear into the static.

I answered the call to prayer and ran toward the mosque.

We haven't gone very far on the beach when Jesus says, "Let's take our shoes off."

"Good idea," I say.

"Warren, take off Dodie's first."

"I can," says Dodie, who plops herself down on the sand.

"Let your daddy," says Jesus.

"Okay," says Dodie.

She has on sandals. No socks. There's sand already between her sandal and her foot. I wipe off her foot. Which is kind of ridiculous. Dodie laughs because I guess it tickles.

I sit down next to Jesus on what looks like the beginning of a small dune. We don't have many dunes left around here. Too much RED, which is Real Estate Development.

Jesus takes off his Timberlands. I take off my Wellcos. We both stuff our socks into our shoes.

Jesus digs his feet into the sand.

"That feels good," he says.

The sand where we are is soft and still warm from the day's sun. I prefer my sand wet and hard and cold. But he's right. It does feel good.

Jesus reaches behind himself and pulls up some kind of vegetation that's so dry it sounds like it's catching on fire as Jesus snaps it out of the sand. It's a few twigs covered with rough green leaves and little moon-yellow flowers.

He hands it to me. "Take this to Bethie."

"What is it?" I ask.

"Poverty grass."

"Poverty grass! *You* take it to Bethie. *I* wanted to bring her an *orchid*."

"I know you did," says Jesus. "But the orchid would have died. Besides, this is better than an orchid."

"Poverty grass?"

Jesus holds it gently in his hand and brings it close to his dark eyes. "This is the first thing that grows on a dune. If it's left to grow, it puts down new roots. When its vegetation dies every year, that decay makes humus with the sand. It turns the dead minerals into new soil. That's when the beach plums start to grow. And the black cherries and the Japanese dune roses."

"Where?" I say.

"Right here," he says, and puts the poverty grass into my empty hand.

"So you're saying there's going to be a sand dune here?" I ask.

"A whole new world, Warren," he says. "If people let it."

Jesus gets up. He lace-ties his shoes together so he can wear them around his neck. I do the same thing. I have to put down the champagne bottle and hold the poverty grass in my mouth while I do it.

Dodie carries her sandals in her hands and claps them together as we walk toward the bonfire.

I can't believe it was only this morning that I started out here. It feels like a lifetime ago. I still don't know how I got here this morning. But I know exactly how I got here now. I remember everything about this day.

In the night that's not as dark as the morning was. Which is not a metaphor, Seth. It's just how it is. With the moon and the Milky Way poured across the sky and the way the distant bonfire looks like small red mountains dancing on the black infinity beyond it. I still prefer the dark to the light and the moon to the sun. But I don't mind company now. I prefer it. I feel like a father for the first time. And that in Jesus there's finally someone I can trust. Who won't leave me.

"There's nothing to be afraid of," I say to Dodie.

"Of what?" she says.

"The dark," I say.

"It's not dark," she says and starts to skip in the sand to prove it.

"Be careful," Jesus says to her.

"She's fine," I say to him.

"Of the bird." Jesus points to what looks like a small rock with a beak on it.

"A bird!" says Dodie.

"Do you know what it's called?" Jesus asks her.

"A bird!" says Dodie again.

"I mean . . ." says Jesus.

"Louis," says Dodie. "Serena!"

"Who?" says Jesus.

"Swan," says Dodie. She points to the constellation in the sky that Jesus showed us. The Swan. The Northern Cross.

"Who read you that book?" I ask her. "With the swans in it named Louis and Serena?"

"Ryan," she says.

"My mommy once read it to me," I tell her.

"Granny Dot," she says.

"Yes," I say. "Your Granny Dot." I put my hand on Dodie's head. I touch my mother again. This time in the flesh, not in the grave.

Jesus says, "Wait." I think maybe I've done what I'm supposed to do and finally my mother will actually appear. Right there next to me on the beach. As alive as Jesus.

But Jesus keeps pointing to that same little bird. It's white with what looks like a black noose around its neck.

"It looks like a rock," I say.

"It's a plover. A piping plover. It's all alone. Except for that crow. And —"

"What crow?"

"Over there." Jesus points down the beach.

"I don't see it."

"That's because the bird's as dark as night."

"But you can see it?" I ask him.

"My eyes are used to it. The dark."

I still don't see it. "What's a crow doing here?" I ask him.

"It must have killed the plover's mate. That's why the plover's standing there alone. Plovers are never alone. And over there . . ." Jesus points toward where the water washes up onto the sand.

"Hey, I can see those," I say. "Gulls."

"The gulls want to eat the plover's eggs," Jesus says.

"What eggs?" I ask.

Jesus leads us a few steps up toward the dune. He kneels in the sand and pushes aside some poverty grass.

"Look," he says.

"Egg," says Dodie.

There's just one. It sits in the middle of a tiny nest. The nest isn't made of poverty grass or any other kind of vegetation. It's just sand lined with little pieces of shell. It's a home made out of the home of the dead.

"There are usually three or four in a clutch," says Jesus.

"Do you think the gulls ate the other ones?" I ask.

"You'd see the gulls' prints if they did," says Jesus.

"An only child," I say to Dodie. "Like you and me."

"Egg," says Dodie. She reaches out to touch it.

"That's all right," says Jesus.

"Nice egg," says Dodie.

"Can she have it?" I ask Jesus.

"No," he says.

"But the gulls will eat it."

"Probably." Jesus rises to his feet. He pulls up Dodie by the hand. "But look at the plover," he says. "See how she's leaning to one side and touching her beak to her feathers? She's trying to get the gulls' attention. She's pretending she has a broken wing."

"And what will that do?" I ask.

"The gulls might attack her instead of her egg."

"And then what?"

"You never know," says Jesus.

Dodie lets go of our hands. She runs toward the gulls. They take their eyes off the plover and look at this little girl coming toward them, her arms in the air over her head. "Go 'way!" she shouts.

Off they fly.

The plover watches them too. When they've disappeared into the darkness of the sky, she turns around and hops back toward her nest.

Dodie turns around and starts running down the beach toward the bonfire. Laughing and flapping her arms like a bird.

We follow her. Jesus walks slowly enough so we don't catch up to her. I don't know if it's because he likes to watch her like I do. Or because he thinks she's safe here and we don't have to hold her hands any longer.

He says to me, "You have to let her go."

"Go where?" I ask him.

"You know what I'm talking about, Warren."

Yeah, I know. "I already let her go," I said.

"True," says Jesus. "But you got her back."

"For a day," I say.

"That's all anybody gets," he says.

"How about you?" I ask him.

"That's all I get too."

"I meant —"

"I know what you meant," says Jesus.

"So?"

"Make the day last, Warren," he says.

"Then we better hurry," I say.

Without waiting for him, I start running down the beach. My boots bounce off my chest. The champagne bottle moves in the air like the hand of a clock that takes back the time it loses. The poverty grass brushes against my jeans with the sound of someone whispering.

Jesus doesn't run. But he keeps up with me.

I walked into the mosque with my hands on my gun.

One other thing I knew about the difference between Shiites and Sunnis was that they prayed differently.

Shiites kept their hands at their sides.

Sunnis held their hands near their chests.

I kept my hands on my gun.

I could see from the entryway into the prayer hall. The entryway was dark. But the prayer hall was lit by lamps on the walls and candles in holders and shafts of light from the dome as narrow in the dawn as the flight of bullets through the air. The red in the carpet looked like blood. The carpet covered every inch of the prayer hall. That's all there was in it. No pews. No pulpit. No paintings or statues. Just a rug on the floor and light that broke the day.

Next to me in the entryway was a fountain. But there was no water falling in it. And no water collected in its basin. Just sand.

Across from the fountain was a bookcase. But there were no books in it. My father would have liked it. He used to say that an empty bookcase holds more wisdom than all the libraries in the world.

I stood in the entryway and waited. I didn't know what I was waiting for. But I knew that if I went into the prayer hall I'd get shot.

That's what I wanted to do. Not get shot, I mean. I wanted to go into the prayer hall. Not to pray. I wasn't much of a prayer. I was more of a believer. I didn't like to ask for things. I liked to accept things as I got them. That's what made a good soldier. The chaplains would have you pray, but that's because they were afraid for you being afraid for yourself. A good soldier walked with God. A frightened soldier asked God to walk with him.

I wanted to go into the prayer hall because it looked so empty. I wanted to lie down on the carpet and look up at the light coming into the sky and think about how Seth was dead. I wanted to learn to be alone again. But I didn't want to be alone again.

Of course I also wanted to take my gun and kill everyone who had killed my friend. It wasn't just Juba. It was these people who used to live next to each other and now killed each other. Who cut off heads and hands and tongues because their holy book told them to slice off everything right down to the fingertips. Who raped a teacher and then defiled her body and then strung it up by the feet outside her school in Ghazaliya where the children learned from her what no child should ever learn. Who went into battle with black masks over their faces because they thought God wouldn't recognize them. Who killed themselves and didn't realize that everyone who killed themselves hurt the people who loved them more than they hurt the people they hated. Who thought terror was warfare, except war was the highest calling and terror was the lowest. Who believed that Muslims had the right to kill non-Muslims because they weren't Muslims. Who wanted to conquer the world though jihad. Who wanted each and every human being to bow toward Mecca. Who made me kill them but didn't make me love it because I already knew that there was no greater love than to do what you had to do to protect the ones you loved from the ones who threatened them. I had learned that you have to kill to live. And that you have to live to kill. But I didn't know if I could keep on killing and keep on living.

I was about to step into the prayer hall when a man appeared beside me.

When we get to the bonfire, I want to introduce Jesus to everybody. I want to say, *Say hello to Jesus. I just spent the whole day with him.* But who would believe me? He looks like just another guy, like a lot of the other guys here. People in jeans and T-shirts. He's older than most of them. But he fits right in.

Besides, I don't recognize many of these people. They must be friends of Ryan and Bethie.

People Ryan met at work. Pharmacists maybe, but happier than there. Girls who worked behind glass counters selling talcum powder, but not to anyone back from Iraq, because soldiers didn't want to be reminded that the sand there was like talcum powder, and some soldiers who wrote real letters put real talcum powder on their fingers because of the sweat and then had to write "Not anthrax" on the top of the letter.

Young mothers Bethie met with Dodie. A lot of girls around here become young mothers and go around with surprised looks on their faces. They almost never get married. I don't know why. I should have gotten married to Bethie. And she never even had a surprised look on her face. She always looked like she expected Dodie. It was me who failed her.

These people here look happy to be here. I wish I knew them.

I wish they knew me.

Most everyone's barefoot. Some of them are close to the flames and some of them are at the edge of the dark.

The flames keep jumping into the sky like the hands of some rapper. Sparks fly off to join the stars. Some of the sparks fall into the ocean.

The ocean waves breathe against the shore. In and out. You think they maybe keep the Earth alive and it would suffocate without them.

Tables are set up in the sand. They're covered with the trays of food from our refrigerator. And platters of other things like vegetables and nuts that other people must have brought. And tiny little plastic cups. They have clean white tablecloths that move in the ocean breeze and take some of the red out of the flames to become paintings painted in the air before us by the fire and the wind and the fingers of God on the clean white cloth.

"Who *are* all these people?" I ask Jesus.

"Guests," he says.

I see my father. He's wearing a suit. The only other time I've seen him in a suit was the day we buried my mother. Except for church. When he still went to church. He looks really nice in his suit. Even without his shoes on.

Next to him is Dodie. She's down on her knees in the sand. Playing with Dippity Pig. Dippity's on a leash. But my father isn't holding it.

My father's long arm is reaching down to Dodie. One of his fingers is touching her hair. Like he just wants to be sure she's really there and isn't going away.

She's laughing and talking to Dippity. Dippity's looking at her and nodding. She whispers something into the ear Jesus healed. She holds the ear up in the air the way Jesus did to make it look like Dippity could fly. Dippity closes his eyes and smiles while Dodie whispers to him.

"You got a permit for this fire," somebody says to me.

It's the same cop who gave Jesus his speeding ticket.

"I don't know," I say.

"It wasn't a question. I was telling you. You got a permit for this fire." He holds up a piece of paper. "So where's the wine?" he asks.

I hold out the empty bottle.

"For this whole crowd?" he says. "It won't even be worth my while setting up a sobriety check up there on 1A."

"There's nothing in here anyway," I say.

"Sure there is," he says.

He raises my hand with the bottle in it up to the half-moon. "See?" he says.

I look at the half-moon through the bottle. It's floating in champagne.

"How did you do that?" I ask Jesus.

"Do what, Raphael?" asks the cop. "You putting new wine in old bottles?"

"How did you know?" says Jesus.

"I know you," says the cop.

"Everyone knows me," says Jesus.

The cop shakes his head. "Not with how fast you drive," he says.

"Speed of light," says Jesus.

"Speed of light," says the cop.

He turns to go. Then he turns back. "I'd change my shirt if I were you," he says to Jesus. "You don't want to be wearing a shirt with a bullet hole at a wedding."

"You're right," says Jesus.

He lifts off his shirt. Then he takes the bottle and the poverty grass out of my hands. "Go ahead," he says. So I take off my shirt too. For a minute we're standing there with our shirts in our hands and I'm hoping some girls might catch us and want to strike up a conversation. Or even Bethie maybe. If she's not too busy getting ready to get married.

Jesus says, "Forget it," and puts down the bottle and the poverty grass in the sand and puts on his old shirt.

I put mine on too. As soon as I do, I feel something strange. I feel like the hole over my heart is letting my life escape into the sky.

I put my hand on Jesus' arm.

"I've got you," he says.

I believe him completely. But I still hold on.

A man comes up to us. He puts a hand on my other arm. As soon as he touches me, I know who it is.

Mr. Smith has still got the hair sticking out, except in the summer and on the beach it curls up a bit and points back at his head like it wants to tell everyone how smart Mr. Smith is. And I can just make out he's got the little line on the end of his round nose where his reading glasses fit. But he doesn't have the big stomach anymore. He's wearing one of his same old shirts with the buttondown collar but it hangs off him and now it comes halfway to his knees.

"Mr. Smith!" I say. I know it's dumb, like you're telling someone who they are. Or that you recognize them. I want him to know that I still recognize him.

"War!" he says back.

We're like two happy dead guys who meet up in Heaven.

Mr. Smith and Jesus let go of me at the same time. Like they're going to shake each other's hand. But they don't. They just stand there looking at each other.

Finally, Mr. Smith says to Jesus, "Who are *you*?"

"This is my friend Ray," I say the way I'm supposed to, though I don't like lying to Mr. Smith, even if it's for Jesus.

"Ray?" says Mr. Smith, like he doesn't quite believe me.

"Raphael," says Jesus.

"Ah," says Mr. Smith. "Do you paint?"

"Not on canvas," says Jesus.

"Houses?" says Mr. Smith.

I can't quite picture Jesus with brushes up on a ladder. Not when he *is* the ladder. The top of it reaches to Heaven, and the angels of God ascend upon it.

"Kind of in the air," answers Jesus.

"Oh, you're a skywriter." Mr. Smith smiles when he says it.

Jesus laughs. "You might say that."

"So you fly?" Mr. Smith asks him.

"He hardly knows how to drive," I say.

"Never flown in my life," says Jesus.

"Well, a lot of great art disappears in the making," says Mr. Smith.

"You must be Ed Smith," says Jesus.

"I'm sorry . . ." I say because I realize I didn't introduce him. Then I realize: "Ed? Your name is Ed?"

Mr. Smith looks at me like *duh* and he says to Jesus, "Do you know your namesake's painting called *The Transfiguration*?"

"I've seen it," says Jesus.

"In Rome?" Mr. Smith asks him.

I would like to go to Rome. At least for the pizza. Me and Ryan.

"It's in the Vatican," says Ray.

"Is that where you saw it?" asks Mr. Smith.

Jesus shakes his head. "In a book, I think."

"Well, Ray," says Mr. Smith, "then you'll remember that in the top half of the painting Jesus is floating in the air before a transcendently luminous cloud. Now that might very well represent Heaven, so beautiful is it. But the bottom half of the painting is dark and full of chaos. But it isn't Hell. Is it, Ray?"

Jesus says, "No, it isn't."

"What is it, then?" asks Mr. Smith.

"I can't say," says Jesus.

"Can't? Or won't?" asks Mr. Smith.

"You got me there," says Jesus.

"How about you?" Mr. Smith asks me.

"I'm fine," I say.

Mr. Smith laughs. I'm happy to hear his laugh again. "I'm glad to hear that, War. But what I was asking you was what you think the darkness and chaos represent."

"You know I haven't seen that painting," I say, because Mr. Smith would know that.

"But you've seen the world now, haven't you, War?"

"I sure have," I say. "Texas and Iraq anyway."

"You've seen the *world*," Mr. Smith says. I think I know what he means. There's Heaven. There's Hell. And there's the World.

"I've seen the world," I tell him.

"Then you know what the painter was painting," says Mr. Smith.

"I can guess," I say. And I'm hoping no one will ask me to.

"It was his last painting," says Mr. Smith. "When Raphael died, his body lay in state beneath it. Do you know who came to see him like that?"

I don't know who Mr. Smith is talking to.

"Who?" I ask him.

"The girl he was going to marry," says Jesus.

I didn't know how the man got there. He was wearing a long robe. It was black with gold trim. His head was covered by a *ghaffiya*, which was kind of like a turban with a tail hanging off the back of it. He had a short black beard. His eyes were dark and gentle.

"Are you the imam?" I said.

"Who else," he said.

"Where is everybody?" I asked.

"Hiding from you."

"Good," I said.

"What do you want?" he asked.

"I have to search the mosque."

"Why?" he asked.

"To find who killed my friend."

"And if you find him?" he asked.

"I'll kill him," I said.

"You won't," he said.

"Find him?"

"Kill him," he said. "No one can kill him."

"Why not?"

"He's immortal."

"Like Jesus," I said.

"Exactly," said the imam. "Now take off your shoes."

"Why?"

"You can't come into the mosque with your shoes on. Let me help you."

He went down on one knee and unlaced one of my boots and then the other. He took off each boot and then my socks and folded each one before putting them into my boots. He put my boots into the bookcase. Then he slipped out of the sandals he had on under his robe. He put his sandals next to my boots in the bookcase.

"I thought you usually leave your socks on," I said.

"Not today," he said. "Now we must wash."

He turned to the fountain.

"There isn't any water," I said.

"There hasn't been for weeks," he said. "We wash with sand."

He reached into the fountain and came out with a handful of sand. He rubbed the sand around in his palms like a bar of soap and motioned with his head for me to get some sand too. I did. It reminded me of being in the desert. In my mind I saw Abed being blown up off the bicycle seat. The sand was rough but it felt good. It felt like if I kept it up I could make my whole body go away. We used to use dental picks to try to take the sand grain by grain out of our weapons. You never knew with sand.

"Good," said the imam. "God wishes to purify you so that He may complete his blessings upon you. And you will be grateful."

When he was done, the imam put his hands over the fountain and shook them just the way you shake water off your hands. I did too. The sand flew around the sides of the fountain and then grain by grain rolled to the bottom. Gravity.

"Isn't it dirty now?" I said. "The sand?"

He shook his head. "Sand purifies us. We purify sand." He showed me his hands. "When we have water," he said, "we also wash our face and our feet. One doesn't want to wash a beard with sand, however. Come."

He motioned me toward the prayer hall.

"Your gun," he said.

"What about it?" I swung it around in front of me.

"Keep it with you at all times."

Jesus is standing at the shoreline with Bethie and Ryan. Their bare feet are in the water when the waves are up. Bethie shuffles from foot to foot the way she usually does. I can see her footprints with each little sideways step she takes. They're the most precious things on Earth to me. I feel I'm the ocean water that fills them up with each small ripple of a wave. I've become part of the Earth and have sought out the one I love. I fill her footprints with everything I am.

Jesus motions for me to join them. I walk over to them and realize that I'm not making footprints myself. And there I was hoping Bethie would want to throw herself into mine.

"We need you here for the rehearsal, Warren," Jesus says.

"What do you want me to do?" I don't have a clue. I was never any good at these public ceremonies. Not that I ever went to one. Except my mother's funeral. And that was pretty private.

"Don't you have something to say to Bethie?" Jesus kind of prompts me.

"Bethie, you brake my heart," I say.

She looks at me like I've lost my mind. "What the h—— is that supposed to mean?"

"Nothing bad," I say to her. "Just that my heart broke open and all my secrets fell out. And you — you're the keeper of my secrets. Forever."

She gets tears in her eyes. "Oh, War," she says.

"And I'm the keeper of yours," I say.

I turn to Ryan. "You too," I say.

"I don't have any secrets," says Ryan.

"*Her* secrets," I tell him. "Bethie's."

"Just give her the bouquet, Warren," Jesus says.

I hand Bethie the poverty grass. She looks at it like she wonders what I'm doing when all of a sudden her eyes open wide. Her fingertips brush my palm as they close over the dry bunch of twigs. I go to grab her hand in mine. But it's gone now, holding the poverty grass. She's smiling down into it, tears still in her eyes.

"It's the most beautiful thing I've ever seen," she says.

"It was the least I could do," I say, because I don't know what you're supposed to say when you give something stupid to the girl you love on her wedding day.

"You never brought me flowers," she says.

"Or poverty grass," I say.

"Or an *orchid*!" she says and holds it out proudly to show Ryan and Jesus.

I don't know what she's talking about so I look down into her hand myself. There, swelling out of the center of the poverty grass, is the lady slipper from the bog. Its pure white angel's wings are as open as I want Bethie's arms to be to me.

"I thought you said it wouldn't last," I say to Jesus.

"What am I, an authority on flowers?" he says.

"On love," I remind him.

"And flowers," he says.

We rehearse until almost midnight. The thing is, we don't practice anything. We just stand there with the tide coming in, talking and not talking. Everyone else is kind of partying. People must have brought wine, because there's wine on the tables and people are drinking it from the small plastic cups. Or maybe the cop brought it. To drum up business. I offer up my champagne bottle to Bethie and Ryan and Jesus. But Bethie says, "Not before the ceremony!" Ryan says, "Hey, I could kind of use a drink." Bethie says back to him, "You never had a real drink in your life." And Ryan says, "That's my point." Bethie says, "And take off those ridiculous sunglasses — it's dark out, Ryan!" "I thought it was the shades," says Ryan. "You don't need sunglasses to be in the dark," says Bethie. Ryan slips the Wiley Sabers off his face. He has on a big smile behind them.

Jesus just shakes his head. I don't know if it's to say he doesn't want any wine or he can't believe Bethie and Ryan and how they're already acting married and Bethie is the one driving their car down the highway of love.

"Go ahead." I hand Jesus the bottle.

"I'll drink it with you later," he says.

"In your father's kingdom?" I ask him.

"If you say so, Warren," he says.

So I take Ryan aside. I say, "Sorry, man."

"Me too," says Ryan.

"What are you sorry for?" I ask him.

"Not being your best man," he says.

"But you are," I say.

"Yeah, but I get to sleep with the bride," he says.

"It's about time," I say.

Ryan blushes. "So we have your blessing?" he says.

"I don't do blessings," I say.

"Then what?" says Ryan.

"Just take care of her," I say.

"I will," he says. "What about you?"

"If you take care of her, you'll be taking care of me."

"That's not what I meant," Ryan says.

"I know," I say. "But it's what I mean."

I go to hug him. When I put my arms around him, he seems to dissolve inside them. But he's right there in front of me. I'm holding him against me. I realize that it's not Ryan who's disappearing. It's me.

I followed the iman. As I was about to step into the prayer hall, he put his hand on my arm. "Right foot first," he said.

He went before me and took the first step. Right foot first.

He walked quickly across the red carpet. I stopped in the middle of the room. I looked up at the light. I looked up into the dome at all the windows and tried to see where someone might be hiding. But there was no place anyone could hide. We were alone there in that large room.

The imam went to the opposite wall. There was something that looked like a door or a passageway. The imam stepped inside it and then turned around to face me.

"This is the *mihrab*," he said. "It faces Mecca. It is the door to paradise. This is where I pray."

The imam looked up at the light from the dome. "It is still early morning," he said. He stood very straight with his hands around his mouth. *"Haya 'alas-salaah. Haya 'alas-salaah,"* he called out like a battle cry. "Come to prayer. Come to prayer. *Ilaya 'alal falaah. Ilaya 'alal falaah.* Come to the good. Come to the good."

I moved a little closer to him. It wasn't that I couldn't hear him. Or that I wanted to pray with him. It was that I wanted to come to the good. I wanted to find a world that was good. Or a place in the world that was good. I also wanted to get a good look at the imam while he prayed.

"Prayer is better than sleep," he said. "The sun is only up. But the time to pray is now. Prayer is better than sleep." He looked right at me and he said, "This is addressed to the lazy ones. Not to you. You're awake. This is our most sacred prayer of the day. Because it begins the day. And only those who have awakened to God will hear it."

He turned away from me to look toward paradise and prayed. As he spoke, he put his hands by his ears with his thumbs kind of stuck in his earholes. If he'd waved his hands it would have looked funny the way kids do who do that to make fun of one another. But this made him look like he was listening for something that he was probably never going to hear but he'd keep listening anyway. Then he folded his arms beneath his chest. His arms were so long I could see his fingers crawl up over his ribs. When he hugged himself I saw the stripes of his 7N14 cartridges crisscross his back beneath his robe.

Not much before midnight Mr. Smith comes over and says to me, "Put me on a table, War."

I know he's looking kind of frail, but I don't think he should lie down there with the empty wine bottles and the almost empty plates of food.

"Maybe I can find you a chair," I say.

"I don't want to *sit* on the table, War. I want to *stand* on it."

I help him up onto a table. He looks a little shaky so I hold on to his ankles. I can feel him kind of swaying up there. Then he takes a deep breath that I can feel all the way down to his feet. He stops shaking completely as soon as his voice cries out into the darkness of the night and the small light of the stars and the red flames of the fire. His voice is deep and loud and takes away all the sound of people talking and the ocean pounding so that the only sound in the world is Mr. Smith crying out, "Here's the bridegroom! Here's the bridegroom! Come everyone, come to meet him!"

Everyone starts walking over to the shore. The moment Mr. Smith's done bellowing, he starts to shake a bit again. I hold on tight to his legs and start helping him down. I knew exactly what he meant about the bridegroom but I'm not sure everybody else did and I'm feeling a bit bad for Bethie, who's his daughter after all. I'm even about to say something about it when Mr. Smith kind of drops into my arms and says, "Let's go give away the bride, War."

. . .

Mr. Smith and I walk her down the aisle. It's not much of an aisle. It's just a path in the sand that Jesus made down to where he stands with Ryan. Ryan isn't any more dressed up than usual. But he did button the top button on his shirt. It makes his shoulders look strong and his face stand out. Ryan looks nervous and happy and scared and sad and kind of like an angel I decide who's come down from Heaven.

And Bethie . . . Bethie stands between me and her father looking like an angel who could have come from nowhere but this Earth. She's got on a white dress now. It's like nothing I've ever seen on her or imagined on her. It makes her stand out from the night like the moon above.

She's got one hand on my arm and one hand on her father's. It's like Dodie walking between me and Jesus, holding on to both of us. But Bethie's hand that's on my arm is very light. She's barely touching me. I think she's letting me go. The thing is, when we get to Jesus and she does let me go, I still feel her hand on my arm. I feel it tightening on my arm. Even when I see that now she's standing next to Ryan and Ryan is holding that same hand. She's let me go. But she hasn't let go of me.

Jesus stands between Bethie and Ryan, but behind them. He has a hand on each of their shoulders. He looks out at all the people and then at me and then at Mr. Smith. He nods at Mr. Smith and says, "The bride's father has a few words. But first I want to welcome everybody to this happy occasion. We're here on this beach to celebrate Bethie and Ryan and to mourn Warren. Mr. Smith?"

Mr. Smith turns around to look at us. Then he turns back to look at Bethie and Ryan. Then he turns back to us. He has a big smile on his face.

"When my beloved wife died, my little girl became the woman in my house. Then she became the woman in War's house. And now she's about to become the woman in another man's house. And his wife. I'm glad I lived long enough to see her loved and loving and loved and loving again. We're all born twice, after all. The man Bethie lost was a man we both loved, who loved the man she now loves who loved the man she lost and who loves her. I could not be happier for her or for myself. Those of you who know me — and I see some of my old students out there, to whom I now apologize in advance . . . those who know me know what I'm about to do. That's right! Poetry! War had his favorite poet. I'll get to her in a moment. But he also liked a man named Wallace Stevens because Wallace Stevens said that life consisted of answering two questions: How to Live? What to Do? War learned how to live, which was for him a most difficult lesson after his mother took herself away. And he learned what to do. For him, they were one and the same. He gave his life so we might live. And where do we live? We live in what that same poet called 'an old chaos of the sun.' That's where War died — where the sun lives in chaos. War's *favorite* poet was Emily Dickinson. In her very first poem, she wrote about a storm walking on the seashore, like this seashore, humming a mournful tune, and a wave that looked to see the moon, just like that wave there beside us all here tonight. In the same poem, a boy and a girl get married. Their spirits meet together. They make their solemn vows. When they do, the boy stops mourning. The girl stops feeling sad. The night is married to the day. Here are lines from how the poem begins, and here is how I end:

> *"The bride, and the bridegroom, the two and then the one,*
> *Adam, and Eve, his consort, the moon, and then the sun . . ."*

Mr. Smith steps away, coming toward me. But then he turns back and looks out at the audience again. He raises one of his pudgy hands and says, "Speaking of the sun, I saw an angel standing in its light. Not my daughter. Though she's an angel to me. But an angel of the Lord who called out with a loud voice" — and here Mr. Smith clears his throat and takes a deep breath and speaks again like he had when he was standing on the table, loud and strong and deep —

"crying out to all the birds who fly in the midst of Heaven, the souls who live in the midst of Heaven, 'Blessed are you who are invited to the wedding supper of the Lamb.' "

Mr. Smith spreads his arms out over everyone who's there. His hands are shaking. Jesus comes to him from around behind Bethie and Ryan. He takes Mr. Smith's hands in his own and slowly lowers them. Then he guides Mr. Smith back to where I am. He puts Mr. Smith right next to me. He says, "Take care of him." I can't tell if he's talking to me or to Mr. Smith.

I could have shot him then. But I'd never shot anyone from up close. Not that I had anything against it. But sniping is the killing of the enemy from a long distance with one shot. And I was a sniper. I wanted my distance from him. Not in meters. This was Juba, and I felt too close to him. I felt he was me, in a different uniform with a different God. I was going to kill him, but with the knife my father had given me. With my treasured sharp deadly little Olsen.

Besides, I enjoyed listening to his prayers and watching him move. The words were full of those *A* sounds you heard in their language. It was like when you were a little boy and the doctor told you to open your mouth and say *aahhh*. My father would do that. He'd make me go *aahhh* and he'd look down my throat and he'd say, "I can see all the way in you and everything looks good." He used to do that with his patients too, at least when I was there. He'd open up an animal's mouth and stick his finger inside on their tongue and he'd say, "Say *aahhh*." None of them said it except when a lamb said, "*Baahhh*." I'd laugh my head off. One time he brought a lamb into the kitchen and made the lamb say, "*Baahhh*," for my mother. She didn't laugh until I did. Then you couldn't stop her. My father said, "*Baahhh*," when the lamb stopped to keep us going.

The imam kept repeating things like *Allahu Akbar*. Which I thought meant *God is great* but he was translating for me, *God is greater*.

And *Anna Muhammadar-rasulullaah. Muhammad is the Messenger of God.*

And *Laa ilaaha illallaah.* Which he got me to say over and over because it was like singing a song. Not the kinds of songs we sang when we swept in on these people and needed the songs we brought with us. All us young American boys and girls come to protect our country from what had already happened to it. The slaughter and the sudden death and the murder of innocent people falling on fire from the black windows of the sky. *Laa ilaaha illallaah* was like something you'd sing to a baby. You weren't telling a baby, *There is no God but Allah.* You were telling a baby, *There's nothing to be afraid of.*

While he prayed, the imam danced. Or so it looked from where I watched behind him and couldn't help but move as he chanted. I didn't do exactly like he did. But still his body was a magnet drawing mine with it and his voice was so full of prayer it opened up and swallowed me.

He would bow, with his long body like a thin tree in an easy wind. Then his hands would go to his knees and he would stay there bowed as he prayed. Then he stood straight again. I thought he might turn around to confront me. But he suddenly fell to his knees like I'd shot him. His body flowed out in front of him but stopped when his forehead touched the floor. He kept his hands flat on the floor near his head. He prayed and sent his words into the center of the Earth. He was completely vulnerable. He was someone whose head was about to be cut off, except here they did that when you were sitting back on your shins and you couldn't hide your fear from whoever had his fingers tangled in your hair. Then he sat up again. Then he went down again. I went down with him. Not on my knees. Just kind of following him. As much to keep track of him as to let him lead me. He stayed for a long time on his knees with his face hidden. Praying. Then he came back up and sat again with his left foot folded under. But this time instead of keeping his head straight ahead he looked over his right shoulder and said something and then he looked over his left shoulder and said something. Then he stood up and turned around and looked at me.

He said, "I was speaking to the angels on my shoulders. We all have angels on our shoulders. The angel on our right shoulder keeps track of all the good we do. And the angel on our left shoulder keeps track of all the evil we do."

"What were you saying to them?" I asked.

"As-salaamu alaykum wa rahmatullah," he said.

"What does that mean?"

"May there be peace upon you. And the mercy of God. You say it to me."

"May there be peace upon you. And the mercy of God."

I went for my knife even before he opened his robe. I could see how his Dragunov had been chewed up by his ejecting shell casings. It was a beautiful beat-up old gun. He pointed the silencer at my heart. As my knife comforted my hand, I swear I could see his bullet all the way from Mecca to me.

Jesus stands before Bethie and Ryan. He looks out over us, to the sea beyond and the Isles of Shoals and off to the east where I went and where I died and where I came home from. Now I know how I got here. Jesus didn't find me on the beach. He brought me home. Free shipping.

He says to everyone there, "You can't really mourn while the bridegroom is with you. You can be sad for your loss but not for the soul of the one you've lost. Warren went to a place in the world where those who abide will die by the sword. He might have left, and lived. But he stayed, and died. Like every soldier, he died for others, though his death was his own. I got to spend today with him. As I will spend your last day with each of you. I set before him the way of life. And the way of death. We walked together. We ate together. We drank together. We visited his family. And now it's time for him to visit God. He won't see God the way he saw his father and his daughter and Bethie and Ryan, or even his mother. No one sees God. No one has ever seen God. God is known only through his son. As Warren's father is known through his son. And Warren is known through his daughter. No one comes to the father except through the child. We're all part of all that went before and all that lives forever. Warren kept asking me today if this is the only world. It is. There are trillions of other rocks and fires in the universe. But there's only one world where God walked in the body of his son. And where we walk in the image of God. Male and female, as God created us. And blessed us. And named us Man."

Jesus walks back behind Bethie and Ryan. He takes their hands in his. He says, "You two are now the hope of mankind. You are Eve and Adam. Adam and Eve. Just as your father said, Bethie. The bride and the bridegroom. The two and then the one. The moon. And then the sun. We live in light and dwell in darkness. We give birth and we slaughter. But we're always striving toward perfection. And when that which is perfect has come, then everything that is imperfect will be done away with. Until then, we must live as we live. Love as we love. Die as we die."

Jesus is talking to them. But he's looking at me. A huge smile lights up his face. He looks happier than he has all day, and his happiness doesn't leave him but spreads out from him and comes to me and into me and fills me with more joy than I have ever felt in my life.

"Repeat after me," says Jesus. "Together."

I know he's not talking to me. But the way he now looks at Bethie and Ryan, I'm able to look at them too. Their backs are to me, but I can see into their souls.

"I will betroth you to me forever."

"I will betroth you to me forever."

"I will betroth you in virtue and honor."

"I will betroth you in virtue and honor."

"I will betroth you in love and mercy."

"I will betroth you in love and mercy."

"Now you know the Lord," says Jesus. "Now you are married."

Jesus looks at me. He shakes his head and holds up his hand. "Now you may kiss the bride," he says to Ryan. "Now you may kiss the bridegroom," he says to Bethie.

They do what he says like it was an order and not just permission.

Everybody applauds. I do too. Harder than anyone. But my hands make no sound. They pass through each other so I almost end up hugging myself. I don't care. You don't have to make noise in order to be heard.

When it's quiet again, and the kissing is done at least for now and the clapping has died out into the gentle sound of the dark waves on the shore, Jesus says, "Warren, I live in you, and you live in me. I give you eternal life. You will never perish. No one will ever take you out of my hand."

Which is why I could feel his hand in mine as I was lifted up and taken forever out of sight.

Deaths

Specialist Warren Harlan Pease, 20, Greenland, New Hampshire, US Army. Specialist Pease was killed with a single shot to the heart while defending the Musab bin Umair Mosque in the Talibiya suburb of Baghdad, Iraq.

Specialist Pease was a Master Sniper and Senior Sniper Instructor.

His body was received by the mortuary affairs unit at Camp Anaconda, north of Baghdad. There it was prepared for shipment to the United States. An honor cordon of several dozen troops saluted his remains as they were carried, feetfirst, to the hold of the C-5 cargo plane that delivered his body to Dover Air Force Base, Delaware. There mortuary affairs workers and casualty assistants identified, autopsied, embalmed, dressed, wrapped, and casketed his body. He was clothed in full dress uniform.

Specialist Pease was buried beside his mother, Dorothy Gookin Pease, in Spring Hill Cemetery, Greenland, New Hampshire. Engraved on his headstone are the words

WOMAN, BEHOLD YOUR SON

Weddings

BETHANY HELEN SMITH was married in North Hampton on June 21 to Ryan Louis Clark. Raphael Santi conducted the midnight seaside ceremony.

Ms. Smith (who will keep her maiden name) was homeschooled by her father, Dr. Edmund Smith. Dr. Smith walked his daughter down the aisle. Her mother is the late Helen Gilbert Smith. The bride's daughter, Dorothy Pease, was also in attendance.

Ms. Smith is a homemaker.

The bridegroom is the son of Mr. and Mrs. Frank Clark of Greenland. He graduated from Exeter High School. He is employed at Walgreens Pharmacy in Exeter.

The couple will honeymoon on the Isles of Shoals.